THE BURIER

A Novel of
The Lord's Millennial Kingdom

by Dorothy Gable

They will set apart men to travel through the
land regularly and bury those travelers remain-
ing on the face of the land, so as to cleanse it....

– Ezekiel 39:14

The Burier

A Novel of the Lord's Millennial Kingdom

Copyright © 2021 by Dorothy Gable

ISBN: 978-1-7376490-0-7 (softcover print edition)

Cover Design by: www.bookcoverdesign.us

Author Photo by Eric Misko – www.eliteimages.com

This is a work of fiction. Any resemblance to actual events, people or circumstances is accidental and not intentional. This biblically based novel brings unfulfilled prophecies to life.

▶ Character List

COLORADO

Asher Wilson . . . . .laborer for Gary Benson, friend of family;
from Zebulun

Charlene Benson . .daughter of Gary, friend of Asher

Daniel. . . . . .pastor's son, friend of Charlene

Frank Benson . . . . .Gary's twin son who is raptured

Gary Benson . . . . . .owner of Benson Construction

Millard . . . . .one of the 144,000 rescued by Owen in Denver

Owen . . . . .Denver lawyer, friend of the Bensons in the
Millennium

Patty Benson . . . . . .Gary's first wife who is raptured

Quinn Benson. . . . .Frank's twin brother, joins the Antichrist's brigade

Sallie. . . . . .Owen's secretary in the Millennium

Vera Benson . . . . . .Gary's millennial wife

ISRAEL

Andrew . . . . .brother to Kish; road builder from Dan

David, Esther . . . . .neighbors in Zebulun

Deb, Philip. . . . . . .fishers on the reclaimed Dead Sea; from Reuben

Jael . . . . .a burier with Asher; from Simeon

Kish . . . . road builder; from Dan

Lazarus. . . . . Deb's brother; from Reuben

Leon, Marta. . . . . . . .leaders at Kadesh-Barnea, friends of Asher

Lester . . . . .Asher's tenth-generation grandson

Leon, Rose. . . . . .workers at Hamonah

Marta . . . . .Andrew's wife

Nehemiah . . . . .fifth-generation grandson of David & Esther

Shachna . . . . .Hamonah supervisor of the buriers

Zephath . . . . .Priest at En Chaika Healing Center, son of Zadok

Jerusalem, Israel

Elchanan, Zamira. . .older couple saved during the Great Tribulation

Bethany . . . . .Isaac's wife; meets Elchanan, Zamira and Isaac at
Petra

Giselle. . . . . .from Judah

Hannah . . . . .Menachem's wife

Isaac . . . . .grandson of Elchanan, friend of Asher; from Judah

Menachem. . . . . .Elchanan's son

Uriah . . . . .Levitical lawyer, pastor in Jerusalem

Terms

Shining Ones — those who were resurrected and help the Lord administer the planet. These glorified ones believed before Christ's
first coming, during the Church Age, or died in faith during the
Great Tribulation.

The Temple Mount — Zechariah 14 describes the changes to central
Israel when His foot touches the Mount of Olives. A large plain is
created, and the Temple is constructed on the highest part near
Jerusalem.

Wanderers — believers who survived the Tribulation to enter the Millennium and have trouble adjusting to their new life.

PART ONE

The Early Days

►1

ASHER MICHAEL WILSON shifted his knees and faced the uplifted Temple district in the south, a large plateau created for the Temple, lands for the Prince, Levites, and the city—Jerusalem. The Temple walls glowing in the light of the pillar of fire radiated His glory. As the rising sun crested the horizon on his left, the pillar that marked the night sky became a luminescent cloud reaching into the heavens.

He remembered the canopies that had shielded them from the sun during the first days after Armageddon. Felt, but not seen, he had absorbed the glow that emanated from the heavenly Jerusalem hovering over the ancient city pockmarked by war and fractured by the transformation of the land around Jerusalem and the Temple Mount when Messiah's feet landed on the Mount of Olives.[1]

Asher lowered his gaze. The sun's first rays danced along waves of tall grass and budding flowers that marked the shoulders of the Highway of Holiness[2] and outlined the shape of a femur's head protruding from the ground. The Lord's highway of peace ran from Assyria in the north to Egypt in the south. As Isaiah had predicted—perfect peace between the three—Assyria, Israel and Egypt.

Lowering his head to shield his eyes, Asher knelt, took out a soft brush, and cocked his head slightly to imagine the position of the remainder of the bone wedged beneath the new growth of the Millennium—the Kingdom of the Lord.

All knew it would last one thousand years—as the prophet John had written in the book of Revelation, reaching past to the end of time itself. Those who entered the kingdom witnessed the beginning of this new epoch, as if awakening from a nightmare where demons ruled the world and walked boldly across it.

He looked up. *"Holy, Holy, Holy, is the Lord God Almighty. Great and amazing are your deeds, O Lord God the Almighty! Just and true are your ways, O King of the nations!"*[3]

Gripping his trowel in his left hand, he nudged the tool along the angle of the femur, pushing against the resistance of the dirt and growth that held it in place.

"Your judgments are true and righteous all together; for You avenge the blood of Your children and take vengeance on Your adversaries."[4]

With a practiced hand, he forced the bone up into the light of the sun, reached for the linen cloth sanctified by the priests, sons of Zadok, and carefully held it to catch the freed bone.

"It is by your mercy LORD, that we are not consumed. Great is Your faithfulness.[5] Cleanse me from all sin and set me upright before You, Lord, as I take the bones of the fallen. To You God has given the right to judge, to give life and to take life. Amen and amen. May You cleanse this land and our children remember You always."

A three-note melody sounded from the radio tucked in the side pocket of the saddlebag. Asher turned toward the sound coming from his packs resting by a slight rise. The sun's rays poured into his eyes with a blinding light and a pulse ran through him. His heart raced. Sweat poured from his forehead…

—⁓—

Splashing in the cold water, he fought against an eddy pushing him to the middle of the river near Carbondale, Colorado. The stream, swollen with spring runoff and recent rains, propelled him toward the center. Floodlights searched the water's surface. Asher dove, grasped a branch and thrust upward to breathe. The lights angled through his eyes into his soul. Still blinded, he curled below the water, pushed away, trying to shoot downstream and across to another tangle of fallen logs and branches. But they were there.

Asher fell back and shook his head, feeling the rough grass, pebbles and dirt beneath his palms. He rolled to his knees, trying to recover from the vision. No, not a vision—not like the ones many seemed to have. He had experienced a few during the time of the building of the Temple and the gathering, the choosing. No, these were panic attacks, or so they seemed—vivid, waking dreams of the time before that refused to leave.

His radio sounded again…this time followed by a voice. "Asher, are you there?"

Thankfully, the bone had fallen on the linen, and the spot had not been violated. He brought the edges up and over. The ritual—as Natan had shown him—had not been ordained by the Lord Himself, but he followed it as it had been handed down to him by the other buriers.

Remembering his mentor and friend, he worked to settle his breathing, walked to his pack for a cloth to wipe his brow and dust off his hands. Straightening up, he answered. "I'm here."

"Where?"

"Near the Highway of Holiness. Found marker 138."

"Tomorrow's assembly day. Do you have a scooter?"

Asher smiled at the donkey foraging close by. "My Chamor." The animal raised its head and approached. Cradling the long face to his chest, Asher listened to Shachna, his current supervisor. "Come in immediately. It's been four days. What happened?"

Four days? Asher swallowed. *I thought I had another day.*

"Where's Jael?"

Blinking, he stared off in the distance, his recent memory returning.

"I took two of his markers. He had three more left. Decided to separate." He released the switch and looked along the highway. Jael's close-cropped head could be seen just past a distant rise. "Just coming up on his scooter."

"You clear the markers?"

"I finished with mine."

"Come back to Hamonah[6] and make yourself ready."

Asher signed off, packed his belongings scattered around the remnants of his campsite and attached them to the pack saddle.

Jael stopped in front of him on the raised highway. "I thought you'd be on your way by now. What took you so long? I finished my six."

Asher shrugged, the will to fight buried under the lethargy that came after an attack.

"Found it? Leon thought 138 had to be a false report."

"Was wedged between some boulders. Walked a grid to find it."

"Last night?"

Asher took a breath. With the sun seven times brighter and the moon as bright as daylight used to be,[7] he found it easier at night to see the slight bumps and exposed ridges from uplifted bones. The night was better than the day for panic attacks as well. He had hoped the isolation of searching for tagged bones in the wilderness would have reduced them.

"Think you can make it in time on your donkey?" Jael leveled his gaze at Asher. "You know, with fewer areas awaiting cleansing, they're going to let some of us go tomorrow. I wouldn't want to be late if I were you."

Asher said nothing. Jael knew he had failed at his other jobs building the Temple and working the quarry. If they were only interested in numbers, Jael would be at the top of the list to keep his job.

"Well, my six bundles are ready to be delivered. Need any help?" Hardly waiting for Asher to answer, he revved the scooter and headed south.

Asher watched him leave. They would have to go to the burial depot first to hand over the recovered bones. The mass graves occupied
a large valley where ancient Samaria had been, north of the plateau
created by the Lord when His feet touched the Mount of Olives. The
bones that remained after the fire of the Lord and the carrion feast
were cast into a pit without ceremony or mourning or remembrance.[8]
The rebuilt town of Hamonah, first erected after the great Northern
invasion right before the abomination of desolation, stood sentry at
the mouth of the valley.[9]

"No," he answered to the tingling air, alive with sparkling light and
colors. Flowers burst forth, carpeting the hillsides with yellows, reds
and purples. Birds sang and even the bees' humming seemed to carry
melodies. No longer did weeds grow, mosquitoes bite, or bees sting.[10]
He held out his hand as a bee landed on his palm, cleaned its gossamer
wings, and almost seemed to nod before flying away. Peace between
all—man and the land and all that flew or walked or crawled. Peace
between God and man. The air around the highway breathed life and
energy from unseen angels guarding it. Rarely did one see them, but
they never masked the serene peace and settled joy that rested on those
who walked the Highway of Holiness.

The perception of peace called to him, but he could only bear it for
a time. The night before he had camped just past the borders, feeling
more than seeing the heavenly shimmer emanate during the darkest
part of the night. As he had walked the grid, he prayed, leaning into
the one—the presence that he knew guided him to find the overlooked
bones and cleanse the land. At least he could do something.

He turned, slipped the bundle into a side pouch with the others
and lifted the packs to Chamor's back, sighing. *Lord, let me know Your
peace.*

Chamor had a stiff trot but a smooth canter. Asher tried to keep his
focus over the miles. He resisted the urge to recall his lost day when
a budding disorientation threatened to emerge. Shaking his head, he

studied the road, straight and smooth that ran from Syria to Egypt—connecting three nations who no longer warred among themselves. Now three—Egypt, Israel and Syria—worshiped the Lord God Almighty.[11]

In his mind Asher recalled the lines of those who had gathered from the nations—many wounded, lame, blind, deaf—arriving on planes or ships or in caravans. The joy of the presence of God, what had once been only momentary feelings that quickly passed, enveloped the ones gathered from the nations. Visible angels and shining ones [12] helped the new arrivals find shelter and food. Unbidden, he remembered the presence that had protected him through the last days of the Great Tribulation, and how he had been led to walk east until he came to the Mississippi River, hundreds of miles away from Colorado. There, they had told him he was of the tribe of Zebulun and took him to Israel.

Having survived without a scratch, he had found his place and met Isaac, a refugee from a town near Jerusalem. When he had told him he was a builder, Isaac had helped him find a job working on the Temple. Elchanan, Isaac's grandfather, had welcomed him into the friendly family with a large house on the south side of Jerusalem.

They had covered many miles. Asher said, "Walk, Chamor," and pulled back gently on the reins. The donkey slowed to a trot and a fast walk—urged forward by the scent of water from a nearby flowing stream that widened into a pond.

Asher directed his mount to a level spot by the pond, removed his tablet and released his donkey. More revelation had been given since that day, but Asher was working through the earlier covenants—for the first time beginning to understand God and His rescue program through the ages. The first books and the second books of the time right before the seven years had been kept as reminders of what had passed. With the new age of Christ, new revelation poured forth,[13] but Asher had to rely on others to help him piece it together. Elchanan had been one. Perhaps he could visit him again.

After a break of reading and praying, Asher resumed his journey south as the Highway veered slightly west and closer to the Western Sea.[14] Edges of the wall of Jerusalem, just south of the temple, and its taller buildings became visible. He looked beyond the walls and thought of heavenly Jerusalem again, knowing his friend Daniel lived there now in his glorified body. His heart raced, his breathing fast and shallow, as he fought against the image of his friend bound and held in place, waiting for a blade to fall.

Drawing closer to the road to Hamonah, Asher pulled Chamor to the side. He swung to the ground, letting the donkey nuzzle his chest. The soft fur and warm breath pulled him back to the present. *It was my fault they caught Daniel. I told him we had to go back for more berries.* Ignoring the pain, he tried to shut down the memories and resume their journey. Pushing hard, he reached the road to Hamonah on the left and saw Jael's head in the distance and heard the putt-putt of the scooter.

Jael pushed the bike to top speeds. Asher followed, not being drawn into a race. Let the man arrive first. Let him brag that he had brought in more than the others. Asher shook his head, shutting down that thought as well. Jael reminded him too much of Thomas who had joined their little group—himself, Daniel, and Charlene. Gary, Charlene's dad and owner of Benson Construction, had sacrificed himself to help them escape shortly after the world leader had violated the Temple and had erected an image for all to worship.[15] They had all mourned the loss of Patty, Charlene's mother, and Frank, her younger brother, who had been taken by the Lord in the rapture.

Asher had to lock away his memories of Charlene as the returning buriers filled the roadway. Jael shot past to be closer to the front of the line for the burial depot a short distance past Hamonah. Having little incentive to return to his small room with cot, bedstand and lamp, Asher headed to the stables, untacked Chamor, brushed his back, cleaned his hooves, and released him into a pen with a water trough and fresh grass.

Asher stood in line, watching the men talk among themselves. As if in a glass cage, merely observing, he saw the swollen packs or bags in their hands or over their shoulders. One or two smiled when their eyes met. He pasted a smile on his face. Those near him did not speak, looking as tired as he should be feeling.

Talk of supper floated by. His ears perked up when a few discussed some of the rumors, but they were only rumors. "Wait until it happens, son," his mother used to say. "Don't waste today with tomorrow's troubles."

In the dining room his good friend Isaac found him at a table with two others. "Well, you have returned."

Asher nodded and smiled. "At least I get out. You still like computer work?" He smiled again with his friend's signature shrug.

The tall Israeli leaned closer and said quietly, "Hang with me after?"

"Got nothing better to do."

"Yo, Asher! For real? Marker 138 wasn't a ghost?" called a burier from a nearby table.

Isaac let fly a retort in Asher's defense. "No ghost. Not for this one," he said loudly, patting his friend's back. He added, "So, you found one of the fabled missing markers. If Shachna is wise, he will let you find all the markers eluding us."

"Yeah, but they look at counts." He stirred the fresh soup filled with rice, greens, tomatoes and other vegetables he didn't have a name for.

"Don't listen to Jael. Anyway, you'll get the credit."

Asher sat back, his spoon slack over his bowl. *Why bother?* But he resisted that retort. Isaac deserved better. "You move into your inheritance yet?" Of the tribe of Judah, Isaac's land nestled in a beautiful hollow south of Hamonah.

"I've finished my house." He lifted his brows.

Asher smiled, "So, you have news?"

"Yes, so quit dawdling. Eat up and let's walk."

In a short time, they exited the dining hall. Asher followed his friend along the walkway and west around a slight mound. "Your news…" His voice froze when the modular dorms came into view. "When did they move the trailers?"

"You've been gone that long?"

"Shachna resupplied us north of the Galilee. The courier collected our bundles and brought more tags to find. They said we didn't have time to come back."

Asher almost laughed. *What's the rush? We have a thousand years!* Pushing down a familiar fatigue, he waited for Isaac to make his usual comeback, but his friend nodded in understanding. "So, what's up?"

The tall man with dark eyes and short curly hair lifted one brow. "Well, I have important news. You did hear me say that I finished my house, or were you listening?"

"I really have been gone a long time."

"Took some leave, since…" He stopped at a secluded spot. "I'd like you to come to my wedding next month."

"In the city?"

He nodded, "At my grandfather's courtyard. It's the perfect spot." Isaac searched Asher's face.

"Of course, I will be there."

Isaac drew out a small, square invitation with flowing calligraphy. "Asher, whatever happens tomorrow, I know you're one of the best finders. Praying they don't transfer you." Wanting to press for more, he hesitated to push his friend.

"It'll be okay. Whatever happens, will happen."

"Asher, live! You're of Zebulun, of the south.[16] Your land is green and well-watered. Find the one you can wed and have a family; make a home."

He looked away. What could he say? This was his friend. "Good advice. Tell me of your plans."

They walked and talked. Asher shared his bundle of sweet figs, and they drank sweet water from a clean well. They headed past the make-shift town and up a small rise to watch the sun set and the signal fire of the Lord appear just past the outline of the Temple.

"I set the stones for the Western Wall," Asher commented.

"That you did." He smiled. "Where we met. I kept the records of the workers."

"Always the office guy."

"Someone has to do it!"

"And what will you do in your land? Farm? Grow grapes? Tend sheep?"

He smiled. "What I know. Do their bookwork so they don't have to. Just because we're in the new era—the Kingdom—doesn't mean we don't specialize, optimize, do what we do best."

Asher turned back to the setting sun, and his hand on Isaac's shoulder clenched.

They pulled him from the river, stripped him naked, seeming to dance with his meager belongings strewn about. Wolves surrounded him, grasping, tearing, pulling him to the back of a van and on to the warehouse where Daniel had been taken.

He breathed in to still the trembling and drew back from Isaac. "Sorry," Asher mumbled, flushing at losing control in front of his friend.

The man rose and embraced him in a hug. "My friend, go to the Lord for healing."

"Of what? I survived without a scratch."

Not wanting to argue—they had had this conversation before—he released Asher and said, "Some wounds are deep. You are and will always be my friend. Never forget that. Don't hesitate to call on me, and I will help you. He does not ask us to walk alone."

Asher's shoulders tightened. The ball in his gut turned. Nodding, he stared at the dimly lit night sky—what in the time before would have been a dull, cloud-covered day. Burying his feelings, he turned, smiled, and nodded. "The same to you."

The sound of evening prayers and singing floated their way. They stood side by side, looking at the Temple in the distance that had only existed in ancient parchments—a Temple filled with the glory of the Lord. The outer Eastern gate was kept shut since through it the glory of the Lord had come to fill His Temple. At the inner Eastern gate, before the altar, the Prince of the Jews, a descendant of the resurrected King David, led the worship.[17]

"And to think we are granted the privilege to see these days."

Isaac's comment needed no response. They worshiped together.

2

ASHER SHIFTED HIS backpack and climbed the first rise to Jerusalem. The city sat on the higher section of the plain that reached from Geba in the north to Rimmon in the south, running along the west side of the Eastern Sea.[18] Only the Temple itself was higher.

That day weeks ago, Asher had felt nothing as he had stood in the assembly not hearing his name called for the ones chosen to continue at Hamonah. He was not surprised. Isaac, stating his relief that he had not been on the list, turned to his friend. "So, now we will see what the Lord will do and how He will lead us."

Shifting his pack, Asher lifted it up from his shoulders and swung it down onto the flagstones. His eyes rested on the cloud by day above the Temple.[19] Nothing. He felt nothing. His future did not exist except for seeking water, food, and a place to sleep.

Thankfully, the city was quiet, almost as if it had paused. *Lord, help me be a good friend to Isaac and help me make it through this wedding.* His heart warmed slightly, looking forward to seeing Elchanan, Isaac's grandfather.

He peered down the narrow street. The crowds in the city thinned out later in the day as it was between feasts. However, he spied a group of visitors heading in his direction.

Something miraculous had happened to all who had been brought to Israel during the first 75 days; everyone knew and understood Hebrew. Elchanan had told him it was a form of classical Hebrew that almost had been lost. A pure language had been prophesied, and so it had happened.[20]

Their accents revealed they were primarily English speakers. He stood back near a light stone wall, guessing they were from the former United States.

"Young man," a woman said, "Do you know the way to the Bethel Hostel?"

Asher smiled. "I do," he said in perfect English and gave the directions.

"Where were you from?" she asked.

They huddled around him and continued their questioning when he mentioned that he had been a burier. Describing the work as patiently as possible, he paused. One he suspected who had been older in appearance asked the last question: "What will you do with your life?"

If only I knew. So many seemed to have a ready answer. "As the years of a tree, so shall our lives be.[21] That we bring glory to God and dwell in His midst…" Asher blinked away threatening tears.

"From the ends of the earth we hear songs of praise, of glory to the Righteous One," the man said, quoting Isaiah 24:16.

"Have you been in His presence?" the first woman asked.

Asher tilted his head. "As all of us, we came before Him and were found worthy to enter the kingdom because He knew us. The Spirit of God dwelt within us. But…" he glanced toward the Temple's upper chambers visible past the city's buildings.

"May you seek His face and find your way," the leader said, with a glance before he urged the group on to their hostel.

Asher knew the man understood, empathized with him. *Why do I not seek out the Lord directly?*

"Friend! Friend!" Isaac called, running toward him.

"Don't fall running downhill like that!" Asher called back, laughing, remembering Zamira, Elchanan's wife's admonitions.

"Okay, Grannie! When did you begin talking like the aged?"

"Hey, we need some mature voices around here," Asher quipped in response.

"You told them you were a burier, and that was it?"

"Slipped out, but I don't mind sharing about the wonders of our land." His land—it was his. He even had a piece assigned to him. An instant thrill shriveled away under an ever-present foreboding.

After the embrace they turned and headed up the last hill to Elchanan's lovely estate near the southern edge of the city. Yellow stone carved into large rectangular blocks surrounded the courtyard and covered the two-story structure adorned with wrought-iron balconies overlooking the southern plains. An ancient tree surrounded by white stones stood near the courtyard entrance.

Asher shook his head. "Does it ever bloom?"

"Missed it. You have been gone a long time. Come on! They're waiting for you."

He paused, looking at the tree. Amazingly, the ancient tree, twisted, with old scars of limbs that had died years ago, reached to the heavens with scattered branches of green leaves. Yet it stood. *The years of a tree.* A shudder ran through him.

"Asher! You've come!" Zamira embraced him first. Her firm hand on his shoulder moved him past the front entrance and to the sitting room with two sofas, modern-looking armchairs and glass tables. The juxtaposition of ancient with ultra-modern grabbed his attention yet again. In the larger cities, steel and the remnants of glass skyscrapers shared avenues with traditional buildings and homes of stone and mortar with rooftop porches, some bursting with flowers. Rebuilding still proceeded at a quick pace.

Elchanan, the patriarch, rose and embraced him. "Asher has arrived. Friend of Isaac and burier." He turned and made the introductions. Asher smiled and nodded at Menachem, Elchanan's only surviving son, and tried to remember the names of Zamira's sister and her remaining family.

"Tell us, burier, where do your paths lie now?"

"Well, my land is south, of Zebulun," he said.

"And what do you think of the blossoming of our land? So different than before. Had you lived near the Galilee?"

"The land of Zebulun and the land of Naphtali, the way of the sea, beyond the Jordan, Galilee of the Gentiles—the people dwelling in darkness have seen a great light, and for those dwelling in the region and shadow of death, on them a light has dawned."[22] The words flowed out.

"The prophet Isaiah," Zamira's nephew said.

"As said by Matthew," Menachem said. "But our friend Asher had lived all his life in the United States, though you would never guess it by his speech. In New York City? Surely, you studied Hebrew as a boy and had your bar mitzvah. You knew Hebrew before?"

Asher shook his head. "My mother and father lived in Ohio. She knew she was a Jew and called me Asher. My father agreed until he learned Asher was a Jewish name. Then he called me Mike, my middle name."

"Also, a Jewish name."

"Michael was also common with my father's people. I had no religious upbringing." He paused. "What of the wedding plans? I have never been to a Jewish wedding."

Isaac looked to his grandfather.

Elchanan drew breath as if to speak, but a middle-aged woman spoke first. "We must keep the traditions. Not let them be forgotten. So, they skipped a witnessed marriage contract, the *ketubah*," she waved her hand. "But Bethany's veiling can be done at the *kabbalat panim* reception."

Isaac explained to Asher, "The bride and groom each hold a brief reception before the ceremony, but Bethany has no family."

"How is that possible?" Asher blurted out. He closed his mouth when all conversation stopped, and many averted their eyes.

"She was from an ultra-orthodox family," Elchanan said. He nodded at the group. "We can speak of those who are gone. Bethany sheltered with us at Petra."

Asher remembered the story well—the day of the abomination of desolation, the day the Antichrist seemingly rose from the dead and entered the temple to sacrifice and forced the priests to worship him, the day the false prophet came with squads to murder all who would not bow the knee. They turned not back to their homes but fled east to the mountain strongholds of Petra as the angels of God guided and protected them.

The conversation flowed, going back and forth, until Isaac stood. "We decided to be apart for a week. It's almost done. We will fast on the day until we eat together as one after the wedding. Bethany will wait in the eastern room, and I will be in the west." He listed the rest of the service, finishing with the witnesses and signing of the marriage covenant before the magistrate. The ceremony would be led by Uriah, a Levite, a friend of Elchanan and a lawyer.

Sighing, he gestured to Asher to follow him out to the darkened courtyard while the family settled the matter of the food and catering.

"I could watch with her."

"Bethany's friends will help her. They were from reformed families and are the only survivors. You working?"

"Odd construction jobs here and there." His eyes scanned the receding hillsides going down to the plain. More homes and buildings had been restored along with signs of fresh construction. "This is a good time to be a builder. My current job will end soon. Do you know of any projects in your village?"

"I do. I can make the introductions after the wedding."

"Aren't you taking a honeymoon?"

"Just a few days by the Eastern Sea, but we both want to get back home." He looked to the northwest, seeing their growing mini-metropolis in his mind. "She's a biologist and a great researcher—looking forward to seeing the transformation of the Dead Sea. She already has a job with a local start-up."

"And you?"

"Independent accountant. They need someone to keep up with the new laws and regulations."

"How does that work?"

"The interim leadership crafts the statutes, but the King's overseers have to approve them."

Asher nodded—the Shining Ones—the people who had a part in the first resurrection and had received their immortal bodies (the church, Old Testament, or Tribulation saints).

"He'd been martyred by the false prophet's forces. Of Judah, but not of this region."

"Have you met him yet?"

Isaac shook his head. "It seems they only appear to the leadership or for emergency situations. Most days you'd hardly know they were about."

Asher would have asked if he could feel their presence, but Elchanan joined them, hugging both young men before they sat on the short wall.

"Is it settled?"

"For now, until my cousin notices a deficiency. I'm sure she'll find a way to rectify it."

"Or Zamira distracts her," Isaac said with short laugh.

"So, your plans?"

Asher glanced at the grandfather, who now looked barely thirty-five. "Work odd jobs."

"But don't you want to get settled? Who's taking care of your inheritance?"

"Rented it out to neighbors. I could go back and work for anyone wanting to build." He shrugged his shoulders and asked about Uriah, the pastor who would be leading the ceremony.

Isaac glanced at his friend but didn't have a chance to encourage him to seek a future.

Zamira stepped through and the sounds of many voices still talking filtered out the door. "Well, time to settle down for bed, or none of us will be ready or happy tomorrow. Isaac, your room is good?" Seeing the nod, she gestured to Asher, "Come, grandson, to your guest room, and I will see if they left you everything you need." She winked at Elchanan and led Asher into the house and up the stairs as if she were a teenager again.

"So, you feel young?"

Zamira smiled and inspected the bedding, linens and towels. "So little, but then," she sighed, "it seems we need much less now."

He nodded. "It means so much that you have taken me in."

"Family now," Zamira waved her hand and disappeared down the hall to the stairs.

———∿∿∿———

Asher stepped through the process—groom's reception, the veiling in the center hallway. Each walked to the canopy circled by many chairs, filling the courtyard. Horn, lute, violins and guitar provided the music. A vocalist sang one of the Psalms from the First Covenant. Now that he understood Hebrew, he felt the rhythm, rhyme and meter of the ancient songs. Stirrings in his soul rose up, but he contained them. Losing control in front of Isaac's family would be embarrassing.

They read the covenant for their vows, blending new with old, pledging themselves together to love, cherish and protect each other until the Lord separated them. Both Isaac and Bethany had insisted on those words instead of the usual "until death do us part" in acknowledgment of their assurance that they would be together throughout the thousand years.

Asher could not allow himself to feel or remember. Stepping aside when they walked to the reception set up in two rooms on the first floor, he found himself by the wall.

"Not hungry?" Menachem asked and stood by him. "It will be my turn soon. My Hannah and I signed a *ketubah*."

"Traditional?"

"It's fine with me. We worship the Lord in our own ways. It was important for her father."

"Is she?" He glanced at Menachem, wondering how old he really was. "Is she as old as you?"

"Old," Menachem laughed, "is relative now. No, in the time before she would have been as old as my daughters," clearing his throat, he continued, "but now we are all young, as if newborn in the Lord. So, you need to find your bride." Seeing Asher's face pale and his eyes slide away, he asked, "What was her name?"

Staring at a distant point, he answered, "Charlene."

"Was she killed? Is she a shining one now?"

Asher shook his head. "I don't know. I guess so." He sighed, and said woodenly, "We were separated. I never saw them again." That was not the full truth, but he could not voice what had happened and keep it together for the reception. That would not honor Isaac's and Bethany's joining. "Shall we? Is there a place for bachelors in His kingdom?"

"We are one in the Spirit and the King! Follow me. Let us sing and dance, rejoicing in new life! To life!" He headed out to the courtyard. Tables and chairs had been pushed back to make way for dancing. A mini-orchestra sat in the near right corner. Menachem and Asher watched the couples separate and encircle one another, then become a pair and a group again. The music, undergirded by violins and strings, delivered a rising beat. Without realizing it, he found himself clapping along with the crowd. Hannah joined them, standing close to Menachem's side.

A woman with long flowing hair and dark eyes stood before him and extended her hand.

"Go, Asher! Live!"

Nodding, praying he could remember the steps, he copied the other dancers' movements. They twirled and clapped and stepped and jumped, until, as one, the dancers melted back to join the crowd. The music shifted to a traditional beat. All clapped in time as six men with long black coats and tall black hats moved together in a line, punctuating the beat with heel or toe, turning, bending. During a brief pause, a group placed glasses of wine on their heads, and they continued their dance, without spilling a drop.

After they joined the crowd, solo dancers stepped forward, one by one. Feeling the beat, calling out with the crowd, he imagined a dance, blending traditional Jewish with some break-dancing moves. He stepped to the open center when those near him urged him forward. Moving with the music, beginning with the traditional steps, he segued to American moves, back to traditional and with a rising beat, began his short breakdance routine, twirling and jumping. Ending with a flourish, he bowed slightly to the next one. That performance broke the ice, and many came forward with their own unique dance steps.

Standing near Menachem, catching his breath, his dance partner pulled him into a hug and whispered her name, "Giselle."

"Asher," he said back.

"Wait for the couple's turn." Seeing his furrowed brow, her smile broadened. "Just follow me, and I'll do the fancy moves. Game?"

"Yes," he heard himself say. "But let's not go first."

Asher studied the routines of the couples, letting the possibilities engulf him. When she reached for his hand, he stepped to the center. They walked with measured steps, drawing a circle. Back and forth, they flowed. When they moved out to arm's length, she began to pirouette or jump. Sensing her next move, he lifted her up and around.

Before he knew it, they were done. He met Elchanan's gaze and returned the smile. Life coursed through him.

▶3

CHARLENE WATCHED HER father, Gary, look deeply into Vera's eyes. "Dad, did you send in the application for our reservations for the Feast of Booths in Jerusalem?"

"What? Oh, yes," he said before looking at his daughter.

"He did. Wouldn't let him overlook that task." Vera winked at Charlene and smiled broadly.

"Okay," Charlene cast a knowing look at her dinner date, Owen. "Vera, do you have something to show us?" She watched her father and Vera exchange glances and extend their joined hands. She leaned forward to see the engagement ring. "It's beautiful."

Owen nodded. "We expected it." Looking at Charlene, his eyes crinkled. "Just didn't know when you'd do it. Have you set a date?"

"That's what we wanted to talk to you two about," Gary said.

Charlene's mouth went dry; a rush of heat rose up.

"Honey," Owen said to Charlene, "You're clenching my hand."

"Sorry," she mumbled and tucked it in her lap.

"Yes," Vera said, "we wanted to have a special ceremony, when you two could..."

"Right," Owen looked at Charlene, "just the right time for a ..." he stuttered, "...wedding."

"Excuse me. I have to go to the lady's room," Charlene spoke as she rose, not waiting for a reply. They had dropped hints. Her father had remarked on the growing number of newlyweds with babies on the way. Owen had begun to call her "Chary-bee," "pumpkin" and "honey." She liked and admired the upright, yet friendly, lawyer, but something kept her frozen, living alone in a small apartment above the New Colorado town offices.

They smiled sweetly when she returned. "Did you have a date in mind? A month, next year?" Her voice trailed off.

Her father had married her mother on a Colorado mountainside in the dead of winter on a ski slope. She remembered the photos, now long-burned or ravaged by the years of war and sorrow. She turned her head to dab her eyes and looked out the restaurant window at the blossoming, windswept plains and rolling hills of New Colorado. *Every mountain laid low, and He lifted up the Mount, the City of God, that it might be the tallest.*[23]

She looked at Gary and Vera and Owen. "I'm so happy for you. I know Mom, in the heavenly Jerusalem, is rejoicing at your life together. I want to be there for you. I do."

"And do you…?" Owen's voice hesitated.

"I don't know what I'm to do—what He's calling me to do, why He saved us and brought us through…" Her brows drew together. "This time of peace, time to make families, rebuild…the future lies before us, but…" Charlene shook her head. "I don't know where I'll be even a month from now."

"But, Charlene, surely your place as executive administrator to the mayor is secure no matter who wins the election. The city will flourish; the future is ours." He laughed. "We have a future now, and I want to live it with you."

Charlene drew in her breath. She didn't want to hurt him but couldn't voice what she did not know herself—what held her back.

"Of course, when you're ready." Owen coughed, knowing he had pushed her as far as he could. Charlene was worth the wait.

"Thank you. I'd like to have it figured out too."

Her eyes tracked back over the plains. Her heart recalled Jerusalem right after the Day of the Lord. She imagined what it must look like now with the Temple completed as they looked forward to the second Feast of Booths. "Imagine, Dad, building the Temple or even working on the outer buildings. What a sight!"

Gary patted Owen's shoulder. "Give her time. She'll be ready. She will."

―⁓―

Charlene made her way to her little apartment where she changed into comfortable jeans and a lightweight shirt. With one last look at her still sitting room and small kitchen, she closed the door and headed down the back stairs. Storage buildings, craftsmen's shops and tool sheds lined the second street. She walked up the slight rise to a grove of trees. The new city, nestled a short distance from a small river, overlooked rolling plains for miles with no towering mountains in sight. Small fields made patchwork patterns here and there. Houses, some finished, some just begun, dotted the landscape not far from the fields. She heard the whisper of the wind running over the wheat, the crackle of hard cornstalks rubbing in the breezes and crickets chirping.

Turning her head, she felt the last of the sun's rays with the slight breeze of the evening's softer heat and waited for the moon to rise. The brief moment of darkness—the darkest it would be—the time between the sun, seven times brighter and the rising of the moon, seven times as well. She faced the moonlight and followed the lighted path before her. Her city had a future. The possibilities grew with each family's settling nearby. God had brought just the right mix of farmer and trader, craftsman and baker. With the help of the Lord, ruling from Jerusalem, and His overseers, the shining ones, she knew this place would thrive with or without her.

She surveyed the plains laid out before her. "Lead me, Lord," she prayed. She had hoped against hope to catch a glimpse of Daniel, but the crickets chirped, a dog barked in the distance, and she heard a few calls carried on the wind. "Daniel," she whispered, "you are now a shining one and with the Lord." Her heart had jumped within her when she had seen him in Jerusalem. He sometimes appeared to help but did not come on call. Some said King Jesus did not send them to towns where their old friends lived. She understood, but nonetheless, her heart tugged.

"Lord, show me," she said. She stepped down the path, walking past the buildings to her place. She did not need to turn on a light but dressed for bed and slid under the covers. Her future lay before her in shadows, uncertain, not ready, formless and void—felt but not seen, heard but not spoken. In time God would show her.

She fell asleep.

———

The house was warm with the scents of flowers in the air. A child's cry pierced the room, and Charlene bent to lift her wiggling daughter with dark curls and blue-gray eyes to the ceiling. She looked out the window to see the distant glow from the City of God. In her heart she knew it lay north of their estate. Setting the child down, she said, "Go call your father. Supper waits." Charlene heard hard soles on flagstone steps. The door burst open, and her heart leapt in her chest. Her husband's tan skin glistened in the evening sunlight and with broad arms, encircled their daughter in a firm embrace. His dark eyes met hers, the corners wrinkling with a ready smile.[24]

———

Charlene sat up with a start. The dream collapsed, but the image burned into her soul. "Asher, where are you?" Fleeing the bed, she paced before dark windows. "I never found him. Not a sight. No word. His name not on any list." She shook her head.

The day of the disappearances, the day their lives changed, never to return—the four of them: Daniel, the pastor's son and friend from the church teen group, her father, Asher and herself—were bound together. In the beginning of the Great Tribulation, they were separated when her father led the police away to keep them safe. Joining up with him shortly before the Second Coming had been thrilling. That was when she had met Vera. She had told them of Daniel's capture and Asher's disappearance. She assumed the Lord had allowed Daniel to approach them so they would know to stop searching for him. However, they had found no sign concerning Asher.

Charlene stood motionless, peering past the windows to the dimly lit night. *Lord, deliver me.* Nothing else rose up.

The rest of that night consisted of tossing and turning. A few hours before her alarm, she resigned herself to the fact that Owen had to know. She wasn't being fair to him.

Midmorning, Charlene exited the interim mayor's office, printed out the latest by-laws and regulations for Owen's review and headed down the street.

Sallie, his lovely assistant, nodded toward his office. "He's in. Would you like to see him?"

Owen still had a private law practice, but he mostly consulted with the town mayor and the board of supervisors on crafting laws that conformed to the Lord's statutes as proscribed by the overseers assigned to this region—what had once been the State of Colorado.

"Latest?" he asked, flashing his usual smile.

Charlene wondered if he struggled with what they were to become as much as she did. "Yes," she stepped forward and handed him the file with the thumb drive. The sideways tilt of his head communicated that he understood she could have emailed it. She had to admit she enjoyed their stimulating conversations about law, government, and how to frame justice through legislative dictates—a task harder than she had imagined.

"Have time to talk?"

Her fleece, she exhaled a breath. "Yes, The Watering Hole?"

"Freshest coffee."

"And best millennial fruit smoothies!"

"Pricey!" He laughed, set the papers to the side, and rose.

"We have time. They don't need them today. Check them over and send your assessment that I'll attempt to frame into an appropriate response for the mayor."

"Always the diplomat. Too bad your dad didn't run for mayor."

"Maybe when the current flurry of construction dwindles, and he gets bored. Believe me, the day will come."

"And he will have let the first mayor flounder so he can swoop in and save the day."

"Something like that. I suppose, even with the demons out of the way, we'll still have disagreements and problems. Guess that comes with being human."

"Someday you'll be in charge, Charlene."

She slid her eyes away and headed for the door.

The Watering Hole was a few blocks down and already the place to be in the mornings, lazy afternoons or in the evenings to listen to the music of a traveling band or choir. "I still get a thrill remembering last week's a cappella group singing the new Psalms of the Lord."

Owen added, "Why I am so looking forward to going to Jerusalem for the upcoming Feast—even if it is more than half a year away."

Charlene ordered her usual smoothie, a concoction of local fruits mixed with those from the trees that grew along the river emanating from the Temple that had healed the once-dead sea.[25]

They sat at a table overlooking the street. "Getting busier all the time," Owen noted.

Charlene gathered herself and met his gaze. "I had a dream." Everyone had dreams now—some more than others. She had ones many others also had of the joy of the coming kingdom and of the life of faith.

Owen waited.

She looked away again. "I dreamt about Asher."

Owen knew Asher's story. "I thought he was just a friend. I know he's lost, but…"

"I thought so too, but I can't forget him…" She took a sip. Not looking up, she continued, "I think I have to admit that I love him." She looked at Owen and added. "I don't know how he feels about me. By the time he disappeared, Thomas was acting really weird. I didn't leave him soon enough. Maybe if…but no matter. What happened, happened."

Owen reached over. "We tried all the lists here and at the capital. When we go to Jerusalem, you can check at the Registration Center. I believe they hold the records for all who entered the Kingdom. It's still too hard to search this far away—with the satellites not yet in place." The last war—Armageddon—had destroyed all the near-earth satellites. Local towers provided some service, but communicating with distant continents was hard. "In the meantime, you can go through those courses I sent to you."

Before he could take a breath and elaborate on his plan, Charlene looked at him. "Owen, what do you see me doing in the future?"

"Joining my team. As a former public defender and defense attorney, I assumed I had been rendered irrelevant. Then I realized I could serve a purpose as a law analyst along with providing legal counsel for contracts. Someone still has to help people get a fair shake. The business is only going to increase, and you have a mind for the law."

"I take that as a compliment since you've always stood for truth and justice."

"Yes, so go through the courses. The licensing process is simpler. You no longer need to have seven years of college."

"I'm not sure that's a direction I want to go," she blurted out. "I saw our home in Israel, south of Jerusalem. I was with our daughter, and Asher came home for supper."

"It was that sort of dream," Owen replied, tight-lipped.

She knew what he meant. Many dreams were vague or worshipful, but some were true visions or leadings. "I…"

"Got it. I know what you're capable of doing if God so led. With a good legal foundation, you could go far in government, but I accept we must follow His lead."

"Psalm 37—may the desires of my heart align with God's path for me."

Owen sighed and looked away. "I hope I receive a vision, a direction. Counting on that trip to Jerusalem."

They both nodded. Even in paradise it wasn't easy to find their way.

———

After work Charlene printed her completed missing person request for Jerusalem's Registration Office. The next day, she walked to the post office during her mid-morning break. Her heart tugged as she watched the envelope drop into the international bin.

That was it, then. She would find out—perhaps fears of learning he had died and was now a shining one had kept her from filing her request sooner. She shook her head, considering the other possibility. Terror of terrors if he had been a pretender like Thomas…perhaps he wasn't even alive. Turning from an instantaneous shudder, she paused by a growing oak tree.

It was as if she was back with their group huddling in the basement—Dad, Daniel, Asher and herself. Before the troubles grew even worse, before she had lost her father and had found Thomas. They were arguing about the order of events. It was still early in the seven years, and Asher pulled from passages in Ezekiel and Daniel—the great northern invasion. Dad settled the group down and patiently worked through the parts of Revelation that had already been literally fulfilled. However Asher continued his obsessive study of the last chapters of Ezekiel. He knew the Savior. *He had trusted Christ. The changes in him were evident every day—his morose darkness had turned into a quiet gentleness and care. He must be alive!*

"Charlene! Charlene! Where are you headed?" Owen said again as he drew near.

"I finally filed a request with the Jerusalem office to find Asher. Maybe I was afraid of what I would learn, but I have to know."

Owen nodded. "For the best."

▶4

Asher caught up on his sleep. Elchanan's nearly empty house was a pleasant refuge from the busier streets. Awakening long before daylight, Asher stepped around the wall to a terraced patio with low walls. The house and courtyard were near the southeast corner—not far from Dan's Gate. He stepped through to the farms and gardens east of the city. A narrow trail, twisting its way down to the next terrace led to a grassy common area with benches, olive trees, ornamental bushes, and beds of flowers.

He welcomed the dimness of a new moon, reciting a few new Psalms he had just learned. Growth was evident everywhere. Some trees seemed to grow as fast as the bushes. Looking at the verdant gardens, who could have imagined that after Armageddon it had been a barren wasteland. For a month he had observed the growth shortly after he had arrived while working on the Temple's western wall. Now, it was Eden restored, and his heart tried to imagine his part in the new world.

Usually, he made his way back and slept in—Zamira calling him "lazy one" with the mischievous tone of an eight year old. But a settled tiredness from a good day's work of retiling a roof the day before took over, and he wedged himself at the base of a tree. The fire by night rose up with a sound like the rush of angels' wings and scents of lavender, lilac, peony and other varieties he could not name.

He walked beside a flowing river, rather small, but more than a stream. Knowing it ran year around, he spied an orchard on the right, stretching for miles—of all types and kinds of trees. On the rise, in the distance a town flowed across the land, with terraced gardens, courtyards and natural amphitheaters. In one, a rabbi recited from the book of the New Covenant. A small group listened, asked questions, and discussed the law of the Spirit of life. As if he were present, he found himself by a small group listening to a singer lead the songs of faith. Peace, joy, and vibrant life filled his heart.

The sound of a branch breaking, and the first rays of the sun collapsed the vision. Asher stirred. *Where was that place? What did it mean?*

He leaned forward, gathered his feet underneath him, and greeted the gardener approaching with a cloth bag and pruning shears. "Shalom!" he called out the standard greeting.

"*Shalom aleichem,*" the woman answered—"Peace be unto you. Early admirer?"

Asher laughed. "It is most beautiful in the light of the pillar by night."

"Ahh, God's peace rest upon you," she said, continuing her way down the path.

Once she was out of sight, he retraced his steps, now well-known from many nights of wandering. *Wandering. Where am I going? Where am I heading?* He resisted thinking of the rest of the questions. Today, he had work, and they needed him early. He could not be late. Also, he could not lose control. Three weeks he had been with Elchanan and Zamira, and they let him know he could stay for as long as he liked and could return anytime.

Elchanan was at his glass table on the lower patio. "Sleep well in the Garden of Dreams?"

Casting a sideways glance, he nodded and sat down on the white iron chair filigreed with vines. "Garden of dreams?"

"Many have visions there. But no matter if one does not come. He chooses when they come."

"How do you tell the difference?"

"Sometimes it's clear—as if you are walking in future days—a vision. Other times, they express our heart's desire, inner longings or deepest fears. Do you dream?"

"I do, sometimes they're not dark like the nightmares. The dreams from the Lord feel different. You're right."

"And of your nightmares?" Elchanan probed.

Asher looked at him for a moment. "You've changed. You're not pushing me to find a wife and settle down. What happened?"

Smiling, he shook his head. "A wise doctor of the law and the prophets reminded me that the Lord is patient and kind; waiting for those like you to be willing to come."

"Like me? What do you mean?"

Elchanan cleared his throat. "It was nothing."

"No, do you mean there are other wanderers who can't find their place?" Seeing the quiet assent, he nodded back. "I think I met some at the Hamonah graveyards, just before they let me go. It's as if we knew not to ask about each other's plans. No one talked of their land, home or family. So, your friend, what did he say is the answer?"

"Some will find their way…in time. Some must see the Lord Himself for healing."

Asher pushed his chair back, gnawing on his lower lip. *Why am I afraid? Why do I turn away, cling to sorrow, and wrap myself in misery?*

Elchanan's soft voice broke through. "He said in time you will be ready and when you are, you have a welcome here. You do not walk alone."

Asher nodded. They both turned hearing Zamira's call for breakfast. "So, tell me of today's job."

Asher settled the bricks in the heavy canvas bag slung over his shoulder. Grasping the railing, he climbed up the ladder to the second-story roof and walked confidently to the broken chimney at the far end. The old bricks had been cleared and carried down the day before. Settling the bag on a flat wooden table perched over the rooftop, he stacked the bricks in neat piles. The mortar was in place as well and he worked, brick by brick.

The wife called the family to the midday meal, and he knew it would be an insult to his host to keep on working and refuse the hospitality. He scrambled down and followed their two children through the door. The floor had new tile, the wiring had been updated, but the simple butcher-block table could have been made by Joseph, Jesus' earthly father.

The boy was six and his sister four. It had taken Asher a while to get used to children again, but it shouldn't have surprised him. They had been born during the Tribulation and had entered the kingdom as innocents. He studied the earnest face of the precocious boy who asked many questions.

Uriah was a Levitical lawyer—well versed in the law and the prophets. He knew the first covenant, what had been called the Old Testament, had mastered the second, the former New Testament, and had been taught the meaning of the New Covenant from the King and His priests as it was revealed each month.

After the prayer, Asher asked his question: "So, are the sacrifices only memorials or if they are for atonement, what about our Lord's death on the cross and resurrection?"

"They do not pay our sin debt. Only the sacrifice of the Just One can do that. But they are not memorials or reminders…" He cast his eyes on his children. "While they are a good visual of the price of our salvation…" He shushed his young son. "We are saved sinners with bodies touched by the curse of sin. Even though most of the curse has been rolled back, the curse-stain of sin remains. For our Lord to dwell with us on this earth, the area and worshipers must be cleansed, covered to make atonement, that we might worship before Him. Otherwise, our sin-stain would defile the Temple when we enter. So, we bring our sacrifice. Do you remember?"

The children nodded, their eyes shining. "They were so bright."

"Yes, they saw some shining ones with the priests. They say the priests' faces glowed when they left the Temple."

"But surely we do not need to have them wear a veil—not like with Moses."

"Yes. But we must be ceremonially cleansed to enter the Temple and meet with Christ. Also, the cleansing is for Israel and the nations."

"I helped build the outer wall," Asher said, his voice soft with memory. He looked at the couple. "Do you find it hard to draw near to the King?"

"A part of us remembers our flesh, but with the Spirit, we can." He would have said more, but he remembered to be patient. "To make atonement is to make reconciliation for men."

"He is our peace. When we have Christ, we have peace with God." Asher nodded. "When we wrapped the recovered bones in consecrated cloth to take them to the burial site, that was to stop the defilement."

"And what was your burial prayer?" the son asked.

Asher repeated it. Looking at the children, he explained, "Only God is the giver of life. Only God has the right to take life. His judgments are just, righteous and merciful. *'Vengeance is mine,'*[26] says the Lord. We must remember that when we see the pits of destruction." Though they were mostly cleared, some still remained.

"For the Father judges no one, but has given all judgment to the Son. And he has given him authority to execute judgment, because he is the Son of Man. He is the one appointed by God to be judge of the living and the dead."[27] Uriah quoted the verses with a distant look in his eye. He cast loving eyes on his children. "For the Son of Man came and paid

our ransom that we might be one with Him, with God the Father and His Holy Spirit."

All nodded.

After the moment passed, Asher said, "Thank you for the meal. I should be finished soon." He rose with a nod to excuse himself.

Asher ascended the simple ladder and walked to the chimney, kneeling by the rising column of bricks, to measure out the top and lay in the grid to keep out unwanted intruders. The fields below him, out of focus in his peripheral vision, stretched out. A distant hawk's cry pierced the air.

The valley below, gutted and still smoking from an attack the day before, was still apart from a small group emerging from a steel building. A tall, black youth walked deliberately with his hands bound behind him. Asher winced when a guard's shock stick drove Daniel to one knee. Another wrenched him up by the arm, and they walked to the guillotine. Frozen, Asher watched, unable to turn away.

As he grasped the chimney tightly, the sharp edges of the bricks cut his hands. Burying the memory, he blinked, focused, and looked at the buildings on a lower street. He was in Jerusalem. The time of terror was past. Repeating some verses, he worked at stilling his breath, trying to stop the shaking of his hands.

Deliberately, he looked only at the work in front of him. If only he could live in the world that he had seen the night before.

Not taking the time to rest or pause, he completed the chimney and brought everything down before Uriah could assist with clearing the roof.

"Done already, Asher?" Uriah asked.

The man's six-year-old son stood nearby, staring at him wide-eyed. "How did you learn to do that?"

Asher forced a smile. "When I was in the States, I helped build houses on the slopes of the Rocky Mountains. The lots were too steep and fragile for heavy equipment, so we had to bring up everything ourselves. The work made me strong."

The boy felt his tanned arm and giggled. "Can I learn to do that?"

"Of course. Learn the building trades, and maybe someday you can repair the Temple or its walls."

"Did you work on the Temple?"

"I did in the beginning."

He shook Uriah's hand, gathered his items. *It was too close to have an attack in the city.*

"Come to our midweek fellowship time. We would love to have you."

He had attended a few weeks ago but found it hard to concentrate. Shrugging his shoulders, he mumbled, "Perhaps. We'll see."

Zamira was busy in the kitchen, and Elchanan was working at the power authority office. Asher left the borrowed tools in the storage room, walked up the stairs, and stuffed his few items in a backpack. Hovering by the bed, he retrieved his journal, pulled out a page, wrote a brief note and left it on the nightstand. One part of him reasoned he didn't want to make trouble, but he knew that was a smokescreen. He couldn't be working on roofs or scaffoldings in the city if the attacks that so overwhelmed his senses continued. He would be putting others at risk. He prayed they would understand that he had no other choice.

Asher headed out of the city gate to the gardens. He paused at the dreaming tree. One part of him longed for release, but the feeling that he would never recover could not be shaken.

▶5

Asher headed north on the highway until he was well past the Temple district. He walked quickly for hours—not risking a stop or thinking or considering other options. After weeks of hoping and praying he could be normal, he had nearly lost it on a pastor's rooftop. If not for the solid chimney, he might have fallen to the lower levels of the city.

He shook his head to clear his thoughts, focusing on distant points. Asher followed the highway north until well past Isaac's village and took the next trek west toward the ocean with no destination in mind.

The next day, out of water and hungry, Asher paused at a crossroad to read the signposts. Tel-Aviv lay to his left. He turned east toward a small village, New Rosh Hayin, not far from the road. Asher found the public water tap and filled his canteens in the square. It was midmorning already.

Slaking his thirst, he sat on a bench and brought out one of Zamira's bagels. Rebuilding Jerusalem and the areas around it had taken priority. Asher gazed at the shells of concrete and steel denuded of siding, windows and doors. The main road was clear and new construction could be seen, but areas he surmised that had once been filled with homes were now sporting tall grasses, but without thorns or thistles.[28]

Some carts drawn by horse or donkey shared the two-lane road with small cars or straight trucks. Piles of fuel and kindling from the great war occupied lots across the street.[29] Most vehicles had been converted with fusion generators, but some gas- or diesel-powered vehicles still existed—mostly heavy construction equipment.

He turned his head to see a man driving a one-horse cart with a large plastic water tank.

"Shalom," the man said, slowing as they approached the water station. "Hold Chaika?"

Asher nodded, clucked soothingly, and patted the shoulders. "*Chaika*—life," he said with a soft voice. He drew the horse forward and to the side to help bring the fill hose closer to the connection.

"Like horses?"

"Some, but I liked my Chamor." Patting Chaika absentmindedly. "Sometimes I had to keep my donkey from following me like a dog."

"Well, this one's a wanderer." The man hooked up the hose and waited for it to fill. "Caleb, and you're?"

"Asher."

"Not from around here? More come through every day, but most head for the city."

"Coming back?"

"Oh, I don't know. Different reasons. What brings you here?"

"Passing through, but always looking for work."

"If you can handle horses… Drive a team?"

"Not really, but I can learn. Know how to tack and clean out the hooves. Have done construction here and there."

"Where?"

"Started in Jerusalem, but…"

"Yeah, time to move on. Day work, depending. Not always regular."

"Place to rent a room?"

The man nodded toward the far road lined with businesses and buildings. "Yep, good kitchens too. Unless you cook?"

Asher laughed. "I don't even try."

"Okay, you've got a job."

—⁓—

Work kept him busy. Everyone was trying to complete as many projects as possible before the rains came. After a brief visit to Tel Aviv, he continued heading north to Haifa before turning inland. The eastern plains of the northern section given to Dan stretched out for miles with tall grasses, olive groves and growth following streets and rivers.

He paused on a rise, imagining how wonderful the plains must look to those who had experienced the destruction of the armies. Perhaps in the stillness, he could find healing and rejoin humanity. Somedays it seemed he was better, but then an attack would come out of nowhere. The worst one had been in a small village south of Haifa when he had relived a flashback in a crowd. When he came to himself, he tried to reassure them, but he could see the fear in their eyes.

He ran to the safety of the wilderness, found a hollow and huddled against the colder weather. The chill he felt wasn't even close to the frigid cold of the higher elevations of the Rockies, but he had become so acclimated to the warmer climate, it felt brutally cold. *Where can I go? What should I do? I am alone.*

Trying to warm his hands over a small fire, he was unable to forget Isaac's cozy home or Zamira's welcoming kitchen. Asher cried out to God. *Lord, I can't exist like this! Why is there no place for me?*

The answer came—this was his choice.

But, Lord, why can't I forget?

The Holy Spirit whispered that he held onto the past like a starving man clutching a loaf of bread.

Your way! I surrender, Lord. Lead me! He wanted to promise he would obey but doubted his own ability to stand against his wall of fear.

The heat of the small fire finally warmed him, and his eyelids drooped. Sleep came—a short time of escape.

Moonlight shone upon him, and he stirred for the first time after many hours. The night animals and crickets sounded a soothing lullaby, but from habit, his mind was awake. *Okay, Lord, where You lead.*

He packed his bag, rose, shouldered the pack, and waited. The light of the moon began shining on a road running northeast. Feeling nothing else, he began to walk. One part of him was disappointed God had not sent a clear vision with directions. He held back his laugh. *God, You don't work that way.* It almost seemed as if he were to wander, so he did—from small village or a gathering of houses to the next, helping here and there.

As if frozen in time—neither going forward or back—he walked, seeking what he did not know.

—⁓—

The simple one-room house had been created out of spare pieces and parts. A person with old eyes emerged and shared his simple meal. Asher brought out the last of his cakes from one of the larger villages. After the sup and sipping tea, the host brought out a rough journal and pulled out worn pages.

Asher leaned forward. "Another Division or a Psalm?"

"Division." After saying his opening prayer of covering, he glanced at Asher. Seeing the expectant nod, he read, his Hebrew melodic with a cantor's rhythm.

Asher answered back with similar divisions.

They let the last syllable die away, savoring God's Word. "He does not leave us blind, with no knowledge of what He does," he said.

Asher nodded, "He teaches us as friends, not servants; children, not aliens or strangers."[30]

"Will you rest here a while?"

Overcome with fear that he would descend into another attack or vision, hesitant to shelter, he heard himself say, "I wander...I do not know where. I try to turn from what happened to the future, but I cannot find my way."

He saw the man nod.

"Peace be unto you. You are welcome to stay inside. There is a sweet stream behind the house and soft grasses in the glen."

"What do I seek? Why is there no place?"

"Only you can answer that." He met his gaze. "But you do not wander alone. The Holy Spirit is waiting for you to let Him in."

Asher sat up. "I hold Him aside?" Seeing the nod, he searched within himself. "Charlene." He added, "I fear she is lost to me forever." His eyes mirrored what he could not say aloud—how could he survive the Millennium without her by his side?

The man's gaze bore into his soul. "He is our all in all."

"He is our all in all." Asher lowered his head praying, pleading with the Lord to help him.

"Lay it down at His feet."

Asher nodded. Naked before God, he could not argue, bargain, or justify how he had treated his friends. Tears ran down his cheeks.

His host extended his hand.

Asher felt the joy and peace that came so seldom and seemed so fleeting.

"Soon, He will call you back. Until then, go your way."

Unmasked the angel released his hand, stood, and faced him before he disappeared.

His eyes opened and refreshed somehow; Asher saw light shimmering down the left road. Lifting his pack, he resumed his journey.

Cresting a rise, he surveyed the plain before him in the dim moonlight. For the first time, he felt almost settled, wanted—his breath froze—sought out. He remembered the Good Shepherd who had left His flock to find the lost lamb. He was that lamb. How God loved him. Tears forming, Asher knelt and thanked the Lord, confessing his stubbornness and rebellion.

What had the angel said? He was to go his way until Christ called him back. If *back* was Jerusalem, going forward led north.

6

CHARLENE READ THE letter from Jerusalem, her hand shaking. Slipping it back into her purse, she could hardly wait to show it to her father and Vera at the evening fellowship.

Owen met her on the corner. "Charlene? What happened?"

Holding her breath, she pulled out the letter and watched her friend read it. His eyes shone. "I'm thrilled for you. He's alive, but…"

Charlene nodded. "He's missing! How is that possible?"

"We have our missing here…" Owen began, but she seemed distracted.

"How can I wait now until the feast? It's two months away!"

"I'll go with you…" Owen offered, then added, "If you don't mind."

"That would be great." She turned, thinking of her schedule and what the new mayor would say. "I haven't told Dad yet."

"Understood. Mum's the word." He nodded toward the city offices.

"I'm going, no matter what."

"If he won't change your leave time…"

"I'll resign. It would be a relief, actually."

Owen nodded. He had had his own spats with the new mayor who seemed to be set on dragging the town back into the past. "I think we both need some perspective from New Colorado."

Distracted with submitting her leave request and thrashing over what to wear, Charlene arrived at the fellowship shortly after it had started. Slipping into a seat near Owen, close to Vera and her father, she could only nod. The news had to wait.

After the final prayer and song, holding hands, Gary leaned across and lifted his brow. "What's the surprise?"

"Dad, you know me too well." Charlene laughed.

"Did the mayor promote you to recreation supervisor?" Laughing, he shook his head when she gave him a hard look. "I almost regret not running, but then, after seeing who they picked…" He shrugged his shoulders with a smile.

They had recently wed, and Vera clasped her husband's hand. "We have news too."

"Shall we?" Owen suggested. They knew their favorite place.

"Not the Walnut tonight. Our place, and Vera has the nacho fixings ready."

"My, it must be good news! Not a word?" She laughed and followed Owen to his car.

She settled back in her parents' new home—built for many children if the Lord so provided. She remembered that discussion. It had taken little time for her to call Vera "Mom," but she still shared her heart's desires sparingly.

She followed Vera into the family room with wide sofas and slide-rocker chairs, carrying the aromatic tray of Vera's super nachos. Gary barely waited for Owen to finish saying grace before he said, "I…" he held his wife's hand. "*We* have won a land claim southwest of here."

Nearly falling out of her chair, Charlene looked incredulously at them. "And I thought you were going to announce that a baby was on the way."

"We'll have time for that, but the way things are going in town, I realized I don't have a lot keeping me here." He held Vera's hand. "A new place for new beginnings. There's a whole continent to explore and discover. New, remade, reborn. So, your news?"

Charlene pulled out the letter. She met her father's gaze. "Asher is in Israel. They say he has land in the southern Zebulun territory, but they don't know exactly where he is right now." She glanced at Owen. "You mentioned others are missing?"

"Mankind has longed for paradise on earth—a utopia where everything is going to be fine. Now we have it and some, realizing they're going to live for one thousand years, well, the thought can be intimidating."

Vera leaned forward. "I think some can't quite forget what they went through—that they survived or who they lost."

"More than that," Gary added, "Without a vision, the people perish. In the past we had something to fight against. You know many reasoned that man was not designed for paradise."

"Not sinful man, but in Christ, we can thrive in utopia." Owen looked at them. "I will go with Charlene to Jerusalem to help her search for Asher. I was thinking of asking to see the Christ for a life vision. I love the law and thought practicing it as I used to would be enough, but now I find it as unsatisfying as being a public defender. No, I need direction from the Lord Himself. We'll meet you there at the feast."

7

THE LAND FOR the tribe of Dan lay along the northern border with Syria. Asher walked the Highway of Holiness to the border overlooking the plains of the neighboring nation. He gazed at a region not separated by guard towers, barbed-wire fences and machine guns. *"In that day there will be an altar to the Lord in the midst of the land of Egypt, and a pillar to the Lord at its border."*[31] The Lord's pillar marked the entrance into Syria as well. Peace truly reigned.

A reception center straddling the border flew the Egyptian, Israeli and Syrian flags. People could walk through the good-sized hexagonal building right into the other country. He stepped through and onto Syrian soil. A small group made its way up the road and called out greetings in Hebrew with an Aramaic accent.

"Shalom aleichem," he answered.

The three men and two women gathered round him. "Are you of Israel?"

"I am of Zebulun."

"Have you seen the Temple?"

"Yes, for a time I worked on the outer wall."

"Is it finished? We can see the Lord, yes?"

"Yes, the Levites will guide you through the cleansing and offering for an audience. Many in Jerusalem teach the law of God and explain what it means for us today."

"But what of the bones?" A man held up a small tracker. "It is said that if we see a bone, we are to put on this thing." He waved it.

"Most of the bones have been found. You do not have to look for them. If you do stumble on one because they sometimes work their way above ground, set it on the highest nearby spot and activate it. Place it firmly so it doesn't wash away, or we could have a hard time finding the marker."

"Are you a burier?"

"I was. But now only a few bones are left. Most of the sections have been cleansed." Asher answered their many questions.

Ending with suggestions for places he could visit in Syria, Asher nodded and thanked them. He walked to the nearest diner, drinking in the rolling hills with fields and growing trees. The country was thriving—just like Israel.

Asher returned to the reception center and headed to the nearest Israeli job center. Pausing, he registered for the first time—during his journey north he had not needed to register but had found odd jobs by asking for work. Scrolling the possibilities, he printed the directions and information for a road-building company needing equipment operators.

Asher headed south on the main road, surveying the empty grasslands pockmarked by clumps of mostly destroyed buildings with piles of the invading army's wreckage. *They will burn the fuel from equipment of the invading armies for seven years.*[32] Past a little village to his left, a newly created gravel road headed east. *Did only a few from the tribe of Dan survive? Probably most are living along the coast.* He wondered about the people who once inhabited that region but remembered that during Armageddon and the Second Coming, the topography of the planet had been reshaped. Checking the map provided with the directions, he turned to the east and followed a road, changing from gravel to dirt to barely being graded.

Asher rounded a bend and spied a spare office trailer sitting by itself by the edge of the road. Surveyors' markers laid out a road charting a course through the eastern section of Dan's territory. No one answered his knock, and the door was locked.

Shifting his pack, he headed down the partially graded road. In time he could hear the intermittent sounds of heavy machinery.

Harsh voices filtered over the hum of engines in neutral. Asher couldn't make out the words. A large man with broad shoulders and thick legs leaned into a slender man standing by a grader. "You made this section too low, and that one too high. Look at the dip. Where's the crown?"

They argued back and forth until the worker stomped off. He paused by Asher. "Looking for work? Watch out. He'll cheat you any way he can!"

The large man swung up into the cab of the grader and parked it by the side of the road. He scrambled down and looked at Asher. "What do you want?"

"Still hiring?"

"What do you think? Have experience?"

"Did some grading at Hamonah."

"For the burial pits?"

"Yeah."

"That's it? I need experienced road builders." The man rubbed his chin, sizing up Asher and the unfinished road. "But…" He swung his head around. "We can settle up at the end of the day at the office." He stepped closer to Asher. "Agreed?"

Seeing Asher's nod, he gestured for him to follow him to his truck to go over the plans. Kish demonstrated the controls for the bulldozer, grader and compacter. "We're laying down a good base. Here, the ground is solid and doesn't need any additives. I'll let you know when we need to add stabilizers if the soil has too much clay. To raise up the low spots Michael created, bring over some loads from the dump truck, grade and compact until we have a good roadway with proper crowning."

They walked the section, and Asher bent down to feel the dirt. "Seems softer here. Probably why it dipped under grading."

Kish nodded. "Compact it, add a few loads. Keep at it until it's right."

Asher worked the section, found Kish, listened to his instructions, and repeated the process until he declared it good enough. The sun was already setting, and Asher wondered how he would see with the moon not set to rise for a while.

"That's it for the day. Jump in, and we'll head back to the office."

The makeshift trailer had a folding table with two benches in the front that doubled as the office. A mini-kitchen ran down the right side and a toilet/shower was on the left. Four bunks occupied the back of the trailer.

Kish reached for a box on the far bench and pulled out a contract. "50 shekels a day with room and board. Flat rate. Your first day was half, so you'll get 25 for today." He entered the date, starting times and pushed it to Asher across the table. "Write your name, district you're from and sign it. That indicates your acceptance of the contract. Any questions?"

Asher entered his information and signed it. The pay wasn't bad, but not great either. However, it would keep him busy.

"Zebulun, huh? That's a long way to go. You want to bunk here?" Seeing Asher's nod, he added, "Okay, pull out the beans. Cooked rice is in the fridge, and the canned vegetables are in the cupboard." Seeing Asher's blank stare, he added, "Go on. It won't cook itself."

Kish turned to his paperwork he pulled from his box. He read while Asher stumbled his way through the kitchen finding pots, utensils and dishes.

They said little while they ate. When Asher pulled out his copy of the latest divisions of the New Covenant, Kish looked at him. "What? You a priest?"

"No, all need to hear the Word of the Lord."

"Well, don't read it to me. I know all I need to know."

Seeing his closed face, Asher put his pack on the farthest bunk and exited out the back door with his Bibles. The moon was up. Finding a good spot, he settled down to stare at the hills, thinking through what he had read. To live in this world so different from the life he had known took time to understand.

—∿∿—

They reached the worksite just as the sun peaked over the horizon. Asher was glad he had slept the night before. His nighttime wanderings would have to be put on hold. Pulling down a cap to shield his eyes from the sun, he walked to the tailgate where Kish had the maps spread out.

"Now, can't be slow like yesterday," Kish said in introduction for the day. He pointed to the shallow valley created by two rises on either side. "I'll bulldoze the first cut. We have a deadline, so bring it to grade, but don't take forever."

Asher figured it wouldn't be wise to argue that the boss also wanted it done right. "I'll do the best I can. In the end, getting it right the first time will be faster than redoing a rush job. I will get faster at it—but how long it takes also depends upon the land." He didn't wait for Kish to spout his retort but went to the bulldozer and scooped the first load for the bed.

It didn't take long for Kish's bulldozer to disappear around a bend. When Asher finally caught up, he could see the boss far in the distance. By midday Kish drove the bulldozer back and began to leave piles for Asher to grade. They worked well together, or so he had thought as there were only a few places where he had to regrade.

"Better be faster tomorrow," was all Kish said on the drive back to the trailer. "Next week we'll move the trailer closer to the jobsite. By then we have to have it done for the gravel mix. That's coming in five days."

Asher nodded. He glanced at Kish, hoping he didn't have to cook again, but the man ordered him to heat up the same food they ate yesterday.

While they ate, Asher asked, "Are you of Dan?"

"What's it to you, Zebie?"

Biting his tongue, Asher shrugged. "No family?"

The string of resulting curse words slapped Asher in the face.

"I don't have any family either." He finished his meal as quickly as possible, did the dishes and disappeared into the night. The sliver of a waxing crescent moon was gone, and he welcomed the darkness. He pulled his blanket from his pack, recited some verses, and curled up for sleep.

—◦—

Kish was sullen, morose, difficult and impossible to please. Asher found ways to keep as much distance as possible from the man. He wanted to flee, but the Lord held him there. Awakened in the early hours, he slipped out to survey the shadows of scrubby olive and oak trees barely larger than shrubs. It seemed as if Kish had placed the trailer in the most barren, ugliest spot.

Why am I here? Why do You keep me with him?

Asher turned, hearing the gurgling of the small river nearby. From what had God rescued him? Could he not help this one? The idea stunned him. It didn't seem like he had made any kind of impression on the miserable fellow.

But what else would I do? If I just exist to survive? He turned to view the dim hulk of the trailer. *Life is more than food and clothes. You will supply my needs. If this is Your plan for me, You will have to show me how.*

The selfishness of his life flashed before him. *How else can I work past my memories if not by turning to help others?*

—◦—

Kish pushed to complete as much road as possible. Asher didn't dare ask why. The day before the Sabbath, he knew he had to seek fellowship. At the end of the day as they sat at the table, he stated, "I'll take a day tomorrow to go to town to worship God and pray with other believers." The words died away. He marveled that he had spoken to the man as if he did not believe—but he must; he was a resident of the kingdom.

Kish responded with curses.

"Then I will request my pay."

"Pay? I don't owe you anything!"

"But you promised 50 a day!"

"That covers your room and board."

"You said **with** room and board."

"That's not what the contract you signed stipulates." He turned as if to pull it out.

"Don't bother. I see you never intended on paying me. Why, I should charge you for cooking, cleaning, hauling water and fixing your equipment. How about that?"

"All part of *work*," Kish replied, his voice cold.

Asher rose, packed his bags and left. The rainy season had started, and clouds blocked the moon's light. "Great! Just when I need to see at night, it's dark!" Shutting down the curse words forming in his mind, he trudged on. A brief flash of lightning before the rumble of thunder urged him forward. He did his best to quicken his pace but failed to find any shelter before the heavy rains started.

Asher gathered his jacket around him, pulled down his cap, tucked his pack under his arm and walked, head hunched into his shoulders. The cold rain sent shivers along his spine. Eventually, he made out clumps of bushes not far ahead. He stepped to the tangle of thin trunks and sparse bushes and crouched down in a small hollow. Sitting on a pile of branches, he waited out the storm. Thankfully, the thunder and lightning had already passed.

The next day was not as bright with thick, heavy clouds. His first rainy season he had had the luxury of shelter and warm meals at

Hamonah. The town should be close. He prayed that walking would warm him a little.

The small town by the main road in the sector had not yet erected a sign. Asher could not recall having even heard their name on the one shopping trip he had made with Kish. He did remember the location for the worship center on a side road halfway down the main street.

Asher heard singing before he reached the short street. Various autos and small trucks filled the parking slots in front and along the main street. He stepped past to the sheltered lean-to for the horses and donkeys. Knowing that he drew closer to fellowship warmed his heart.

Asher stepped onto the raised sidewalk and headed for the door in the middle of the side of the town's printing and newspaper building. He stepped inside and stood along the back wall until his clothes stopped dripping.

"Shalom," a tall man greeted as he approached.

"Shalom," Asher replied not meeting his embrace. "I'm still wet from walking."

"Anyone with you?" The man furrowed his brow. "You're with Kish?"

Asher shook his head. "I walked all night." With the New Covenant the Sabbath was the day of rest worldwide, but each area observed it differently. Some were observant, like this little village, with all shops closed and worked halted for 24 hours. Kish barely recognized the day, muttering that his competitor would still be working.

The man brought him a chair. A young woman offered a cloth for him to dry his head and shoulders. Another approached with the First and Second Testament readings, along with the month's division and Psalm.

"Thank you," he said softly, touched by the warm generosity and fellowship. At first, he followed the hymns, some ancient, some only a century old, along with one he had never heard before. It sounded Jewish with hints of Spanish classical guitar and Celtic melodies. The words sank into his soul of the new time, the new life, the new way now that Messiah ruled from His throne in Jerusalem.

Life enveloped him with the Spirit's love, warming him from his center. Hope rose and the joy spread until he could hardly wait to see what God would do next. Where would he go? What was he to do? However, his time for walking north was done. The time had come to head south on the Highway of Holiness.

A cantor began, "Oh, how He loves you and me. Oh, how He loves you and me. He gave His life, what more could He give? Oh, how He loves you. Oh, how He loves me. Oh, how He loves you and me."[33] They sang as one through each of the stanzas. The earlier ones, from the time before, spoke of the Savior's sacrifice and resurrection. The new ones spoke of His coming to dwell with His people.

The teaching pastor rose and began the words for the remembrance, the bread and the cup. They passed the halal bread and a wine goblet. Each tore off a piece and took a sip. All stood for the division of the coming, with the hallelujah songs of praise. "Complete, God with us. Our hope we see fulfilled before our eyes."

The assembly had an additional song of praise for God's Word that poured forth from Jerusalem to cover the world. *"For the earth shall be full of the knowledge of the LORD as the waters cover the sea. For the earth will be filled with the knowledge of the glory of the LORD as the waters cover the sea."*[34] Without a break, the cantor sang praises from Psalm 136. *"Give thanks to the LORD, for he is good,"* he sang. The people sang in reply, *"for his steadfast love endures forever."*

The leader sang out each of the original verses and without stopping, continued onto the new verses that spoke of the light of the Lord that destroyed the wicked nations, that cast down powers and principalities, that shattered the hold of sin and death to bring in an age of truth and justice. *"For his steadfast love endures forever,"* they sang in response to each couplet. "For his steadfast love endures forever."

Asher sang with them as one. He knew he had a purpose and a life and a hope. The details were blurry; the path unseen, but he could feel it just beyond his mortal sight. At the end, he glanced to his right at a young woman with an infant in her arms and a toddler by her side. She pulled a handkerchief from her pocket and wiped away the tears, just as Asher had done.

The teaching pastor urged them to sit. He began to speak of the power of love above all. *"If I speak with the tongues of men and of angels, but have not love, I am a noisy gong or a clanging cymbal. And if I have prophetic powers, and understand all mysteries and all knowledge, and I have all faith, so as to remove mountains, but have not love, I am nothing."*[35]

Asher listened to the familiar verses. As he hoped, the pastor continued with the new verses on love given last year by the King of kings Himself. That love Asher knew. That love he remembered. That love he felt, sitting in a plastic chair in the back of a simple room set aside each Sabbath for worship.

With many buildings still not finished, it doubled as a seamstress's shop. Asher stared, unfocused on the worktables pushed to the side and the covered sewing machines. Hearing about forgiveness, he tried to keep his focus on the preacher. Forgiveness he had received. Forgiveness he needed to extend to another.

The pastor moved past that rabbit trail to his main points concerning God's love before wrapping it up. The cantor ended with announcements about the upcoming Sabbath trip to the Temple the week before the feast. "We will go a week before as those from many nations will be coming. However," he described their midweek trip where they could take part in the festivities.

A woman who sat beside him rose. "All are welcome to join our lunch. God bless you!"

Asher hung back, but a couple approached and introduced themselves. "Are you with Kish?"

"Not any longer. I worked for him for a while." He paused but decided not to spread bad news about the man. "Anyway, I need work. I'm out of money."

"Did he pay you?" the man asked.

"No, he lied about the terms of the contract, and I didn't bother to read it."

"Not unexpected with that one. The third man on the right is the magistrate. File a claim with him."

"He tricked me. Like I said, I don't think I have a case."

"Things are different now. The Lord's judges can decide in your favor if he was deceptive. But you can't win if you don't file."

Asher shifted, staring off into a corner. He could not forget the message he had just heard—God's love and forgiveness. *Do You ask this of me? To forgive him?* He knew his burden of sin that God had released was far greater than a few weeks' wages.

He straightened. "As the Lord has forgiven me, I think He is calling me to forgive that man." Asher recited, *"Put on then, as God's chosen ones, holy and beloved, compassionate hearts, kindness, humility, meekness, and patience, bearing with one another and, if one has a complaint against another, forgiving each other, as the Lord has forgiven you, so you also must forgive."*[36]

A man standing to his left said, "It's time we dealt with Kish."

"The Lord wants me to forgive him and release his debt to me." He could not escape the argument that swirled around him. Pausing, he said, "Even in these times, we must love one another. Can we not find a way to show him our love? Christ loves him. He paid his sin debt, and Kish must have accepted that free gift or he would not be with us."

"They're all mean, stingy men!"

"There are others?"

"He has a brother. They even hate each other. That's why he is alone. He's trying to grab his brother's road contract with the territory."

"So that's why he works as if the demons were nipping at his heels."

"And they are. Bitter family!" a man spat.

"And yet we now live in the Kingdom with righteous judges and our God to direct our leaders. Does that mean we don't have to extend love to one another? How else will we witness the beauty of faith to our children, grandchildren and their grandchildren?"

"He's right," the group leader said. "But it's hard to love difficult people."

"I know." Asher stepped back, thinking. "Perhaps we have a hard time going forward because we have not forgiven those who harmed us in the past?" He met their gaze. "Perhaps, more than ever, to live in the new life, we must choose to live by the new life of Christ?"

Many nodded. Asher turned back to the line. He joined a lively family of five along with a couple and a few singles. He basked in the warm fellowship.

The cantor and his young wife who appeared ready to give birth, approached Asher as he was getting ready to leave. "I heard what you said about Kish and showing kindness to those who are not easy to love. Right now, we can't imagine the nations turning against our Savior, but it is in the Scriptures."

Asher nodded. "Before many doubted that what we have seen, as the Word predicted, would come to pass. But here we are. The heart of man, even with God can drift to sin, even without a corrupt world system." He extended his hand, but the man stepped forward and hugged him.

"Complete the Sabbath with us."

"Thank you. That would be a blessing." He hugged the young wife, holding her hand a little longer. "So young to have gone through such terrible times." She looked barely out of her teens.

"We sheltered in Petra. God was kind and merciful."

"Do you know Elchanan and Zamira? They're good friends of mine."

"Yes, were you there?"

"No, I was in the United States—in the mountains. To see someone you called friend turn on you was hard. Glad your time was better, although I imagine it was not easy."

"It had its challenges, but to know His coming would be soon... The fig leaves had blossomed. The time had come. God's Word will never pass away."

"Amen," Asher replied.

———

Their fellowship was sweet. Along with the respite of a quiet home, Asher felt reborn. The next morning, he gathered his pack, a little heavier with gifts of bread and cheese. His canteens were full of sweet water. The husband slipped some shekels into his hand.

"Thank you. You are living love to me. May God guide you in loving others. Maybe we will meet someday in Jerusalem."

"In Jerusalem."

Asher waved and headed back to Kish's worksite. He had no illusions about his reception, and he was not disappointed. Kish grumbled, swore and told him to get out of his face.

Happy to oblige, he continued south along the valley, musing over what had happened. Being with Kish had opened old wounds, and the anger that bubbled up bothered him.

Am I holding on to hate? Am I like Kish?

Asher could not forget the men who had tortured him at the center in Carbondale where Daniel had been killed. He had tried to work through forgiving and releasing the anger. Image after image surfaced until he remembered Thomas whom he could not forgive.

Mile after mile he walked, turning away from his exercise of inner reconciliation. As the rolling hills gave way to open plains, he saw the road-building equipment before he heard it. Drawing closer, he paused when a man resembling Kish but a little taller and slimmer, walked up to a worker to berate him harshly.

Asher turned east until he reached the Highway of Holiness and stood a distance off, feeling unworthy and unclean.

He found a good spot, sipped water and munched on a dry cake of nuts and figs. Distant, cold and aloof, his peace with God lay shattered in his heart. Now that he knew and understood what the Lord required, he began to argue. "How can You expect this of me? Haven't I suffered enough?"

The answer: *"In your struggle against sin, you have not yet resisted to the point of shedding your blood."*

Asher turned his head, squeezing his eyes closed. Rubbing his brow, he looked up. "I can't do this!"

He felt in his soul: *"You can't do this on your own."*

Perplexed, puzzled, tired, he rose and walked parallel to the road but not on it.

►8

AFTER TWO LONG weeks, Charlene and Owen boarded the plane to New York where they would transfer to the Jerusalem flight. Theirs was an overnight flight arriving in Israel shortly before noon the next day.

Charlene knew she had to sleep. She needed to sleep but doubted her swirling emotions would let her.

Once on their way, after supper and reading for a while, Charlene and Owen talked softly. Owen shared more of his hopes and dreams for the future. Charlene clutched the armrest. *Asher has to be alive.*

One by one, passengers turned off their overhead lights, and Owen produced a powder—a sleep aid—from one of the healing leaves. Charlene held out her cup of water, and Owen stirred in the powder.

"Thank you," seemed insufficient, and Owen's warm gaze stopped her blubbering. She smiled back. "You truly are a good friend."

Owen tried to joke, "Well, having friends in Israel is always a blessing. I can drop by whenever I want and stay a while." He laughed. "Teasing. Not sure I'd make this trip too often."

"How long are you staying?" Charlene watched him closely. She had resigned her position, pared down her few belongings and packed as if she would not return to New Colorado.

Owen shifted. "I took a month's leave. Something tells me I need to keep my options open."

She nodded and sipped the drink. It was different, slightly bitter, but with hints of pineapple, papaya and lemon.

"How does it taste?"

"Not bad. Good, actually." She glanced over. "You having some?"

"Saving mine for the trip home." He didn't need to add he'd probably be traveling alone. Shifting, they found the least uncomfortable positions and fell asleep.

—⁓—

Charlene roused from a midmorning nap when the plane banked. Breakfast had been filling and after reading a few pages, she had drifted into a light sleep. The low undercurrent of other's voices tinged with Owen's note-taking with his Bible study were hypnotically soothing.

—⁓—

"The land of Zebulun of Tamara, the garden of the south," a voice called. Charlene glanced at the guide welcoming a group emerging from a bus. Pausing, she waited to greet them…

—⁓—

"Charlene," Owen touched her arm. "The Temple Mount."

Shaking her head to remember where she was, she shifted and looked out the window. The plane circled wide, approaching from the south. "Ahh," Charlene breathed in, the southern territories of Gad and Zebulun coming into view. She glanced over to see that Owen only had eyes for the pillar of cloud on the northwest corner of the Temple Mount.

Forcing herself to look away from the land below, she gazed at the wonder of the Temple complex on a high mound, north of a city. "Is that Jerusalem?" she asked, almost in a whisper.

"Yes," Owen dropped his eyes to take in the short wall that outlined the city's perimeter. Some sections had narrow, winding streets while others with straighter roads appeared to be of new construction.

Not wanting to miss anything, Owen looked up toward the Temple. Three tall entranceways with curved roofs resting upon pillars in the shape of palm trees occupied the east, south and north walls. "The Eastern Gate is shut," he said.

"That is where the glory of the Lord entered."[37] Charlene looked at the three inner porches surrounding a raised altar. "The altar. Is it really over 20 feet high?"

Owen nodded, studying the Temple proper with a curved canopy covering the highest structure on the Mount with upper levels wider than the lower. He realized the conversations around them had stopped. Everyone was gazing at the Lord's Millennial Temple. He could almost feel the joy of the Lord and His glory. Many of the other passengers gasped in wonder and astonishment.

The first time they had seen the land shortly after the Second Coming. The region had been barren apart from the remnants of the war. The Temple foundations had been laid, but the walls barely reached above a man's shoulder.

"It's so tall," Owen said.

"It's so green…as if…" Her mind returned to her brief dream of a courtyard with roses, lilies, orchids, irises and gladiolas rimming a ranch-like building. "…the garden of the Lord."

They watched, transfixed as the plane banked out over the ocean for its descent to the airport just north of the Temple district in the land of Judah, close to the Western Sea. She found herself holding Owen's hand.

They sailed through customs. "I expected it to be harder—not that I had ever traveled internationally before."

"They no longer have to ensure that you're not smuggling drugs or weapons or are a terrorist."

Charlene squinted, trying to understand the signs in Hebrew characters. "I really should have worked harder at learning to read Hebrew," she offered.

Owen nodded toward the long walkway for the Jerusalem shuttle. "I believe it's down that way." He picked up his bags and glanced at his friend. "Ready?"

"Lead the way."

The shuttle bus had seats in the back with tall shelves in front for luggage. Owen helped slide her luggage on the racks, and they found a seat. The bus was half full. A couple across from them smiled. "Shalom," they greeted.

Feeling shy, Charlene still hadn't replied with the standard greeting when she heard Owen reach across the aisle for a handshake. "Shalom aleichem. Are you going home or visiting?"

"Returning from London." The man smiled at his wife. "I return with my wife. I was sent here after, you know…" He stared into his wife's eyes. "but I had to go back for her."

"Are you of Judah?"

"Benjamin, but Jerusalem's my home now. I had been a rabbi, but now I am learning the New Covenant."

"I had been a lawyer, but now I wish to know God's law," Owen stated.

"There is no problem with non-Jewish wives?" Charlene added, "I'm searching for a dear friend. We had been in the States, but he was also taken to Israel."

"Of what tribe?"

She glanced at Owen. Her mind went blank.

"Zebulun, I believe."

"Right, it's in the south." She stopped herself in time from saying she had seen it. She had—but in a dream and one that was certain to have been of the future. The brief glimpse from the plane didn't count.

The shuttle continued up the incline to the Temple District, following the road between the Levite and Priest's portions. The Temple was in the center of the district and the London bride, along with Owen and Charlene stared, fixated by the Temple as it came into view.

Charlene glanced at Owen and realized a bridge lay ahead. At first, she tried to remember what river that would be.

As if he read her mind, the rabbi said, "That is the River or the Great River or as some call it the River of Life."

"That flows from under the altar toward the east, then goes south until it splits, and half goes west to the Mediterranean."[38]

"Now we call it the Western Sea."

"And east to the Dead Sea," Charlene said.

"Now called the Eastern Sea." He shrugged his shoulders with a wry smile. "New names."

"Of course." As they drew close, Charlene studied the trees along the banks of the River. "Fruit each month…" She turned to the man. "…meaning they always produce fruit year around?"

"Yes, and there are several varieties."

"Seven," Charlene stated, naming each one. "Even in Colorado in the center of the States, we can buy new-fruit smoothies."

"She's tried them all."

"The leaves," her voice softened. They drew closer, and she could see the varying-colored fruits, leaves, and shapes. Some trees were tall and slender with long, wispy leaves. Other trees were broad and squat with lobed or scalloped-edged leaves. *I want to learn them all. What leaf for which ailment. Which fruit to fix and ways to prepare them.* She sat back stunned, realizing that she wanted to be a healer.

The shuttle crossed the River, and Charlene watched Owen stare at the Temple. He had shared his heart's desire.

"Perhaps you'll stay for a while to learn the new law."

"Perhaps from the Lord Himself…" Owen pondered.

Feeling the stillness, Charlene realized they were not the only ones transfixed by the Temple Mount and the beautiful land.

The shuttle turned left and ascended the rise to Jerusalem, her walls tall and fair, the gates wide and open. The road followed the Western Wall, passed Asher's Gate and approached the arch adorned with bas-relief etchings in yellow stone with an archway emblazoned with Naphtali. Charlene saw in her mind's eye the first gate on Southern Wall—Zebulun.

"Benjamin's portion," Charlene noted, staring to the south. *Where would Asher's land be?* She remembered Asher's tiny Colorado house he had purchased from Old Man Totten on the south side of "Totten's Hill"—as the locals called it. Scrubby, bare at spots, but clear and open as the sky. *What does the land of Zebulun look like?*

Some of the streets were not as narrow and winding as she had expected, but then the road curved sharply into what looked like the older part of the city. A few small round tables with some chairs sat to the left of the front entrance of the bus depot. She sucked in her breath as the bus barely made the sharp turn into the parallel slots for the buses.

Relieved, both began to breathe again when the vehicle came to a sudden stop. The driver called out "Jerusalem" and swung the doors open. Most of the passengers were up and filling the aisle before Charlene and Owen could even move. Smiling at the ones standing by their seats, they nodded, glad to see smiles in return.

"Where are you staying?"

They rose. Owen shook his hand. "We were going to the hostel, but…" he looked at Charlene.

She pulled out the folded letter. "I think this means Elchanan asked us to drop by. But we didn't want to impose."

He studied the letter and handed it back. "Elchanan and Zamira would want you to stay. How did you meet?"

"We have never met, but he said he is a friend of Asher's."

"Oh, Asher, I know him. Has he returned? Is he back?"

Charlene shook her head, trying to hold back her ready tears. "No, we're searching for him. I lost him…during the troubles. Shortly before the end he went out with Daniel to find food, but they never returned." She pulled back and couldn't say anymore.

"We understand." His wife patted her hand. "Many are still searching for their loved ones."

"At least we've confirmed he's still alive," Owen said. "Do you know the best way to go to Elchanan's?"

"Owen, we have to stop by the Registration Office first."

The man nodded. "They will ring Elchanan, and he or Zamira will come for you. It's still early." With well-wishing and shaloms, they filed out of the bus.

Charlene tried not to give into a sudden urge to cry.

"He still lives. If God has brought us this far, He will bring you together. I'm sure of it."

She nodded, trying to have faith. "I trust. I must trust." Unsaid were her reservations. *What if it's His will that we are not to be together? But my latest dream seemed familiar—like the home I saw with Asher.* Shaking off her thoughts, she stepped into the aisle, pulled down her bag and followed the line off the bus.

—⁓—

The two eventually found their way to the Registration Office. Taking a breath, she stepped through the door Owen held for her—always the gentleman. She smiled wistfully and headed directly for the tall wooden counter. "I'm looking for Asher Wilson," she said. His name sounded foreign, almost alien in Hebrew.

The man behind the counter placed a quick phone call, went to his cabinets, and pulled out a file. He furrowed his brow. "This hasn't been updated since we answered your search letter." He typed in the name and waited, watching the screen.

Charlene tried not to chew her lip. It seemed as if he took forever, searching through screen after screen.

"Ahh," he said.

Owen glanced at Charlene and tried to smile encouragingly. Her eyes were tight and fixed on the man behind the counter.

"He registered for a job in Dan."

"That's north?" Owen asked.

"Yes, but it doesn't look like the job was taken."

"How do we get there?"

"It's with a road-building crew in the eastern section. You'd have a hard time finding the jobsite." He glanced at the clock. "You will have to make ready for Sabbath. It's almost upon us. I'll run the updates and let you know what I find. You can check again next week."

"Who should we ask for?"

"I'll be here. Sylvan." He extended his hand to Owen. "So glad to see friends of Asher are searching for him." He looked closely at them. "You're not from Galilee?"

"From the United States," Charlene added.

"Oh, I'll pray for your success. Try not to worry. As a burier, he knows the land well and how to walk it."

"A burier?"

Sylvan narrowed his eyes.

"We're from New Colorado in the center of the continent—the former United States. Rebuilding, restructuring, finding our way. News from the outside world takes a long time to reach us."

Charlene added, "An envoy from Jerusalem did stop by. He brought the latest divisions of the New Law, described the building of the Temple. Some felt called to go and help build."

Owen's eyes shined. "He showed us how to receive weekly updates. Arrive by Monday and Wednesday we pray over them." He pulled out his notebook of the divisions in numerical order.

"Don't you have a Levitical lawyer to teach their meaning?"

"No, but we chose a pastor from among us who understands the earlier covenants and helps us understand the new law."

Sylvan noted Owen's notations and references along the side. "You love the Law?"

"I do. I used to be…well, I still am, for now, a lawyer—man's law." Owen glanced at Charlene. "I once thought I could pick up with what

I had done before in Denver—practice law, but without taking God's Law into account. These laws, going along with the earlier revelations build a framework, a foundation for creating a just society. God's Law, not just for the Temple or worship, but for business and caring for one another as a community."

"You should visit the training center right here in Jerusalem."

"What did the buriers do?" Charlene asked. "I thought that position was only during the first seven months."

Sylvan nodded. "In the beginning all worked to cleanse the land, but after the seven months had passed, men were employed to find and bring the bones that remained to a pit at Hamonah. Asher was an excellent burier. Now the pit is being covered to create a memorial to warn those who will be born during this time that our Lord is a consuming fire." Before he could complete his thought, Elchanan stepped through the door.

"Sylvan, they're here?"

The tall receptionist smiled and nodded toward Charlene and Owen. "Yes, Asher's friends, or family?"

Charlene sighed. "Not family, but very close friends." The words caught in her throat. "We are family." She looked at Owen. "I'm sure we can all be family together…" She looked back at the wiry man a little taller than herself. "Where is Asher?" She knew, with his quiet shake and somber eyes, that he also did not know. Her tears overtook her, and her shoulders shook.

Owen held her close. "Charlene, we no longer live in the days where it's almost certain a missing person has died. The gangs and brigades no longer hunt us. If God brought Asher through the darkness, He will protect him and bring him to us during these days of the light of the Holy One."

Charlene nodded and dried her face. "I know. I do believe, but…"

"Daughter," Elchanan gently took her hand in his. "You are here, and we will search for him."

He glanced at Sylvan. "The latest?" Elchanan studied the printout. "Kish? Do we know that name?"

"Perhaps," Sylvan's eyes were tight. "I've sent out enquiries to see if he's still in northeast Dan. Until then, we will wait until we receive confirmation that he is building roads there. If you leave now, you might miss hearing of his current location."

Elchanan nodded. "Come and celebrate the Sabbath with us."

"Oh, Owen," Sylvan added, "Make sure you meet with Uriah the Levite. You'll find him extremely helpful."

Elchanan nodded and ushered them out the door. "Sorry for the rush." He swallowed his laugh. The pace of life rarely rose to the frenzied hurry of the time before, but the last hours before Sabbath still quickened his steps. "Sabbath is near."

Charlene and Owen exchanged glances.

"Who determines the exact time the Sabbath begins?" Owen asked.

"The priest. When the sun is even with the horizon is when it begins, but a group of Levites establish the exact time as approved by the priest." Elchanan noticed Charlene's wry smile and returned it, trying to focus on navigating the road.

Elchanan parked the small auto in a narrow garage in the lower alley behind the house. They walked up the stone steps.

Zamira greeted them in the courtyard. "Our guests have arrived. Lunch will be ready soon."

Elchanan helped them carry their luggage to their rooms. He gave them a quick tour of the home until they heard Zamira's call.

A wooden table was filled with sliced bread, cheeses, fruits and a pasta salad. Charlene's eyes brightened. She sat in the chair Owen pulled out for her, surprised she felt so tired.

They joined hands, and Elchanan said grace. Zamira leaned forward, pushing the plates in their direction. "Eat! Enjoy!"

"What a feast!" Charlene exclaimed as she smiled brightly and filled her plate.

"As this is Friday, we will have Shabbat at sundown. Our days begin when the sun sets."

Owen and Charlene nodded to their host.

"Elchanan, they know the days! The whole world knows when a day begins and when it ends."

"We also keep Shabbat," Owen added, "but we are looking forward to beginning the Sabbath with you. Our weather service sets the official time for each state. We are a large country, so it changes with each time zone. Do you have a six- or a five-day work week?"

Elchanan smiled, "Well, some wanted six, but five is good. Five is very good. Each town can choose, but many work from Sunday to Thursday; Friday is workday for the family. Many are still building their homes. And Sabbath is worship and fellowship."

Zamira and Elchanan exchanged glances. "He works six days. Okay, so he works half the day on the Friday, but he still works."

He laughed in return and patted her knee. "I am close, anytime, and we have friends to help. We are not alone."

"I know." They smiled, laughed and observed their guests.

"How do you describe your Shabbat? Do you worship at the Temple each Sabbath?" Owen reminded himself not to pester them with too many questions.

Elchanan looked at the couple. "I see Shabbat as family worship to begin the holy day. The rest of Sabbath is set apart to think of God and His love. Worship at the Temple is to live in joy."

"To bow before the Messiah, the King of kings," Zamira said, rubbing her eyes, "is beyond words. We do not go every week to make room for visitors and others from the land. Many travelers come to see the Savior and learn His Law."

"Bible study and group fellowships?"

"Uriah leads those in our neighborhood. Sylvan encouraged you to meet him. He is a wonderful teacher. We can join the group after lunch tomorrow."

"I look forward to it."

They ate the simple, filling meal. "Everything tastes wonderful," Charlene acknowledged and rose to help Zamira clear the table.

"Sit! You are guest." The woman grasped two platters. As she headed to the kitchen, she winked at Elchanan. "Be a good host now."

"I was wondering if you would like to meet Rabbi Uriah."

"That sounds like a wonderful idea," Charlene said. She glanced at Elchanan. "And what does Zamira need to do to finish getting ready?"

He smiled broadly. "Go to the market."

"I will go with her, and you can take care of your business," Charlene declared.

"So, she tells us what to do!" their host teased.

Charlene tried not to blush. "I'll keep her company."

The hours flew by. Charlene stayed close to Zamira's side as they walked along the stone-paved streets, breathing the aromas of scented flowers and spices wafting from an open stall. She struggled to read the signs. "I really need to learn to read Hebrew," she reflected.

Zamira glanced her way on the walk back. "Do you ever wonder why all who entered the kingdom can converse in Hebrew but must learn how to read it?"

"Because the Messiah does not do for us that which we can do for ourselves. He made us to need to work and to have a purpose. And the work at learning to read will only teach us more than if He had given it to us in the beginning. Owen reads very well."

"Practice, my dear. The more you read the Word of God, the easier it will become."

"I know. I was so busy back home." As she gazed up the street, a pulse ran through her upon seeing the curved canopy roof over the Temple sanctuary.

"The sight never grows old," Zamira said with softened voice. "And to think we are granted the privilege to see these days."

"Amen." Her heart flipped again. *O Lord, let me be a part of this fair land.*

———

Zamira let her help. In fact, the woman kept her busy—clearing the dining room table, wiping it down and covering it with a special tablecloth. Charlene dusted and swept. The rooms were already neat, so they didn't need tidying. After that, she helped Zamira in the kitchen. With a sharp knife, she chopped and sliced various vegetables—some she didn't recognize.

"Are you and Owen close?" Zamira asked.

For some reason Charlene felt free to bare her soul. "We worked so well together in town. I was the chief administrator for the interim mayor, and Owen was the resident lawyer. We helped shape the new laws and regulations for the area. At one time I thought we would be together. He was going to teach me law, and I could join his firm, but then…" She slid the celery ends into a small bowl, "I could never forget Asher. At first, he was like the older brother I had never had. Of course, my younger twin brothers were constant pains. But Asher…he looked out for me." Charlene chuckled. "One time he scared off my date. I was so upset, but shortly after I realized he had saved me from a disaster."

Charlene reached for the orange sweet pepper. "I had a dream." She leaned against the butcher-block table and shared her vision. "Now I know I could see the Temple from Zebulun." She had to steady her voice. Her hand shook.

Zamira handed her a soft towel, saying, "Tears are healing balms."

She dabbed her eyes, nodding, not yet able to speak—not embarrassed but determined. She nodded. *O Lord, be my strength.*

"Thank you," she said, smiling through her tears. "I remind myself that God will bring us together in His time, and until then, let us thank the Lord for all He has done for us."

"Amen, daughter." They turned, hearing steps on the flagstones.

Owen smiled and hugged her. "This is why I will always care for you." His eyes shining, he held her hand. "You always find a way to see the light of Christ—no matter how dark the room."

"You're back. Young man, how did you find Pastor Uriah?"

"Very well. Which is it—pastor, rabbi, Levite?"

"They all fit him. I love the imagery of a pastor as a shepherd who tends his flock."

"He is our rabbi," Menachem said, bringing Hannah, his new bride, with him.

"You have come, and we have guests! Elchanan, introduce them!"

Charlene nodded at the stocky man with dark, wavy hair and deep eyes. The young woman by his side was a little plump, but her broad smile, framed with a halo of dark frizzy hair set her at ease. "Charlene, a friend of Asher's, if you know him."

"Hannah. We met briefly."

Owen shook hands with Menachem. "Do you also work at the power authority?"

"No, a banker, or a keeper of records. Right now, I'm managing the common lands for the city." Seeing the puzzled looks, Elchanan's son added, "Places where the workers who live in the city can grow their gardens or raise crops for the markets. Each region is to produce its own food."

"Sounds familiar," Owen reflected, seeing Charlene's nod.

"Although some of the farmers are seeking to expand, I think in time they will adjust."

"As we all will. Now," Zamira said, gesturing them to the dining room. "It is time!" She surveyed the table set for six, two tall candlesticks in front of her place, the cup for the wine and the board with the braided Challah bread by Elchanan at the head of the table. Zamira stood in front of the candles, a lighter in her hand.

Elchanan led Charlene and Owen to the places on the right side. Menachem and Hannah stood on the left. The patriarch stepped to the head of the table, spread his arms in greeting and picked up the open Bible with his left hand and placed his right on the text. His eyes scanned those standing with him. "I am honored to begin our Sabbath with you." The love he felt for his middle son…the one who had been so distant before. Still quiet, but in the stillness, they were together as they had never been in the past. Hannah, so warm and friendly, her energy added to the family. And the new couple, his eyes met theirs. "Peace with God. Peace with each other." He nodded at his son and his new wife. "Peace among the nations."

All said, "Amen."

Elchanan marveled again at God's work and plan, but this was only the beginning. On with the Shabbat. Zamira's eyes reflected her impatience to light the candles. Clearing his throat, he quoted without glancing at the Bible in his hands, *"And on the seventh day God finished his work that he had done, and he rested on the seventh day from all his work that he had done. So God blessed the seventh day and made it holy, because on it God rested from all his work that he had done in creation.'* And thus He gave us Sabbath. A day set apart for Him and for rest. *'Remember the Sabbath day, to keep it holy. Six days you shall labor, and do all your work, but the seventh day is a Sabbath to the Lord your God.'"*[39]

Zamira's lips set, she met each one's gaze, with a slight nod to her beloved. She lifted the lighter, flicked the actuator and cupped the flame to the first candle and then the second. The sound of her placing the lighter on the table echoed softly across the room. All stood a little taller.

She lifted her hands before her, drew them over the lights and then to her face as if to absorb the essence of light itself. After the third time, she covered her eyes, bending forward slightly as she sang the Shabbat prayer—"Blessed are You, God, Ruler of the universe, who sanctified us with the commandment of lighting Shabbat candles."[40]

Elchanan continued with the blessings for the wine and bread. Following everyone's lead, they sat, and the head of the home read from the book of Matthew. "Our Lord said, *'I tell you I will not drink again of this fruit of the vine until that day when I drink it new with you in my Father's kingdom.*[41] We live in this kingdom now. Today we drink the cup and eat the bread not only in remembrance of our Creator, Savior, and sovereign Lord, but in fact, having seen Him. And to celebrate the beginning of this Sabbath with you this day is an honor and a privilege."

And their fellowship was sweet.

▶9

THE NEXT MORNING Owen headed downstairs. Hearing voices from the kitchen, he rounded the corner. Charlene was perched on a chair by the small kitchen table, cupping a mug of coffee in her hands. Her laughter filled the room. "Oh, you're up," she said, with lifted brow.

"How long have you been awake?" Owen waited for the teasing.

"Young men do need their strength. Sleep is good," Zamira answered then added, "Long enough to warm the coffee and bring out the breakfast."

"Do Menachem and Hannah live with you?"

"No, but we love their company for Sabbath. Now…" She turned to dab her eyes.

"How many children did you lose?" The question was out before he could stop it. "Sorry, you don't have to answer. We've all lost family and friends."

"Yes," she lifted her gaze, her smile bright through her tears. "There was no other way. It was their choice. We were in Petra and searched." Zamira brought Owen's mug and sat with them. "We searched, but the presence of the Lord brought peace and His joy. Would we have wanted God to force them—to make it so? And then the ones who died in faith."

"In the light of eternity, being apart is but for a moment." Owen said.

"Yes, a brief separation. To them the privilege to serve the kingdom and dwell in the heavenly Jerusalem. For us, to rebuild, renew, start again." Zamira held their hands. "Menachem and Hannah are a joy and a promise that He does make all things new. And for you?"

Charlene drew back her hand before glancing at Owen and then looked aside. *All things new.* The thought brought a shiver up her spine.

"Yes, all things new, but some are still seeking what that is exactly. Has Jerusalem always been your home?"

"Yes, and we see the new with the old. Most days I see the new community rising from the ashes. Elchanan has his job with the power authority. I will be a mother again."

"And?"

Zamira gazed out the window. "To welcome visitors and friends, those who I do not yet know but are never strangers. To be in the Temple district of this city where the nations will come to hear the Word of the Lord and see His face… I do not see all my days, but I hope and pray it includes welcoming, greeting and hosting those seeking the Lord."

"A wonderful vision." The purpose touched her soul, and Charlene wondered about her future. Before she could ask another question, they heard footsteps coming down the stairs.

"That would be my husband." Zamira headed for the cupboards.

———

They ate breakfast at the larger dining room table, bright with light pouring through the French glass doors, opened to let in the gentle morning breezes. Filled with bagels, cheeses, and dried fruit and nuts, they sat back drinking fresh juice from the month's fruit.

"I still don't have a name to describe this one." Owen shook his head. "I thought drinking it fresh would help clarify it, but this tastes like a new fruit we've never tasted before."

"It is. About a third are new."

"But the familiar fruits seem also to taste different."

"Better—closer to what God had intended from the beginning."

"Exactly." Owen swirled the drink in his cup and drained the glass. "So…" He glanced at their host. "What is it like to worship at the Temple?"

"We have missed the daily morning burnt offering but will leave for the Sabbath offerings soon. As our guests, we will pay for your offering. I have already arranged it with the priests."

"We exchanged our money in New York. Please let us pay for our sacrifices."

Elchanan smiled. "Then I will let them know to extend it to a poor traveler who cannot pay for themselves."

They readied themselves and walked out to the courtyard. Owen fell in step beside Elchanan, asking questions and drinking in the answers. Charlene walked with Zamira, her eyes on the Temple walls and the roofs of the tall gateways and canopy higher than all the rest. The air vibrated with life and the sound of rushing wings increased as they walked north through the city, the Temple Mount rising before them as they drew closer. Menachem and Hannah joined them.

Zamira squeezed her hand, "Many are coming for worship today."

Charlene nodded, keeping her eyes fixed on the Eastern Gate. "Will it be closed?"

"The outer Eastern Gate is always closed because the glory of the Lord passed through those doors to fill the sanctuary, but the inner one is opened for Sabbath."

"In my distress I called to the LORD, and he answered me," Menachem quoted from Psalm 120:1, the first verse for the songs of ascent.

Elchanan recited from the next Psalm. "I lift up my eyes to the hills from where does my help come?"

"My help comes from the LORD, who made heaven and earth. He will not let your foot be moved." Owen quoted from the second verse.

Menachem continued with verse five, "The LORD is your keeper; the LORD is your shade on your right hand."

Elchanan said the next, "The sun shall not strike you by day, nor the moon by night."

Owen completed Psalm 121. "The LORD will keep your going out and your coming in from this time forth and forevermore."

Zamira smiled. "I was glad when they said to me, 'Let us go to the house of the LORD!'" Her eyes twinkled as she recited Psalm 122:1, her favorite verse.

"To you I lift up my eyes, O you who are enthroned in the heavens!" Owen recited Psalm 123:1 as they crested the broad stairs on the very edge of the plaza upon which the Temple area stood. Others flowed by, but they stood, transfixed by the pillar of cloud emerging from the northwest corner of the Temple sanctuary.

The six held hands for some time before looking at one another. Elchanan stepped as if to go right, as they usually did. The city lay south of the Temple complex, slightly below it.[42] Worshippers could enter through the north or south entrances to continue on to the opposite gate. All walked straight through, stopping before the opened inner Eastern Gate where they could see the altar of sacrifice and worship, led by the Prince, a descendant of King David.[43] The sounds of the Temple singers that seemed to blend with heavenly voices gave life to the very air they breathed.

Elchanan looked to the right, as had been their custom, to walk past the outer Eastern Gate and enter the outer courtyard through the Northern Gate. But the crowds to the right seemed to block their way. As if guided by an invisible hand, Elchanan stepped to the left and around the Western Wall.

Along the Western Wall, inside the inner court, behind the Temple sanctuary was a long building over 157 feet long and 122 feet wide. No furniture had been mentioned in Ezekiel 41:12, neither its purpose nor for whom it had been constructed. The rooms, workplaces and kitchens for the priests, Levites and guards had been described in Ezekiel's vision. Of the western building, only its dimensions had been given.

No one spoke as they turned left toward the Western Sea in the distance, its waves catching the sun's light with the gentle breeze stirring the surface. Elchanan and Menachem continued reciting the Psalms of Ascent. Owen and Charlene stared at the tract of land close to the Temple, slightly lower, with houses, playgrounds and small gardens.

"That land is for the priests and their families," Owen shared. He had read and studied the descriptions from Ezekiel 45, but here it was before him.

"The lower lands out to the sea—the Prince's portion?" Charlene's gaze rested on the small neighborhoods of homes, others with larger buildings, but also vacant tracts of streets or vast open areas.

"What you see is a miracle," Zamira said. "Before our land had been brown, almost barren. Only by hard work and toil could any crops grow…bringing water, planting varieties that could thrive in our desert. But now," she spread her hand toward the verdant green all around them. *"You shall eat the fruit of the labor of your hands; you shall be blessed, and it shall be well with you. I will abundantly bless her provisions; I will satisfy her poor with bread."*[44]

They turned right along the path by the Western Wall.

"No mortal lives there," Owen said. He glanced at Elchanan. "Some of the 144,000 sealed servants of God? Perhaps that is their temporary dwelling as they serve the Savior. After all, does it not say that they will follow the Lord wherever He goes?"[45]

"Some things are not for us to know," Elchanan stated.

Menachem drew up to Owen's side. "I imagine that is where the redeemed from earlier ages work for the Lord, perhaps where He meets with them as they shepherd the nations." He shrugged his shoulders. "The outer courtyard is where people can gather to worship, learn from the priests, and pray."

"The inner altar, of incense, the prayers of the saints?"

"Exactly, as these are shadows and copies of heavenly counterparts, the prayers of the saints are offered on God's golden altar before the throne as stated in Revelation 8:3."

As they drew opposite the mysterious western building, they grew quiet, hearing the pillar of cloud and sensing the high notes of angelic voices.

"He placed a canopy above our heads," Menachem said quietly. "Most buildings were too damaged to live in. When Asher wasn't building this wall," he paused facing Owen and Charlene, "he came and helped us rebuild our home—my father's house. It was a special time that I will never forget."

Charlene studied the large yellow-tan stones of the wall. The stones were so tightly packed together, there seemed no gaps between them. *Asher has been here. This is where he worked shortly after arriving in Jerusalem.* She sucked in her breath. He might have been building this wall when she had been brought here during the second 45 days before the Millennium officially began.[46] The thought warmed her that Asher might have been here working on the Temple when she had been with the crowds stepping past the piles of bones and remnants of the war. She shook her head to listen to Menachem and Owen discuss the possibilities. Elchanan and Zamira walked hand in hand and rounded the corner for the Northern Wall. She watched them pause and stare off into the distance.

She drew alongside and gasped. The valley heading south to the Eastern Sea was visible in all its glory—a river of blue from the Sea of Galilee that broadened and brightened when the River of Life joined it. While the area north was green and seemed to thrive, once the rivers were joined, the land itself burst forth with overabundant life. Large birds flew below them. Splashes of color from beds of flowers mingled with various hues of the green of grass and bush, tree and vines. The smiles on their faces needed no explanation.

The group joined the crowds entering the northern entrance to the

outer courtyard. The deep voice of the lead cantor, with the chorus singing the response, floated through the entranceway. She had known the
edifice was tall, but standing before it as it reached to the sky with columns decorated with carved palm trees took her breath away. She followed the group as they ascended the steps. The passage to the courtyard
was longer than most homes. Eighty-seven feet, she remembered.[47]

She joined the flow of worshippers as they stepped along the
marbled floor, past a series of small rooms on either side to the outer
courtyard. Yards away a series of tables where priests in turbans and
white robes prepared the sacrifices stood around a similar entranceway behind them that led into the inner court. Stairs leading up to the
altar in the center of the court were visible through the gateway. On
raised steps priests stood in front of the large square altar.

Elchanan and Zamira gestured for them to join a group waiting
to worship before the opened inner Eastern Gate. Singers' voices that
seemed to blend with the glorified redeemed and angels filled the space.
Charlene heard a voice in the distance quoting verses and praising His
name. They watched a lamb being offered, and they stepped forward
before the gate. A tall man stood in white robes and colored sash.

At his call to worship, all knelt as one. They rose and watched
the priest put the offering on the altar with a portion of the flour and
oil. The Prince led the worship. *"Praise the* Lord. *Praise the name of
the* Lord *for He is good,"* he began. *The group responded, "Praise the
Lord. Praise the name of the Lord."* The Prince led with other phrases
of God's grace and mercy. The responsive voices continued until the
Prince raised his hand. *"Praise the* Lord *in His sanctuary, praise Him
for his wondrous works. Praise Him with trumpet, lute and harp. Praise
Him with singing. Let everything that has breath praise the* Lord!*"*[48]
And the people said with him, "Praise the Lord! Holy, Holy, Holy is
His name."

Charlene gazed at the graceful canopy that covered the Lord's
sanctuary. Not only were the open doors decorated with palm trees,

but also cherubim with the faces of a man and a lion. Did she see Him in the Temple? But she felt Him and sensed His joy. "He said this is His footstool where He will dwell with us."[49]

Owen looked into the Temple. "And so He prayed to the Father, *'And now, Father, glorify me in your own presence with the glory that I had with you before your world existed. The glory that you have given me I have given to them, that they may be one even as we are one, to see my glory that you have given me because you loved me before the foundation of the world.'* We do not need to see Him to feel His glory."[50] He remembered having seen the Savior in the Valley of Jehoshaphat.[51]

The crowd turned and headed in the opposite direction from the gate where they had entered. Owen spied the tables in the corners of the outer courtyard. He heard Menachem say, "Where the priests or Levites explain the covenants. Uriah often teaches at the southwest corner."

"Have you seen any of the 144,000 God selected during the Tribulation?"

Menachem shook his head. "I saw the two prophets of God who called down fire from the Lord. Did you?"

"I met one of the chosen from Israel, but not the two prophets." They stepped through the Southern Gate. The city spread out below them. Owen stepped to the side, remembering.

►10

COURT HAD NOT gone well that day. His client had pleaded not guilty, but then had clearly implicated himself on the stand. Owen had tried to warn him not to testify—that it was not necessary, but the man was arrogant and proud. The man had lashed out at him in a screaming rage when the bailiffs came for him after the jury foreman declared him guilty. And so he was.

Thankful for the guards, Owen walked through the courthouse and would have left by a side door, but due to the latest terrorist attack, only the front entrances were open. Pausing at the top of the steps in front of the courthouse, he watched a small mob begin to surround a man standing on a bench. *Another preacher or agitator.* Sometimes it was hard to tell the difference these days. It seemed as if anything a person said could cause a mob to rise up.

"The day of the Lord is at hand. Repent or face the flames of fire in outer darkness and gnashing of teeth," the man said, his voice booming across the plaza, swallowed up by the noise of traffic and crowds. Owen was halfway down the steps when he noticed a gang forming with sticks and chains. He headed back to the three guards manning the entrance.

"You have to help him." Owen wanted to shake them out of their lethargy, but that would only get him in trouble. "Well, do you want to have to disperse a mob and account for all the bodies or maybe we could get him out of here before things escalate!"

"Butch, you're up." The site commander almost pushed him to Owen. "Guy's been warned, and he still came back."

Owen didn't wait to see if Butch followed. He hurried down the steps and strode purposefully to the side, stepping close to an agitator. "Hey, you know the rules. No congregating and…" he glared at the leader with a long stick. "I'd suggest you drop it and get out of here."

"Yeah? Who's going to make me?"

"Me," Butch came up to Owen's side. "Listen up! This man is an officer of the court. Move along, or he won't be representing you at trial. Unless you haven't heard, it's getting kind of crowded in lockup." He leveled his taser pistol at the ringleader, who stepped back, dropped his stick and sauntered off. "Okay, you've got a reprieve, a brief one. Get him out of here."

Owen gestured for the speaker to come down. "Come with me." Incredibly, the man obeyed. As they rounded the corner, Owen could see the gang reforming to tail them. He quickened his pace to his car and drove to get as far away from the Denver courthouse as quickly as possible. His efficiency apartment was within walking distance, but sometimes the streets weren't safe to walk even in daylight.

Owen stopped by his neighborhood Oriental takeout, and they headed up to his place. Despite the man's brave words, his hands were shaking. "You look cold. Take a warm shower. Coffee? Hot cocoa? I'll find you some warm clothes."

The man held out his hand, "Millard. Coffee would be greatly appreciated."

"Owen, enjoy your shower."

Owen kept the meal warm, tidied up the kitchen and looked about his sparsely furnished living room. It was just a shower and a warm meal. *Why did I help him? Probably because I can't bear to see someone else beaten to death by a mob.* One time had been once too many. The man was obviously hungry. He ate quickly, and Owen shared some of his. "So, cop said this wasn't the first time."

"Oh, it was for me. Probably ran off another one."

"How many are you?"

Millard met his gaze and tried not to laugh. "Quite a few. Not all in Denver or this country, for that matter, but we are a large gang."

Owen raised his brow. "Let me guess…144,000?"

"Exactly."

"No way." He turned to a small side table where some books were piled. "You mean that Jesus Christ sent you to stand on a bench and tell people they were going to hell unless they repent and take Christ as Savior?"

"Yes."

Owen reached for a lower shelf and pulled out a book near the bottom to put on the table.

"You have a Bible! Are you reading it?" Seeing Owen's nod, Millard lowered his voice. "I had been where you are today. Convinced that modern man didn't need God. In fact, I hated Him because of the holocaust. My family had lost so many. How could I love a God who would allow that to happen? But the world grew crazy, almost as if our advancements and our knowledge had turned into madness."

Owen nodded. "That's why I started reading it. Even with our education and scientific achievements, look at where we are today. The chaos we're living in and our leaders' solutions to our most pressing problems no longer make sense and are certainly not helping anyone." He ran his hand over the Bible's worn leather cover. "My grandmother's. My mom gave it to me when she died. I don't even know why I asked for it, but she certainly didn't want it. Guess I didn't want to see something so precious to my grandmother in the trash."

"May I?" Millard opened to Isaiah. "I had my good uncle's Hebrew Torah. I tried to read it and never lasted more than a few minutes, but in distress, knowing disaster was certain to overtake us, it fell open to…"

"Isaiah 53?"

"Yes, and I read it in Hebrew. Now I hardly remembered the letters from my early Sabbath classes and for my bar mitzvah, but I read it in Hebrew, and I understood it." His eyes grew distant. "The Lord appeared to me, in person and told me that I was of Levi!" He opened the Bible to Isaiah 53 and began to read.

Owen listened, knowing it spoke of Christ, His upbringing in obscurity, and rejection by His own people. The tears flowed when Millard read verse 6, "All we like sheep have gone astray; we have turned—every one—to his own way; and the LORD had lain on him the iniquity of us all."

Millard paused when Owen dropped his head, the Spirit within making him still. Millard handed over a box of tissues as Owen lifted his head. "What happened? Did you meet the Savior? Did you see Him?"

"Yes and no, but…" he raised red-rimmed eyes. "How do I become saved? What must I do?"

"You prayed?" Seeing the nod, he asked, "Did you acknowledge your sin?"

"I did. My sin put Him on the cross. We have all sinned, every person." Visions of the cells full of criminals rose up, but he perceived that from God's viewpoint all deserved to be there. "What now?"

"Did you ask for forgiveness?"

"Inside, but what must I do?"

"Nothing but admit your sin and believe on Jesus to save you. In prayer." He watched Owen close his eyes, and his face brighten.

"He would receive me? I mean I've never been religious. In fact, I despised Christians."

"So did I. Like so many, I clung to my liberalism, convinced it could save us and bring in a just society."

"I'm a lawyer." He reached for the Bible and turned to the last book. "You read Revelation?"

"Yes, after the disappearances, but it didn't make much sense until Christ appeared to me. Now I spend every waking minute trying to warn people and tell them that only through Christ can they be free. Only through Christ can they reach God and His heaven."

"I believe. I also believe you need to leave this city."

"I can't until the Holy Spirit releases me to go to the next place."

"Can you pick a different bench? I'd hate to see your body in the morgue."

"That's not possible."

"Really? You're certain of that! Why would God come to your rescue?" He remembered the mob who had beaten a Christian to death not far from his apartment.

"God's angels protect me. Most people can't see or feel them, but it does stir some of them up against me. No, as one of Christ's chosen, I cannot be harmed by men."

Owen flipped to Revelation 7. "Have you been sealed then?"

"No, but I will be."

"Pretty soon. While I didn't believe even this morning, I did realize that today this book is being literally fulfilled."

"It is. When our task is done, the Christ will take us up to Him where we will serve Him forever." He added, "You are not of Israel, are you? But you will have to leave this city someday. When God calls you to leave, do not delay."

"When?"

"He'll let you know when it's time."

"How?"

"God created us to be in fellowship with Him in our spirit. When you accepted Christ, you received the Holy Spirit, the guarantee that no matter what happens, Jesus will take you to Him—unless you are chosen to survive this time."

"Hard to believe, and with what's coming, I don't see how anyone's getting out of these times alive."

Millard laughed. "If God can create the universe in six days, He can preserve your life. Only by Him do you have any hope of stepping into God's kingdom on earth."

Suddenly, Owen knew what he had to do. He headed for the top drawer in his bedroom and found his second spare key. He returned to the table and pushed it across to Millard. "A spare key. You can stay here for as long as you need. Eat anything in the fridge. I'm usually not here. I only have one bed."

"Couch will do just fine."

Owen nodded. "Will you pray for me?"

———

Owen shook his head, realizing his group had continued on. He turned toward the Western Wall. During that time in Denver, he rarely saw Millard. The man could be gone for days, but he still kept his kitchen stocked. A little more than a month later, he had found a small note on the counter. He had moved on. Owen had prayed for him every day until Christ came. *Where are you?*

In a blink of an eye, a figure emerged as if from the wall itself. He was larger than Owen remembered him being, and he was shining with the glory of the Lord. Owen smiled and stepped forward, but he knew they could not touch.

"He gave me leave to see you. Fear not. The Mighty God has great plans for you and your friends."

Speechless, Owen nodded. He knew in his soul he would see the Savior with his own eyes.

"Soon, but not yet." Millard extended his hand and the blessing of God, His joy and grace flowed to Owen.

Just as quickly Millard vanished, and Owen stared out across the Prince's lands to the Western Sea itself. Content and happy, no longer sorrowful at having lost Charlene, but settled, knowing they would always be good friends.

►11

Owen caught up with the group by the meat market. Charlene looked at him, but he shook his head slightly and drew close. "I'll tell you later."

"Your face is glowing."

"Is it?" He touched his face, but it was the joy and peace in his heart that he felt. They caught up with Elchanan and Zamira in time for Menachem and Hannah to head down a side street to their small apartment.

"They're not coming back with us? Don't they need their things?"

"Their room is always waiting for them."

Elchanan added, "Newlyweds need time together. And they know we will not be alone today."

Owen helped Elchanan grill the meat. Charlene assisted Zamira in the kitchen. They ate in the courtyard. From her seat, she could see the tips of the waves in the distance, splashing white across a blue canvas.

"How do you explain that they still have sacrifices after the Lord of Glory conquered sin and death on the cross and rose again?" Owen thought he knew the answer, but he wanted to hear Elchanan's reply.

"What does Romans 1:17 say?"

"The righteous shall live by faith. We are saved by faith as it says in

95

Ephesians 2:8. 'For by grace you have been saved by faith. And this is not our own doing; it is the gift of God.'"

"Was this a new teaching? Before Christ was salvation by any other way?"

"No, for Paul was quoting Habakkuk. Job was saved by faith, as well as Abraham. Paul made this clear in the book of Galatians."

"Correct, so for what purpose were the Mosaic sacrifices if they did not save?"

Owen looked off to the side. "Hebrews states the blood of animals can never take away sin—only cover it." He surveyed the differences between the time of the church and the Mosaic law. "We are not yet in sinless bodies—not yet glorified."

"Yes, and the taint of sin affects this planet, as well as all who are still in their mortal bodies. For a time, the glory of God dwelt physically in the Temple, as He does today. The sacrifices provide ceremonial cleansing that we might draw near to God in these bodies."

"Elchanan, according to Revelation 20, many of our descendants will not accept the Savior even though they will have the benefits of living in a just society and see God's glory for themselves. Will they be able to approach Christ at the Temple?"

"Yes, if they are ritually cleansed."

"It says that only the saved will be able to walk on the Highway of Holiness." Charlene looked at their hosts. "I imagine the angels guarding it will keep them from it. There are other roads."

"But there is no such statement concerning Temple worship?"

"Not that I know of. However, I doubt if one who does not know God would be willing to worship."

"They might not realize or acknowledge it. Elchanan, parts of the United States used to have so many Christians that many convinced themselves that they were Christians simply because they had been raised in the church and could talk like a Christian. But their lives did not reflect faith."

"Ahh, like the sons of Abraham who considered that being his physical descendant automatically made them acceptable to God."

"Yes, Jesus tried to tell them many times." Owen nodded. "Thank you. That makes it clearer. I know how I long to be close to God but feel unworthy."

"Yes, and that is good to remember. When we are glorified at the end of the age, we will be able to be close with God."

They nodded. Owen looked forward to Uriah's afternoon fellowship.

"But first, a sacred Sabbath tradition!" Zamira laughed, seeing their puzzled looks. "A long-held secret for our success through the ages—the Sabbath nap." She leaned closer to Charlene. "We leave the dishes in the sink and take our rest."

⸺⁓⸺

After a light snack and tea, the four walked along the city wall to the community center. Others greeted them from the growing crowd all headed to the same place. Owen, carrying his case that held the three covenants, his ever-present companion, noticed Charlene carrying her Bible, but their hosts held tablets. "Does that hold your testaments?"

Elchanan nodded. Zamira stated, "I prefer printed copies, but it's easier to navigate and less to carry." She cast a glance at Owen's briefcase.

"Old habits die hard," he said with a slight chuckle. "Do you know which testament he will be preaching from today?"

"It can vary," Elchanan said with a twinkle in his eye.

Owen nodded. Realizing they were drawing closer to Uriah's home, he almost stepped down the narrow street to their right. However, Elchanan, Zamira and the crowd continued down the wider avenue. In the center of the neighborhood's market, at the apex of five roads, a pie-shaped, tan brick building rose to three stories. Broad stairs along the western wall led to an open rooftop veranda. "It's a storefront?"

"A reclaimed building—one that could be renovated. We all decided, almost without discussing it, that this would be our community center." Elchanan reached out for the railing to the steps leading to a roof-top plaza.

"What activities happen here?"

"Rooms for meetings, celebrations, weddings." Elchanan took the first step.

"And our healing center," Zamira added. "In the beginning we had an open kitchen. Today cafés, restaurants, and markets meet that need, but we will always need the doctors."

"Doctors?"

"I guess that would be using the older term. Those who cannot be healed through the medicinal leaves with the help of counselors, go to the Messiah, blessed be His name, who makes us whole."

Charlene lingered at the nearest window showing a dispensary. The sign above the counter displayed the fruits in their colors and shapes along with a list of the leaves. Seeing her group on their way up the stairs, she forced herself to leave and joined the crowd flowing up the stairs.

Round tables filled the back half, rows of folding chairs in front of them faced a simple podium. Owen smiled when he recognized Uriah to the side of the podium, talking to the singers and musicians. Some cradled violins or lutes along with guitars and a percussion box—the new with the old.

He turned his head and followed Charlene to a table on the side. Menachem and Hannah waved them over. His heart jumped with a long-lost memory of family gathering for fireworks in a park, each group seated on their blankets. That family had been lost years before the Tribulation, and no place had felt like home—not like this. Again, he wondered where he was to go. New Colorado, even with the warm fellowship of other believers, didn't feel like this.

"How do you read the screens in this daylight?" Owen asked Menachem.

Smiling broadly, he said, "We select daylight mode. Easy to see. We innovate."

It was true. Owen held Menachem's tablet and navigated through the various testaments. "Maybe I should buy one before I leave."

Charlene smiled knowingly. "But you'd still miss your notebooks."

"I know, I'm hopeless."

"You are same as us." Elchanan spread his arm to the street. "Old with new. We don't have to destroy the old to accept the new. We use the best of what we have and create new along with the old."

They nodded in response. They had seen this so many times—an ancient building of tan brick next to modern structures. However, millennial buildings avoided the cold, sterile look of the earlier concrete, glass and steel architecture.

The crowd settled in the warm afternoon sun—not too hot or cold, but just right—the Eastern Sea twinkling in the sunlight.

Uriah walked to the podium and placed his Bible and notes on the ledge. After a brief welcome, he said, "Second Testament, the book of 2 Corinthians, chapter 12."

Charlene looked forward to hearing what he had to say. The letters to the Corinthians had seemed strange and hard to understand. As Uriah described the complex relationship between Paul and the church he had planted, she began to see the struggles he was trying to resolve.

Following along, she knit her brow, hearing Uriah read from the ninth verse. *"But he said to me, 'My grace is sufficient for you, for my power is made perfect in weakness. Therefore I will boast all the more gladly of my weaknesses, so that the power of Christ may rest upon me.'"*

Owen noticed her consternation but would have to ask her later what the problem was.

Her mind was spinning. *Don't I believe that I have to be strong in Christ? Isn't that in the Bible too? Aren't all believers to be strong in Christ? Isn't the Bible filled with all the things the faithful are supposed to do for God?* She tried to focus on what he was saying, but the rest of his message barely registered.

She smiled with the rest, listening to Zamira chat with Hannah. She barely heard their invitation.

"Charlene," Owen asked, "Tomorrow…supper with Menachem and Hannah?"

"Yes, that would be wonderful." She really did want to get to know this lovely woman better, hear her story and see her home.

They walked back. Elchanan and Zamira said little as they had been together for so long. Owen glanced at Charlene who was still distracted. "I'll buy falafels for all of us," he stated, knowing they were close to his favorite stand.

They held the meal in their hands, sitting around a table for four. "Charlene, what's on your mind?" Elchanan asked.

Owen shot him a look. *So he also saw it.*

Charlene looked at each one, her mind racing. "You all know your Bible so much better than I do. You've got it together."

"Don't you?" Owen said before he could pull it back. "Of all people, you seem to bounce from one problem to another with a positive outlook and hope. I assumed, that you, at least had the faith for these times."

She looked away, trying to rub a tear away before that was also noticed.

"My dear," Zamira laid a gentle hand on Charlene's, "you can share with us. We are all relatively young in our faith for Christ—even those who strictly followed Moses. We have had the opportunity to learn from those like Uriah."

"Who is also learning with us," Elchanan interjected.

"God calls us to act. To be strong. Look at what the apostle Paul accomplished. And he now tells us to be weak?" She pushed back her chair, trying to frame her distress. The only thing she knew was that Asher was here, but she couldn't do anything to keep him safe. The dam burst, and she buried her head in her hands, her shoulders shaking. "I can't lose him again."

"Oh, so you've been pushing it down, covering it up," Owen said with a soft voice. "Honey, God's got this."

She pushed back and walked out to the open market, pacing in front of the shop. Elchanan shook his head. "Let her go. She needs to face this."

"I wasn't trying to be judgmental."

"I'm sure she knows that. You spoke truth in love. Even then the truth still pierces the heart. But this is part of our walk with God—facing the hard times and our inability to carry the burden ourselves."

Charlene headed for the nearest public restroom, splashed cold, clear water on her face, combed her hair and tried to recover. She returned and tried to smile. "Have I been a fraud?"

"No, you tried to make yourself strong in the face of desperate circumstances. But now that you have heard…" Elchanan paused. "…the strength that we draw from is the Lord's strength—not our own."

"Remember, Jesus said in John 15:5 that apart from Him we can do nothing."

They headed up the steps to the courtyard. Owen explained, citing verse after verse, of the inner dance of stepping out to complete a task for Lord with His help and with the Holy Spirit directing, guiding, strengthening. "I met one of those sealed by God. He stayed with me during the month he was walking the streets of Denver. The few chances I had with him emboldened me to share my new faith. I had only been reading the Bible for a month, and it made little sense. After I surrendered to Christ, I could feel the Holy Spirit giving me understanding, but discussing it with other believers helped." He laughed lightly. "Sometimes it felt like the blind leading the blind, but God is so patient with us. I was trying to share the difference between knowing about Christ and believing in Him when I took a moment to ask the Holy Spirit to help me. I began to talk, explaining the concept, almost as if God Himself had been teaching me along with that fellow attorney."

"Did he accept Christ?"

"She…and I don't know. At least she was willing to hear me out. It seemed like she had listened."

"Faith—believing faith—is a gift from the Lord," Zamira said.

"I not only have to trust God to take care of me…" Charlene stared at her friends. "I also need to trust that God will take care of Asher. It's not up to me."

Seeing their nods and answering smiles, she squeezed Zamira's hand. Her smile widened.

▶12

Sᴜɴᴅᴀʏ Aꜱʜᴇʀ ʀᴇᴀᴄʜᴇᴅ the road to Hamonah and sat at the crossroads. Part of him wanted to walk down the road one last time, but he dismissed that impulse. Grabbing a light snack, he drank from his last canteen. He knew where the watering holes were on this route. It almost felt like home base.

Hearing a jeep approach and turn down the road, he shifted to look but couldn't identify the driver. The vehicle passed him and then backed up. A slim figure emerged.

"Asher? Asher the burier?"

He rose. "Leon! Shalom! Yes, this is the real Asher who *used to be* a burier."

Leon reached him and wrapped him in a hug. "Well, only a skeleton crew was kept, and we all have to take speaking rotations. Our last earth mover is in Japan. So, you available?"

Looking at him sideways, Asher held back a bitter laugh. "What? I thought it was for good."

"Contract work. Just this one job."

"Didn't do too well with my last contract. Ended with no pay at all."

"We do better than that, Asher. You know us." Leon studied Asher's face. "Come on. Get you a shower, a meal and a bunk for a night. If you don't want to take the job, that'll be okay too. It's good to see you."

"Same here. Sorry, just…" He turned and followed Leon to the jeep. "Okay, tell me about the job."

"Most of the land has been cleansed. Maybe they could give you a contract for the last sections, but to the point—we need the burial pits covered."

"Weren't they going to be left open?"

"A warning memorial was selected closer to Jerusalem. You familiar with the equipment?"

"Yes." He watched the portable buildings coming closer.

Leon drove to his trailer. "Come in. We're a little cramped with the new baby."

"It has been a long time!"

Asher entered the cozy home and accepted the hot coffee. Rose, Leon's wife, served her luscious pastries.

"Shower. Here…" He walked Asher to their small washing machine. "You can wash your clothes."

Asher basked in the gracious hospitality, but the Lord would not let him forget Kish's utter aloneness. *Is this my future if I do not turn to the light?*

Early afternoon they headed for the office. Asher recognized Shachna, his former supervisor, behind the desk.

"Oh, Asher?"

"Thought he could help finish the last section."

"He could if our equipment worked."

"I might be able to fix it. I'll take a look." Seeing their doubtful looks, he shrugged. "Before the time, I worked for a small construction firm, and sometimes we had to build our own roads. Our company had used machines, and I learned how to keep them running."

But Shachna's face remained a mask.

Asher nodded, hefted his pack. "Well, probably not. Okay, Leon, it was great to see you again."

Leon stopped him at the door. "No harm in looking, right?" Seeing

Shachna's nod, he walked with Asher to the equipment barn. Smells of oil and grease brought back pleasant memories with Gary and Rusty, a mechanic who liked to make people laugh. Shaking his head to clear his thoughts, Asher approached the large skidder and shook his head. The hydraulics were in pieces.

"Have spare fluid? Leaking?" He examined the seals. "Who's been maintaining the Katuba?" Seeing the puzzled looks, he added, "You didn't let Samuel go, did you?" Lifting an eyebrow, he resisted the urge to scold or laugh. "Give me some time with your baby, and we'll see how far I get."

Asher approached the toolboxes. "What happened to the tools?" He put the tools back in their proper drawers and places. "Don't let Sam see it this way. Now…" He grasped what he was looking for and turned to Leon. "This might take a while. I'll find you."

"Report to Shachna. I have to get back to the books."

Asher smiled. "Isaac made it look so easy."

"He did!" Leon waved.

——◊——

The *Beast*, as they used to call the Katuba, was not unredeemable. The hydraulics needed cleaning, the seals replaced, and new fluid added. Asher brought it to life and tested the front dozer blade and the grader slung under the carriage. He drove it through the open door and up to the office.

"Shachna, it works."

"We'll see how long it lasts in the field." Shachna put a form on the counter.

This time Asher took the time to read it. "Seems good enough. Where do I sign?"

"A road builder's coming with his equipment, so can't guarantee how much work we can give you."

"I can live with that. Who can walk me through the job?"

"Jael's on site."

"Oh," Asher collected himself. *Okay, Lord, show me how to be kind with Your help.*

The beast made its slow way—even at top speeds. Asher moved with the bumps and jolts as the large tires straddled the roadway. He rounded the bend and slowed to a stop. The pit stretched out three times longer than he remembered. He recognized Jael as the man exited a tiny shack at the road's end. Asher swung down. "Jael, they sent me to help."

"Oh, Asher, how'd they find you?"

"I was walking by."

"Really? Well," he gestured for Asher to follow him. They walked the long edge. "Decided to consolidate here. Been intense. They want it done before everyone comes for the Feast of Booths."

Asher listened to the specifics, his experience quoting jobs for Benson Construction coming in handy. "I assume they want it done right—not just fast?"

Jael rolled his eyes. "Shachna's a taskmaster."

"Well, it has to be done right or no one's going to be happy a few years from now when bones work their way up."

"I know, but…" he shook his head.

"Hey, Jael, I can do this. Just let me know if I'm adhering to specs, and I'll make it right. But…" he surveyed the large field.

"I know. This would normally take weeks. Reinforcements are coming."

"To replace me?"

"That's up to Shachna."

"Got it." As he swung up, he called, "Jael! Hey, going to need about four more loads of fill. The seed on order?"

"They approved sod. The delivery is set to arrive in ten days."

Asher wasted no time. He brought the beast to life and headed toward the farthest corner to work his way back to the road. Moving the dirt, bringing in loads, leveling, grading brought a rhythm that was almost calming. Turning the field of bones into a grass-covered memorial felt as if he were completing something for the first time in a long time. He had always felt at home with the buriers.

Leon and Rose insisted he take his suppers in their trailer. He tried to help with the groceries, but Leon told him to put his money away.

His few weeks with Kish had brought back rusty skills and built upon them, but progress was going more slowly than he had hoped. He worked for as long as he had sufficient light. This job could not be done even with the brighter nights, and without a full moon, there was not enough light.

———

Two days later close to lunchtime, Asher heard a large semi pull up. He parked the beast and walked to the office. The machines chained down on the trailer bed look familiar. His gut wrenched.

Asher pushed the door open and stepped to the side. Kish's large frame dominated the open space in front of the counter. He listened to Shachna go through the standard contract. Kish tried to quibble.

"That's the contract. Take it or leave it."

Kish raised his brow. "I thought you were dead in the water and needed emergency help."

"We found a driver and a mechanic," Shachna said, a tight smile on his face.

Kish's face paled when he spied Asher standing to the side. His brows drawn down, he tried to change the terms, but Shachna would not budge. "He talk about me?"

"Not at all," Asher stated. "That would be gossip." He stepped closer to the counter. "Kish, they will be fair, and they have bunks, washing machines and…" he glanced at Shachna. "No more dining?"

"Not enough people. Cooks are gone."

"I can bunk in my rig."

"You can bunk with me," Asher heard himself say. "Plenty of room." He assumed the grunt was the only answer he would receive.

Shachna looked at Asher. "Can you show him around?"

"Of course." He glanced at Kish. "Eat yet?"

"No." He shifted his feet.

"I'll show you the bunkhouse, and we can share lunch." He opened the door. "Grab your gear. It's not far."

Kish chewed his lip, but he followed with a large duffel slung over his shoulder. They paused at the head of the narrow gravel lane bounded by six container units. "That many?"

"This place used to be three times larger. It was bustling with buriers bringing their finds, recorders, and pit workers. Now it's a shell. Quiet, though." He headed to the second one on the left. "Best one. Leaks less than the others."

A small kitchenette was offset from the dorm area with a half wall. "Fridge, stove, some pots." Asher passed through to the bunks. "Mine's down on the right. You can take any that are open."

He turned and pulled out his sandwich and leftover rice and beans while Kish chose a spot.

"They deduct much for this?"

"Complimentary. I checked." He slid a plate over. "We can sit here."

Kish didn't say much. Asher didn't want to risk asking a question that would set him off. He rinsed the dishes and slid them away.

Kish found a place to park the semi and backed out the grader. "Drive the loader."

Asher remembered that temperamental machine. He drove it past Kish's to the fill pile. They walked the jobsite, and Asher pointed out the most troubling spots. Kish had few questions. All business, they made their plans and set to work. Asher respected that the man knew his business and worked hard. Trying to ignore the fact he was relieved Kish was here, he worked his corner and Kish his.

From time to time, the man ordered him to bring fill, but Asher didn't mind. Kish had years of experience on him and was an excellent grader.

By the end of the day Asher parked his machine and set his foot on solid ground. He wasn't sure what to say to Kish, but Leon pulled up in his jeep.

"Great timing." He approached Kish with a broad smile. "So glad to have you. Kish? Or should I call you something else?" Ignoring the grunt, he continued, "So, you'll have supper with us. Rose loves having company." He smiled at Asher. "And the baby's ready to play."

Kish looked at Asher.

He smiled back. "Leon's a good friend. We worked the middle strip, but he's doing the books now."

"Yeah, settled, wife and kid already. Come by after you've both cleaned up."

Asher looked at Kish. "She's a great cook. But you can drive into town or eat from your pack in the bunkhouse. Your choice."

"Sure." His nose twitching, he walked with Asher to the bunkhouse and made sure he was in the shower first.

Asher waited, wondering how he would handle spending almost a week with the man, but he reminded himself to let the Lord help him.

———

Leon and Rose were wonderful hosts and shared their stories. "You from Dan? Were you always building roads?"

"Family business. But haven't settled on a place to live yet. Just working here and there."

"Your inheritance?"

Kish snorted and looked away. He turned his head back. "And you, Zebie? Used to being down south instead near the Galilee?"

"Never been there. I used to live in the Colorado Rockies."

Kish look at him. "You weren't native?"

"No, just good accent, huh?" He exchanged glances with Leon. "Anyway, I rented my land to the neighbors. Probably where the goats and sheep are grazing. Seemed empty and barren."

"Bet there's been lots of growth. We're building a town on our land.

The family put it together, and we've started a house. But this job pays well enough, it was worth it to stay here and see it through." He looked at Asher. "It was a privilege to be a burier."

"It was." He ignored Kish's grunt. Laughing, he said, "Guess we're the strange ones."

"Almost therapeutic and one way I could repay the Savior for what He has done for me." Leon's smile was broad and carefree.

"I didn't know you had family," Asher said. As it could be a sensitive topic, he never asked unless someone offered to talk about it.

"My father, a sister, some friends…" He smiled at Kish. "Some couldn't get along, but they now understand life's too short to be at odds."

"Too short?" Asher laughed with Rose.

"Honey, did you forget that we're going to live a thousand years?"

"And how does that compare to eternity? Hey, why did we end up going through those terrible times? Because we couldn't see, we refused to hear, and they didn't do a good job convincing us it was real."

"Who?" Kish asked.

"The Christians. Listen, we have only a thousand years to do it better."

Kish and Rose furrowed their brows.

"He's right. I grew up in Ohio, and the Christians in high school were fruitcakes or milquetoasts. Man, they were in your face or trying to fit in just as hard as the rest of us. And they were all at each other too. Patty, Gary's wife…" he explained to Kish, "My boss Gary and his family sort of adopted me. And their son Frank. They believed and they cared, but it didn't get the rest of us past the jerks some Christians could be."

Kish spouted, "I don't see how any of this is relevant. God's here. We can go to the Temple and see the Prince and King David, the angels and some of the resurrected ones. They say we have the Holy Spirit with us."

Flabbergasted at Kish's statement, Asher couldn't hold back his retort. "You have the Holy Spirit and look at how you treat your brother in the Lord!"

Kish drank his tea and set it down, silent and morose.

"That's the point. The Christians had the Holy Spirit too and didn't do any better than I assume you're doing?" Leon asked.

Asher waited to see what Kish would say. When he pushed back his chair and stood, he rose. "It's fine, Kish. Sorry I said that. You're welcome here. We need each other. Can we?" Seeing him sit, he looked at everyone. "Leon's right. All of us living today…" He glanced at the baby. "…apart from the babies and young children are believers and have God's Holy Spirit dwelling within us. But our children will need to make the same decision we had to make to surrender to God and accept Christ's gift of salvation. How are we going to do better?"

Kish grunted. When everyone waited. "Don't see why you're putting it on us. They make the choice for God or not. Simple. Not my fault."

Leon sat back. "That is also true, Kish. No one is without excuse." He looked at Rose. "The apple cake ready?"

Asher nodded. "Romans 1."

Kish fidgeted, but Leon leaned toward him. "Please stay. It's good to fellowship together. Not that many of us are left."

Rose served the cake and smiled, watching the men devour the pastry. Talking of the time before often brought a chill to her soul.

Asher scooped up the crawling infant and placed him on his knee. "Wonderful, Rose. Thank you."

On their way to the bunkhouse, Asher said, "It's been helpful to eat with them each night."

Kish grunted again and was soon in his bunk.

—◦◦◦—

Parts of the field cooperated, but others seemed determined to resist the top layers. Asher parked the Beast by the side and inspected the hydraulic lines to the front scoop. Kish joined him, and they looked at the aged machine. "Seen better days, but unless we start making more, we're going to have to keep them going."

"I'll drive the beast to the maintenance shed and see if I can fix him tonight. When I return, I'll bring the fill; you can grade."

"Looks like a fool's errand to me, but it's your time. You are crazy!"

That night Kish watched Asher take the front loader apart, bleed the lines and remove the worn hose section. They both shook their heads.

"Replacements?"

"Doubt it." Asher headed to the back and rummaged through the bins, boxes and drawers.

"Have some hose in the semi we could retrofit. I'll get it."

"Thanks." Asher inspected the other parts and lubricated it while he waited. Kish wasn't talkative, but he was civil and not that bad. However, no one would make the mistake of considering him friendly.

The hose Kish had was the wrong size, but they found fittings to make it work. In short order Asher sealed the connections and re-pressurized the system.

"Think it'll hold?"

"For a short time."

Kish glanced at Asher. "I used to have a son like you. Had four sons and six daughters."

Asher turned, waiting to hear his story.

"They all said no to Jesus—even the wife." Kish stared at him. "And to think my brother survived! Guess everyone's surprised we knelt to the Christ, and they said no. You can't tell how nice someone is or try to change their minds. They surrender to God, or they don't."

"Having a hard time seeing your future?" The grim, shattered look on his face answered the question. "I am too. I lost everyone I cared about—everyone I loved."

Kish turned to the door. "Bunk time."

►13

Owen led Charlene to the registration office on Thursday. He had announced they would stop at a café on their way back, but she insisted on getting her new fruit smoothie first. He glanced over, watching her cup the cool drink in her hands. "Before I hear more bad news," she had added and headed for the office.

Sylvan's gaze was brighter, more encouraging. "Good news?" Owen asked the head clerk.

Sylvan put a printed sheet on the counter. "Asher's at Hamonah."

"Hamonah? But that's not far from here. I thought you said he hadn't registered anywhere."

"Not for an official position. Temporary contract workers don't need to be registered. It's up to them to report their locations, but if they don't have family or close associates, some don't bother. However, remembering that Asher was roaming the country doing odd jobs, I sent out a request Monday afternoon." He glanced down at the paper. "Asher worked his way up to Dan, and now he's at the Hamonah burial grounds."

Charlene nearly dropped her cup. Trying to stay calm, she set it on the counter, but couldn't resist squealing with joy and hugging Owen.

"So, how do we get there? Can I hire a driver?"

"Elchanan's still at work, but Zamira will help you find some kind of transportation. Be sure to check in with them and let them know where you're going."

"Of course. We'll do that." She reached for the printout. "May I?" With Sylvan's nod, she beamed. "Thank you! Thank you! He's alive, and I will see him again!"

They walked quickly to Elchanan's home. Propriety held her back from breaking into a run—as well as the realization that she might run over a small child or bump into the scattered crowds at the various markets on their way. Eventually, they entered the courtyard, and Charlene burst through the door.

Owen nearly ran into Charlene when she came to a sudden stop. "What?"

She looked about, listening with every fiber of her being. "Where is she?" The kitchen was empty. No footsteps sounded from the upper floor. Their eyes met. "Outside hanging the laundry?"

"I'll check there."

"I'll go upstairs." She needed to grab a light sweater and water bottle if they were going on a trip.

Charlene met Owen in the courtyard. "Nothing?" She sat on the short stone wall, trying to keep her plunging emotions at bay. "Every time I think I'm drawing closer, the opportunity vanishes—like the mist!"

"Charlene," Owen gently held her hand. "Have no anxiety."

"I know. I know." Charlene tried to still her soul, but tears fell. Lifting her hand to her cheek, she bowed her head. *Oh, Lord, Your will. Whatever You have for me—even if it's not to be with Asher, I am glad for the time we did have together. But Lord keep him safe, preserve him and bring him to the future You have prepared for him…and for me.*

She lifted her head, smiled through tear-drenched eyes. "Thank you." Charlene accepted the handkerchief and wiped her face. "You're right. In God's perfect timing."

Owen squeezed her hand. "Hear that?" He smiled broadly. "She was at the market!"

"Of course!" Charlene rose. Owen opened the gate for Zamira, and they shared the good news.

However, it took time to walk to the power station to use their small auto. Elchanan's smiling face and wave grew small in the rear window. Charlene forced herself to look forward, trying to set her sights on Christ. *Whatever happens, Lord, let me be thankful.* "Abounding in thanksgiving," she heard Owen say—as if he could read her mind. And she was thankful for good friends—old and new. She wondered again about her prayer for Asher—to keep him safe.

⟞∿⟝

The sun was bright in a cloudless sky now that the rainy season had passed. Asher brought the fill, scooping and dropping loads where Kish directed. The man was difficult, but it would be the only way they could get the job done.

"Hey, half that. Need the rest to the left!" Kish shouted over the roar of the engines.

Asher grunted and turned back to scoop up the excess without dropping any more from the bucket. Focused on the scoop, he raised his head and the sun's rays reflected off the side of Kish's grader and directly into his eyes.

⟞∿⟝

His head was clamped in a vise. Four extensions held his eyelids open. Drool ran down his chin, and the sharp prick of a needle jammed into his biceps sent a shock wave up his neck. Pain cascaded up and over his head, but his eyes could no longer produce any tears. The images projected on the screen before him blurred, but he heard the words of the examiner work through the screens, paring down to the location of their hideout.

⟞∿⟝

Kish watched in disbelief as Asher froze on the controls, eyes fixed and unseeing. He slammed his machine into reverse, brought it to a stop and jumped clear of the cab. Some had talked of states like this, but he had never seen it happen. Asher had always been solid. Pushing aside his questions, Kish ran alongside the loader, pulled himself up and shut down the machine.

"Asher! Asher! What are you doing?"

The man looked at him, through him, past him. He shoved Kish off the loader. Before Kish could recover, Asher fell off the other side, rolled in the dirt, scrambled up the bank of a nearby berm and over the top. Kish forced himself up and forward, struggling to catch him.

"Let him go," Shachna said from the grassy border of the pit.

Kish looked at the supervisor. "What was that?"

"An attack. He's one of the wanderers."

"You knew?"

"Well, thought he'd taken care of it. We didn't have many other options. Frontline staff tried to tell them not to let too many go until the site was commissioned." Shachna surveyed Kish. "When, exactly, did he work for you? During the rainy season?"

"I guess so, yeah."

"It was cloudy this year. Sunlight's a trigger. As a burier, he often worked through the nights out in the wilderness."

They both turned, hearing a car drive up.

"Zamira! What a pleasant surprise, and these are?" Shachna stepped forward to greet his good friend.

"Friends of Asher."

"Where is Asher?" Charlene looked about, but the place seemed almost deserted. "You reported that he was here. Is he working at a remote jobsite?"

Shachna took a moment to answer. "Let's go to the office. You as well, Kish. It's time this matter is addressed."

Owen stepped forward. "I'm Owen, and this is Charlene. We've been searching for Asher for a while now."

Shachna made the introductions as they walked. Zamira drove the car up to the office. He stopped by Leon's small office. "Leon, join us."

Kish described the afternoon's incident, and Shachna relayed what he could remember about Asher's attacks.

Charlene sat close to Owen, thankful for his support.

"Had he had problems like that before? Did something happen during the time of Jacob's troubles?"

"Asher was always a dependable, excellent worker. He came to us—to my father's construction company in Colorado." Charlene laughed. "Just drove up one morning, sent by the temp agency. I found out the next day he had just arrived from Ohio and was living in his car. He had never worked construction and didn't own any tools, but Dad needed someone to carry roofing shingles up ladders for a job. Dad's regular helpers had moved away, and he was stuck. Asher showed up and put in a twelve-hour day—just like that." She could see the lack of understanding in their eyes. "The jobsites were over a mile in elevation."

"Almost two kilometers," Owen explained.

"Right, anyway most people can't do much physical labor when they reach our area until they've had a chance to adapt to the elevation. Asher had seemingly been built for elevation and heights. He was fearless."

"Why he did so well on the Temple buildings." Zamira smiled, but she added, "…until he started to have problems."

"Charlene, did something happen after the disappearances?"

"Probably, perhaps." She glanced at Owen. "At first it was my father, Asher, Daniel and I until the Great Tribulation started. My younger brother joined the Leader's Brigade, and friends warned us that he planned to bring us in. Dad diverted them so we could escape to hideouts Asher had built with the help of a Christian friend who disappeared in the rapture…" Her eyes grew distant for a while, but everyone waited patiently. "Well, it grew hard. We had to hide. Couldn't shop or show our faces in town. Thankfully, we weren't near a large city, but it was still difficult with my brother hunting us." She sighed.

"Thomas joined us, and we thought he was a believer, but he acted weird. Searching for food was always risky. After a while, Asher and Daniel scavenged for supplies while Thomas guarded the place. We had to move when a brigade almost found us. Thomas blamed Asher for that near discovery. They had found some berries, but they didn't last long with four of us. We were so hungry. After a long argument Asher and Daniel left to pick more before the birds finished them." She wiped her eyes.

"They never returned. Thomas wouldn't let me out of his sight or search for them. When he developed boils near the end, I finally admitted the truth that he wasn't a believer. God gave me the strength to escape. Incredibly, I found my father along with several others." She glanced at Owen.

"We rebuilt. Owen joined us, but I couldn't forget Asher. Then I began to dream about him." Her lips trembled. "God will keep him safe." Whether it was a question or a statement, she knew it was her only prayer.

"Did Asher say why he moved to Colorado?"

"To get away from his father. His mother had died a few years before, and his dad had told him he had to enlist in the army after high school graduation. He knew it wouldn't be right for him. The day after he received his diploma in the mail, his father beat him in a drunken rage. Asher put everything he had in his car and headed west."

"There are healing centers to help those having problems adjusting, but some might need healing from the Lord. For all of us to have gone through the time of Jacob's trouble, to find the living true faith and then to be a part of this kingdom of truth and grace—it's quite a change." Shachna smiled at Zamira. "Some find their place and spread their love. Others…"

Kish nodded. "Others wonder that God chose them to enter His kingdom. Those who are not deserving."

"None of us are deserving—not one. Even those of us who seem to have it together…" Owen's eyes grew distant. "…are seeking. I thought I knew what I was to do, that I could see my place in His kingdom. I had been a criminal attorney in Denver. After the Second Coming, nothing fit there, and I found New Colorado." Owen glanced at Charlene. "The Bensons are wonderful people and made me feel right at home. But what I thought would satisfy no longer does. Feeling as if I'm just existing, scrambling to find my path, I realized I too need a vision, a dream, a purpose."

Kish nodded, saying nothing.

"Let us pray." Shachna began with Psalm 200—one revealed at the last Feast.

▸14

Asher stumbled into a flowing stream. Small, sharp rocks sliced his palms. Breathing in, he pushed away and fell back. The shallow water rushed around his waist and swirled past nearby boulders. Shaking his head, he looked about. *How much time have I lost?* The quarter moon was barely visible in the sky with the sun lowering on the horizon.

Asher stared at the orb without blinking. He knew. In his soul he knew that normal life in a community would not be possible. Sighing, He pushed up, rose, shook the water from his torso and turned to step out of the stream—away from Hamonah.

—∿∿—

He would wander through the years, being pushed into smaller spaces as the population swelled. Alone, bereft, worshiping the Lord from afar.

—∿∿—

Asher froze. That was his future if he chose it—aware in his soul of God's sorrow and disappointment. "What choice do I have? You should have taken me and left Daniel. He would have handled it better. He'd know what to do, how to live." Asher stopped. The unleashed anger rose up to overtake him, but he fell to his knees.

"No," Asher cried, "No, God. But…" his shoulders shook. He cried

120

out in his soul and heard himself repeatedly say, "Your will be done on earth as it is in heaven…Your will, Lord. Why did I never tell her that I loved her?" He knew why—he'd been unaware, then he'd been afraid, and then there had been Thomas. Even without her, he would live on his land. He would live because that is what his God asked of him, and the Messiah deserved no less of him. "Forgive me, Lord."

Asher rose, turned, stepped through the stream and to the pit. Once there, he stared at the loader parked on the side and Kish's grader a third down from the end. *If not for me, they would have finished tonight.* He looked about. *Where is Kish?*

He knew what he had to do and headed for the office. Asher unseeing, walked past the vehicles parked in front. Taking a breath, he pushed the door open and stared at the empty reception area. Voices filtered from the back meeting room.

Asher stepped to the left and peered down the hall. Shachna sat in the corner chair visible through the door.

"Asher!"

Each step, wooden and stiff, propelled him forward. Sweat beaded on his upper lip, but he resisted the urge to wipe it away. The words stuck in his chest, but he forced them out. "I have to quit. It's not safe. I'm sorry." Before he could turn away, Asher heard a rustle, and a figure came through the door. His eyes widened.

Charlene threw her arms around him. "Asher!"

In shock, he stepped back a little. "Charlene! You're alive! How did you get here?"

She smiled and lifted her face to his. "I love you. We've been searching for you."

"I love you too, Charlene, but I'm broken."

"I heard. Come. You are not alone." She reached for his hand, but he stood, unmoving, shaking his head. "Asher! Believe! Would God bring you through to abandon you now?" She stepped closer and lowered her voice. "We will have a daughter. From the front window of our home, we can see the pillar of cloud of the Lord and the roof of His Temple. I have seen this in my dreams." Drawing closer, she added, "That is why I never stopped searching for you. I had no idea you were in Israel."

He blinked back a tear. "My mother was of Israel. It never came up. Why should I have mentioned it? She had died years before. When they brought me here, during the first thirty days, I learned I was of Zebulun. Our land…" A ghost of a smile began to form. "…is in the south, and yes, you can see the outer wall from the rise overlooking a plain not far from the river that crosses my section." His eyes grew distant.

"Asher, join us," Shachna called. "There's a place for you at the En Chaika Healing Center."

He yielded to her hand and followed Charlene into the room. Perching on the chair closest to the door, Asher surveyed the group. He lowered his eyes when he spied Kish. His heart sank when he noticed Owen next to Charlene, but he remembered the words she had spoken—I love you.

"The En Chaika Healing Center, north of En Gedi on the shores of the Eastern Sea, formerly the Dead Sea."

"But I survived without a scratch."

"Some wounds are not seen. You're on the waiting list." Shachna watched Asher soften and turn.

"There's an opening?"

"It's not that kind of a waiting list. They are waiting for you. I just have to place the call. It's the only way. Did something happen? Something with Thomas?"

"He threw me down the mountain as if possessed by a demon. He said I was cursed. That I had brought the brigade to their hideout. That it was my fault. I left, with no place to hide, and they caught me." He shuddered and tried to turn away from the memories…

Blinded by the searchlights, he struggled in the swollen river. The strong ropes of a net bit into his skin. Struggling to breathe, he thrashed, but could not find the edge to slip free of the net. The mob dragged him up the muddy bank and Quinn, Charlene's younger brother, drove a cattle prod into his side. Gasping from the volts that surged through his chest, around his sides and up his spine, his hand shook.

They watched Asher's unseeing eyes relive a terror long past. Charlene laid a gentle hand on his leg and whispered his name. "Asher, let us in."

He came to himself and tried not to redden. *How can I tell her that Quinn, Frank's evil twin, had reveled in the chance to torture me?* He had entered Asher's cell when no one was about to force saltwater down his throat until he retched. Turning from the memories, he tried to settle his pulse and steady his breathing. Working through the calming verses from Psalms, he longed with all his heart he could overcome this, but the dread never left.

"Asher, you don't have to talk about what happened. The teachers will guide you at the center. Listen, I know I was hard on you, but we had to let you go. You should have told me you hadn't yet gone for healing."

"I thought I was healed. Thought I'd gotten past it. Didn't have any problems like that with Kish."

"Because you were working with him during an exceptionally cloudy rainy season and had fewer triggers from sunlight." He added, "But the Lord has His ways and His timing. You'll have to be brave and bare your soul. Don't shut down to avoid an attack. The counsellors there are experienced and know what to do."

"How many of us are there?"

"Too many. This center is on the western shore of the Eastern Sea."

He acknowledged Shachna's words, but he had to finish. "They took me to the same station where they had killed Daniel. He's a shining one now."

"I've seen him. That's why I knew you had to be alive. If you had died with him, you would have come with Daniel." She added, "Thomas did not believe."

That fact didn't surprise him. "When Thomas threw me down, I thought I saw a demon in his eyes. Overpowered by his strength." He looked at Owen. "That guy was half my size, and I'd always been able to push him around—until that day." His words died away in the still room. Asher recognized the look overshadowing the group. Memories of the evil that they had witnessed were still too fresh for many. "But our God reigns and His presence fills the Temple." He wiped his face. "The joy that day when God came to dwell with me!" Several nodded with him. "If only I could live there and not…"

"Are you ready?" Seeing Asher nod, Shachna rose. "I'll make the call." At the door, he asked Zamira, "Can you drive him to the center? I'd take him myself, but we have a deadline." Seeing her nod, he headed down the hall.

"Sorry, Kish. We'd have finished up if…" He glanced at Owen who smiled at him encouragingly. Hope began to stir within him, but he worked to keep the fear at bay. He glanced back at Kish, remembering bits and pieces of his attack on the bulldozer.

"I don't get it. If God knew you need healing, why didn't He send you there?" Kish asked.

"He is kind and gracious and gives us the free will to choose. God is waiting for them to choose to live and follow His plan for them. It's the same back home. But if the counselors are not able to help them, and they must see the Savior, we transport them to Jerusalem." Owen reached for Asher. "The joy of the Lord can be yours. His future for you will transcend anything you could have dreamed or hoped for. I, too, will seek an audience for a vision, a direction. I am also searching. Asher, I'd like to go with you to the center."

Charlene added, "Now that I've found you, I'm not letting you out of my sight." She blushed when several laughed.

Kish shook his head and rose, striding out of the room. Asher followed him.

"He always that direct?" Owen asked.

"Oh, yes," Leon said. "Come."

They followed him to the front.

Asher surged ahead to catch up with Kish in the parking lot.

"Kish, wait!"

The large man stopped; his brows drawn down. "What?!"

"You saved me. You rescued me! Thank you." Asher tipped his head. "I realized later. I could have driven the dozer right into the grader or the berm. I could have hurt you." Asher looked past the man's shoulder. "Thank you for helping me. Please forgive me."

Kish set his jaw, forming the words of rebuke and condemnation, but a rising compassion stopped him.

"If I had had any idea that the attacks would return, I would never have taken the job. I really thought they were gone, that the Lord had healed me. All those weeks building that road with you was the first time I had been able to walk away from a job on my own terms. Not being driven away because of an attack."

Kish stood stiff and rigid.

"The last little shreds of hope seemed buried once again." He glanced toward the office. "I realized that unless I surrendered to God, I'd spend the next 998 years hiding away, alone, with no purpose. Worshipping the Lord in deserted places in the light of a crescent moon, hearing the call of the owl." Asher peered into Kish's grim face and set eyes. "I have to believe that God has plans even for us. I have to push past my mountain of fear, take courage and go to the center. Nothing else matters but finding His will for me."

"*Perfect love casts out fear.*[52] Only God's love can do that."

"Exactly. What is your purpose, Kish?"

The man shook his head, his voice a thin reed. "I don't know. After I finish this job, I too will go see the King of life."

"I'll wait for you at En Chaika. We can go to the Temple together."

Kish blinked and looked aside. "That would be an honor." He looked back at Asher, nodded slightly and turned to walk away.

A couple coming from his blindside almost ran into him. "Sorry. Can you tell us where the office is?"

"Gary!" Asher surged past Kish to embrace his former boss. "You survived?" He noticed Vera. "Hi, I'm Asher, a friend of the family."

"Vera." Her smile was warm and broad and open. "I've heard about you. They've been worried sick, trying to find you."

Asher nodded, speechless.

"Charlene?"

"She's in the office. You found it." He turned to Kish. "This is Gary Benson, Benson Construction, my former boss. He taught me everything I know about construction."

"Gary." He extended his hand to Kish.

"Kish's a road builder. In fact…" Asher cocked his head. "…you up for helping him finish grading the burial pit—if it's all right with Shachna?" He glanced at Kish. "Unless you have someone you can call on to finish the job," he added, looking at Gary. "The job needs to be completed in a few days."

"By tomorrow," Kish intoned. He leveled his gaze at the slim, rugged American. "Shachna's the boss. Check it out with him." He turned and walked away.

Asher sighed.

Gary shook his head. "Why couldn't…"

Asher shook his head and briefly described his latest accident. He could see Zamira waiting patiently by the car. "Charlene, Owen and I are going to the En Chaika Healing Center by the Eastern Sea. I feel terrible. If not for me, we would have finished the job today, and it has to be done. Would you?"

"Of course." Gary nodded toward the office. "Lead the way to this Shachna."

Asher paused by Zamira. "Sorry, we'll be right back."

Charlene met them at the door. "Dad! I thought you were coming for the feast!"

Gary and Vera exchanged glances. "Well, happy reunion. Actually, realizing we weren't needed to represent New Colorado, we felt compelled to help with the search. The hostel gladly shifted our reservations." He wrapped a friendly arm around Asher. "And you gave us the scare of a lifetime. Not coming back to us! But I see we're late."

"Right on time, if you can help prepare the memorial." Asher introduced him to Shachna.

"Sounds like the providence of God to me. You three head out. Looks like we're back on schedule." Shachna smiled for the first time.

In short order Charlene, Owen and Asher filled Zamira's small auto, and they drove down the gravel road. Gary and Vera waved goodbye.

"My," Vera said, "I didn't expect things to move this quickly." She smiled at Leon who gestured for her to come with him to their trailer.

"Rose will love the company. I think the baby should be asleep by now."

"Looking forward to meeting her."

As Shachna and Gary headed for the burial pit, the drone of Kish's equipment sounded low and steady in the distance.

Gary paused by the Katuba, worn with patched hydraulics and polished bucket where the paint had been worked away. He surveyed the stretch of partially covered bones.

Shachna described the job specifications. "The sod will be delivered tomorrow at noon. The commissioning's a few days before the Feast." He waved to Kish. "He's one of our most experienced road builders from Dan."

"That's how Asher met him?"

"I guess so." They watched Kish walk to them. "Well, I'll let you two figure things out. We'll bring some food along at supper. Sound good?"

"Of course, I understand doing whatever it takes to meet a deadline. Been there before. I'm honored to have a chance to be a part of this."

After a brief discussion, Kish swung his head toward the Katuba. "They call it the beast. Asher's fixed it two times already."

"I'll be gentle." Gary swung up, started the engine, and heard it purr. A few levers were touchy, but the beast moved, and the bucket lifted.

They worked hard into the night with the area lit by floodlights. Leon came with tea and sandwiches. Gary followed Kish's lead and worked while they downed the lunch. He smiled, leaning into the work, anticipating Kish's requests. They finished before dawn's light and the last rays of the moon slipped below the horizon.

He drove the beast, following Kish's to the equipment building beside the man's semi-trailer. "Not too many of these machines left, but we're already gearing up for next generation equipment." Gary swung down and faced the man who looked at him speechless. He stepped forward and extended his hand. "It was a pleasure working with you. Anytime you want a job in Colorado, look me up. I think my wife will be awake soon, and she's going to want me clean and presentable."

Kish twitched his mouth slightly. "The Lord does provide, His ways past finding out. You know what you are to do?"

"Think so. Married last year, and we left our village to start a homestead a few hundred miles west. Think it will be a small village, but we'll see what the Lord does. One day at a time."

"You had a family before?"

"Yes, my wife and son were raptured. My other son, his twin, joined the Leader, and I found my daughter Charlene right before the end. Looks like we're going to have to travel to see the grandkids."

"You starting over?"

"I think that's what He's calling us to do. If we are here today and not up there, then He has a plan and a purpose. Seek your calling, your vision, Kish. Don't be afraid to face the future, for we do it with our Mighty God, the Lord of lords."

▶15

En Chaika Healing Center on the western shore of the Eastern Sea, north of En Gedi, encircled Andrew's Bay with small cottages. Asher rose from the bed in his half of a cottage. He surveyed the small room with a bed, a wicker chair, a nightstand and a desk. He grabbed some clothes out of his duffel and headed to the shower.

The events of the previous day ran through his mind—it was as if a year had flashed by. His grading the pit before dawn's leaving, the attack and finding himself in the stream beyond Hamonah—finally surrendering to God or so he hoped and returning to the office determined to follow God. The thrill of seeing Charlene and hearing her words to him in the hall… But he knew—he knew he was not ready for her to be with him, not yet.

Shortly before noon Zamira and Charlene had walked with him and Owen into the main building—a long, low, open-air aggregation of smaller buildings linked by canopied walkways and open verandas. The lilies and flowering bushes scented the air with perfumes. They had been welcomed by Jonathan, a Levite, and he had watched his newfound love depart.

The parting had been hard on Charlene. He could see the anguish in her eyes. Asher had so wanted to take her aside, convince those in charge she had to be permitted to stay with him, but better judgment prevailed. "I must do this so we can be together. I love you, and knowing you are waiting for me will help me stay the course. Can you pray for me? Uphold me in your heart and your thoughts while I'm here?"

Her tear-stained face was his last image of her as he and Owen stepped past the reception desk, walked down a short hall and through the building to a large veranda. Tan flagstones outlined by iron railings overlooked the slightly lower rows of cottages ringing a small bay. Tall grasses with sprays of white tuffs bent toward lilies, peonies and rose bushes. The songs of birds filled the air, along with hoopoes and plovers running along the sandy beaches. For the first time, he heard the sound of rushing water from his left blending with the gentle lap of waves against tall reeds.

As if Machir, the guide, had read his mind, he pointed uphill to the west. "A hot spring runs down to the bay and joins the living sea." Asher remembered when Zamira drove in that they had passed over a stream with flowers nearly bending down to the water.

Friday morning, emerging from the shower, he grabbed his Third Testament and stepped through the door to the wide veranda facing the bay. Small round tables with chairs dotted the porch. Asher nodded at a man sitting at a table three cottages down. He grasped his Bible and journal and walked down the four steps to a lower ledge and around to face the body of the inland lake.

Asher sat on a nearby bench, angled slightly away from the rising sun. He closed his eyes and remembered Psalm 200 of the new world before opening his Book of the Prophet, the one foretold by Moses.

Memories of the sessions the day before tried to intervene, but he shoved them down, knitting his brow to focus on the phrases and the images the Scriptures conveyed. *Be still before the Lord. I will be in His presence. Lord, help!*

Asher stood and approached the beach, quiet in the growing light. Sand and wave, with distant calls of a hoopoe mixing with a chorus of birds singing.

He bent to select the next stone for the third layer of the Western Wall for the building behind the Temple. But the stone was
not whole. Spidery cracks ran along the top and when he held
the brick that had been hewn in the quarry, it was as if he could
see the breaks snaking through the solid rock. On the outside it
had appeared hard, sturdy, strong, but it was riddled with cracks,
some joining to create weak points.

Asher dropped the stone, and it shattered into pieces. He
placed his hand on the partially constructed wall, and, as if
he could see, he felt the cracks. Turning his head, his mind
bore through to the center. It was wrong—rotten. Not one
stone was fit for this building that would house those chosen
by the Lord.

A whisper of movement behind him reached him and blew
past. An electric shimmering tickled the hairs on his arms. Asher
turned, shielding his eyes from the luminescence of an angel who
approached with a figure beside him.

He had talked with shining ones before, but he had never
conversed with an angel. A shining one strode with him as if they
were close friends. They looked comfortable together.

Asher sucked in his breath. "Daniel? Is that you?" So many
things he wanted to say. So happy to see his lost friend he wanted
to hold him close, but he knew they could not touch. "I am sorry..." he began.

They paused six feet away. "Don't be. God chose me. I was
privileged to die for Him, and now I live for Him. What we saw...
what happened was as it was meant to be."

Asher straightened his back and remembered the wall. "It is
corrupted." Why had he used that term?

"All of Adam's sons are sick, riddled with the cancer of sin."

"Like the wall. The very stones are not fit."

He didn't need to ask. They would convey the message when the time appeared. "Help me hear," he prayed silently.

"But He makes all things new for His purpose," the angel said, his voice soft yet firm, deep yet melodic.

"For I know the plans I have for you, declares the LORD, plans for welfare and not for evil, to give you a future and a hope. Your house will dwell securely in your land. They shall build houses and plant vineyards. For like the days of a tree shall your days be, and that of your children and your children's children to the tenth generation."[53] *Asher nodded as Daniel quoted from the prophets.*

"The cracks will be healed, the breaks mended, and the pathways made straight. Do not fear. Walk with the Lord whose wings overshadow you always." The angel finished speaking, looked at Daniel and as they communicated without speaking, walked away, vanishing in the light of the sun.

—⁓—

Asher shook slightly, felt behind him for the arm of the bench and let himself down. Beyond thoughts, with no words to describe his vision, he sat and gazed at the sun's cresting the rise of what had been the land of Edom. He drank in its energy and warmth as if it contained the love of God in physical form.

He had no illusions that the coming few days of counseling would be easy. But he knew he had to see it through. Asher sat back and turned his head away. No, not in me. *Oh, Lord, not by my strength, but by Yours. May it flow through me. Help me to...* Releasing a long-held sigh, he knew he could not walk this journey alone. That meant he would have to let the Lord in, as well as the counselors, and if in a group session, the others, if he could, and that was his concern.

Lord, You know all things. You already see. I do not have to hide anymore. He sucked in his breath again. Could it be? Could his struggles and surrendering to God's healing help others like him? He remembered what he had said to Charlene—that he would have to be brave.

Lord, help! he whispered in his soul and stood to face the day.

———

The day before had started with a tour after lunch. There had been a group session for all new arrivals with the various bits and pieces of information—maps, room layouts, group and session descriptions, times the dining room and two private kitchens were open, beaches and walkways, library and private conference rooms, along with a new-fruit bar next to the healing room where medicines were prepared from the leaves of the trees by the River.

The next morning Owen found him along the veranda by the cottages. "Ready for breakfast?"

Asher nodded, glancing at the pack slung over the man's shoulder. "You're bringing your luggage with you?"

"This is my soft briefcase with the testaments, notebooks and paper. Machir will introduce me to the priest assigned to the center. He holds some classes here on the new covenant. I hope I have time to ask my questions."

"You have questions?" Though his reply wasn't meant to be a question, that's how it came out.

"Just think of it. Those of us who survived have only known the Lord for seven years at the most. And those weren't ideal times for studying the Word of God. On top of that, with everything different and more revelation from the Christ, yes, I have questions."

Asher almost envied him. "I love to read the new divisions, but…"

"I can't imagine with what you've lived through."

Reluctant to share, feeling open and exposed, Asher gestured to the side path leading to the dining hall by the side of the main building. He said little after that, and Owen fell into step beside him. He had to trust God. *Step by step*, he reminded himself, setting his face to see the day through.

———

Before they parted for their morning sessions, Owen asked,

"Would you like me to join you for lunch?" When Asher hesitated, Owen added, "Not a problem if you need some time alone."

Asher nodded slightly. "I appreciate that. I have no idea how I'll be. I'll find you?"

"Of course, and Asher, Charlene truly loves you. There was a time I thought we could be together, but we're just friends—very good friends. I hope I can be your friend too."

"I'd like that." Having friends sounded good. If he could only let go of the bad times, he knew he could thrive. Turning away from the thought he should be cast out, not brought in, he headed for his cottage.

Asher retrieved his schedule, took his journal and pen, and went up the steps in search of his first session. He tried to resist the desire to run away when he saw the group of six in a small semicircle. Seeing Machir sitting in the center encouraged him to enter the room.

"Asher! This is a new arrival." Machir made the introductions. "The first session is to share what you have learned, prayer requests, discuss problem areas." He smiled at Asher. "So, let's begin with your story."

"Story? Which one?"

"Brief highlights of your early life, the last seven years and what you have been doing during the days of the kingdom."

"I was born at a very young age," Asher quipped, his throat constricted. No one laughed. A few smiled slightly, as if to encourage him.

His eyes widened. Asher focused on a spot on a distant wall. "My mother, I know now, was of Zebulun, from a strict family." He remembered her saying how strict they had been, but he had had no idea what that meant. He only knew that they had never called her. She never brought him to meet his grandparents. It was as if they did not exist. "She was a good mother—not as strict as her folks, but she cared. That's what she said—*I do what I do because I care. If I didn't, I wouldn't bother.*" He sighed, leaving out her words for his father who rarely entered into his life except to yell or curse at him. He dropped his head. "She died my junior year of high school."

"Junior?" one asked.

"My third year." He cast a desperate look at Machir.

"This is important, Asher. Those who had trauma before the difficulties are more likely to develop post-traumatic stress issues. There is no shame in having come from a difficult family."

Asher nodded. "He…he…" remembering the living room strewn with empty bottles, the TV left on, his dad in his underwear sometimes half slumped on the floor. And those had been the good days—when the man had drunk himself into a stupor. "My…" He had never been a father to him, and the rage still burned. "That man," Asher said to Machir, "hated me, cursed me, and beat me. He insisted I join the army."

"Of course," one, a few chairs down, stated.

Machir shook his head. "We do not interject or judge here, Saul."

"Sorry."

Asher nodded. "No offense taken. I lived in Ohio in the United States. Our country did not need all its young men to serve—not like it used to be here. We had a volunteer army. I feared the army would be another four years of abuse. No," he stared at the group. "The last time he beat me, I loaded all my belongings in my car and headed west." His voice softened. "God provided a family—a home. I worked for a construction company building homes in the Colorado Rockies, and it was great. The family who owned the company took me in. It was great until…" He glanced around the room. "How much detail do you need?"

"As much as you feel led to share. This is your session."

"Old Man Totten lived on the far side of the hills down the road from Benson Construction. The family's house was built on the side of a hill. They had an old barn and a pole building for the equipment. I drove west until I ran out of money. Found a job and prayed they'd pay me each day, but that's not how it usually goes. After a day of hauling fifty-pound bales of roofing shingles up two-story ladders, I drove away and parked in a nearby deserted trail. Nothing was in sight. Of course, I ignored the no-trespassing signs. I drove up behind some trees to camp. Got away with it for a few days until the daughter, Charlene, caught me driving in there. Well, told her I was out of money, and she brought me home." He smiled. "Never left after that. Gary taught me everything. I took classes. Soon I could lay a roof, frame in a room, install cabinets, even do most of the finishing work. Had just started to estimate bids."

He sat back. "Old Man Totten finally caught me on his land and warned me off. But I helped him change a tire. Guess he'd been watching me work for the Bensons, so eventually we became friends. He let me buy an abandoned cabin around the side that was way back from the road. The guy owned half the mountain. Something else was different about him. He was a believer."

Asher could see they didn't make the connection. "He was also a Jew, but Charlene's mom and younger brother Frank went to the same church. They had become Christians also. Totten was big on prophecy and prepping—laying up for bad times—like the ones we just survived. Anyway, he asked me to help him build hiding places and storage caches throughout his land, along with high fences. He took me aside and tried to tell me about the Tribulation, but his accounts seemed like fairy tales."

"Nightmares or stories to scare the kids." One guy shook his head. "I thought the pastor was doing it to scare us into faith. Didn't buy it."

"Not until it happened." Asher nodded. "Yeah, we all missed the signs, the warnings. Totten gave me permission to use his land and his supplies if he suddenly disappeared. Well, I did what most of us probably did, tried not to laugh and said thank you. But they did disappear. Daniel, the pastor's son, where Charlene had attended a few times for youth group had been left behind too. He knew about church and the Bible but didn't believe."

"Had he been surprised?"

"He was shocked that it had been real." He looked up at the ceiling. There were some fond memories. "There we were. Dan was alone, so we took him in as well. Gary, the father, Charlene, myself and Dan. He brought with him Bibles, charts, commentaries. Revelation read like the daily newspaper. After the abomination in the temple the Antichrist had let them build, Charlene's other brother tried to hunt us down. After Gary drew the brigade away from us, I never saw him again—not until yesterday.

"We hid out for quite a while in Totten's caves. Thomas joined us. But then we ran out of food and trying to go into town to find supplies was too dangerous. The roving gangs, leader's brigades, along with the fires, disruptions to the climate due to the comets, the water going bad, it was crazy. I couldn't even find rabbits to snare. Things got so bad that we didn't feel we could leave our hideout. Thomas and Charlene kept it while Daniel and I hunted for food. Thomas grew more paranoid and nervous every day. When a brigade nearly found us, forcing us to abandon a site and leave behind our supplies, Thomas attacked me.

"I knew of a place overgrown with wild berries and since there had been a pause with the disasters, I figured we could find something. Daniel and I went, but I hadn't realized the brigade had set up their detention facility just down the hill in the valley. Dan joked that the best place to hide would be right under their noses because they would never expect us to be there. I couldn't agree with him, but that hillside was covered with berries. We harvested enough for almost a week, but then we totally ran out of food.

"There was a huge argument, but I insisted we had to go back." He looked aside. "We weren't so lucky that day. The brigade caught Daniel, but I managed to escape. I went back to let them know what had happened, but Thomas met me on the way. He was livid, convinced that Daniel would tell them where we were. I didn't think he would, but Thomas seemed to think they had new ways to find out. He threw me down the mountain. I hid as best I could.

"I went back to try to find Dan, thinking I could rescue him. What a fool! I arrived in time to witness his execution. I thought I'd be able to slip away once it became dark, but a patrol with dogs and night-vision goggles saw me. I fled to the river, not knowing that it was swollen from recent rains. The current overwhelmed me. Quinn, Charlene's brother, who was part of the team led them in torturing me. They thought it was great fun.

"Later, as they were about to extract the location of our hideout, a rival gang attacked the center. In the ensuing uproar, I managed to escape. Still feeling the effects of the drugs they had pumped into my body, I crawled back to the cave, but no one was there. They had moved.

"What Thomas said, I never forgot. I knew I had accepted the Savior. I knew if I died, I'd go to heaven. But I couldn't shake the knowledge that it was my fault that Dan had been executed. Knowing I had led the brigade to them, I didn't have the heart to try to find Charlene. Figured she was better off without me. It was now toward the end of the seven years, and God must have sent His angels to protect me. There was no other explanation for me to have been able to see the Savior return with the clouds of angels and resurrected believers—His army.

"The Spirit drove me to walk east to the Mississippi where many had gathered. Angels and shining ones were also there. They separated the Jews and took us to Israel. That day I learned that I was of the tribe of Zebulun."

He glanced at the time. If he was normal, he would be praising the Lord, rejoicing that he had been accepted into the Lord's kingdom. He almost asked if he could stop, but he heard Machir urging him to continue. "That I had been rescued and chosen to dwell in the kingdom should have brought joy and wonder and hope and peace. At first, I thought everything would be fine. I didn't realize I was just numb. I assumed Charlene had died with Thomas. I suddenly wished I had told her how much I cared for her. Thinking that I would have to live through the thousand years without her sapped the life out of me.

"But life goes on." He saw the nods. "We found our things to do. I had been in construction, so I worked on the Western Wall." Asher sighed. Now was the hardest part to share. "Why I couldn't forget… why I couldn't let go…why I found myself reliving the worst parts of my life when I had the chance to experience real life and joy and peace…" Asher shook his head. "I would relive scenes to the point where it felt like I was literally back there. Having attacks like that ten or twenty feet up on a wall while laying stone or a girder or a crossbeam doesn't work too well. I didn't even realize I had triggers, but I'd find myself out in the wilderness not even knowing how I came to be there.

"Of course, they had to fire me. I knew that. Sent me to the quarry, and that was worse—the noise. Elchanan and Zamira had taken me in. I hated to tell them. Tried to hide it, but they found out. His grandson, Isaac, helped me get a job with the buriers and that worked for a time." He relayed the rest of the story with his head down, ending with, "And I survived all that without lasting injuries…not a scratch by the time I reached Jerusalem." His voice died away along with his hopes.

"We will pray for you," Machir said and began the prayer. Each took a turn. Asher could only whisper, "Lord, help me."

The one next to him said, "Been there. Will pray for you. You're going to need it."

Another said, "Whether or not you believe it, once you get through this, you're going to wonder why it took you so long to come for help."

The man he had seen that morning smiled broadly. "There is so much hope, Asher. Like you, I knew if I could simply get past my issues, it would be like a dam bursting full of life and promise."

Each attendee had kind words for him.

Machir began to wrap up the session. Asher pursed his brow. "I took up the whole time!"

The group leader smiled. "That was the plan. Glad you were willing to share your story. The first session focuses on the newest arrival, so we can know how best to help you. While you are here, Asher, this group will be your community. Think of yourselves as partners, supporting one another. You will keep Sabbath together."

He dismissed everyone but Asher. "Now you will see Chilion, the center's healer."

"Healer?"

"We combine the healing leaves with counseling and prayer."

"Sounds good." Asher's hopes lifted.

—⁓—

The session was easier than he had thought it would be. Chilion had almost seemed like a doctor, probing, listening to his pulses, looking at his tongue, asking questions about symptoms. He reminded himself to be honest about sleep issues. With his list of remedies and his first tonic, Asher headed to the dining room and joined Owen. The man seemed glad to see him.

"How did your morning go?" Asher asked.

"Great, spent time with the priest, went over the various classes for the testaments. I'll complete the basic lessons here, and if I want to continue, I can do so at the Temple. You know Uriah?" Not waiting for a response, Owen continued, "He's a well-respected rabbi. From the one session I attended in Jerusalem, I wasn't surprised to hear that. If I qualify, I could learn from him."

Asher nodded. "So, I get how it's thrilling to understand God's Scriptures, but what do you intend on doing with that? You're not from Levi—certainly not a son of Zadok."

"We are one in Christ now, Asher. It's so wonderful that God has brought us into His kingdom. I want to do something with this back home. Not sure exactly what, but I don't want to only know civil law or man's law. I want to know God's Law, all of it, so I can teach others."

"So, you have your vision then?"

"No, I have a direction, but not the place, the timing, where and how and to whom. We can see the Savior together to ask for a vision."

"That sounds nice." He liked that. *Just ask for a direction for my life. That's all I really need.* And now that Charlene was back, all was good. Everything should be fine.

They parted, and Asher began to look forward to his afternoon session—until he entered the room and saw Priest Zephath. The man had dark, beady eyes, a pockmarked face with dense black hair cut short. As short and as broad as Asher but he was slightly tubby and stiff in his movements. His Hebrew had the sing-song of a cantor. When he quoted from the Scriptures, which he seemed to do every other sentence, it felt as if the man were talking through him. It didn't even feel like a conversation—not like with Machir.

"Name your triggers."

"What?"

"Your triggers," Zephath repeated tersely. He turned Asher's chair to face the light streaming in through the open veranda.

Asher blinked against the light and tried to angle his face in the shadows. "My triggers were sunlight, bright lights, the cry of a hawk or an eagle, musty odors." He paused, trying to recall others without bringing up bad memories. Sometimes, a unique combination of small events, or maybe some emotion or circumstance working in concert that started an attack. But he must be past that now. Surely, with the right counseling and medicines, he could set them aside. Now that he had Charlene back, all should be good.

Thankfully, their session was short, followed by an afternoon Bible study he had been looking forward to. Asher began to relax and mingle with others after the study as they discussed the coming Sabbath.

He found Owen at a table with three others. "May I join you?" he asked.

"Of course," Owen made the introductions.

"I didn't see you in the afternoon session," Asher stated.

"I attended my first course with Uriah at the Temple."

The two next to him smiled and nodded. "He knew the Scriptures so well that he already passed the basic levels. His Hebrew knowledge is also good."

"Do need work on the grammar and hermeneutics," Owen added. "And you?"

"Day one, always a challenge."

"Have you ever snorkeled?"

"Not really…but I'm a good swimmer." He looked at the group. "Is there a plan?"

"Meet at the beach in front of our cabins after supper Sunday."

"Sure, worth a try." He felt better already. The tonic seemed to be working, and now he had a group to hang with. Asher let the conversation flow around him. He was not alone. The attacks were in the past, and he could see a future.

▶16

SUNDAY AFTER SUPPER the water was warm, the air still. Asher walked out holding the fins and followed the group into the fresh water. Bright sunshine outlined silvery schools of fish darting among fragile fronds growing up to the light. Colored rocks shimmered with the water's currents as the men before him knelt to push off into the bay. He set the mask on his face, and Owen checked the seal. Asher followed his movements and brought the mouthpiece forward.

He sucked in a breath, even though he was still above water to check the snorkel. *It seems sufficient.* Not wanting to be left behind, Asher caught up with Owen still standing in the shallows. They looked at the ledge that dropped off and disappeared into the depths.

"You ever done this before?"

"Eons ago," Owen admitted.

"Well, we can make sure we both come back alive."

Owen smiled, lowered his face into the water and pushed off, skimming the surface with steady, even kicks.

Asher followed, not to be outdone. He slipped his face in the water, noting Owen's direction and glided effortlessly along the top of the water. The other three who were ahead free dove to look at something on the bottom. He followed Owen down.

Feathered fronds, uplifted to the light filtering into the bay, moved back and forth with the currents as if blowing in the wind. He had enough breath to reach the group watching a crab make its way along the bottom. On his way up to draw in another breath, he noticed a school of fish near the mouth of the bay. Light filtering through the water created bars of shimmering particles. The silver sides of the small fish glistened when a scale caught the light and sent it back. Shimmers of purple or pale green danced across the bay.

Asher looked back and gestured to Owen to follow him toward the mouth leading out to the lake. They caught a breath and dove deeper each time. In the distance he could see the shadows of larger fish, but the variety and colors of smaller fish also held his attention.

Eventually they had surveyed the bay and most of the area around the mouth. Asher noticed that various kinds of fish inhabited different levels—some hugged the shoreline closer to the surface while others lived in and among the tiny forest of plants in the shallow areas. He wondered what he would see in the deeper parts of the lake. Owen followed them farther out into the lake.

About to catch up with the group, Asher lingered to watch a long slender fish with pointed teeth lurking in the taller reeds. The sun dipping behind the raised plain, cast a shadow over the bay. Flicking his fins, Asher headed up and away from the shore to find the group. They were no longer visible in the hazy water.

What had they said in the orientation about the lake? Asher couldn't quite recall, but he knew he had to stay away from the fishermen. Trying to discern the direction of his group, he returned to the surface. *Their snorkels should be visible.*

Asher cleared his snorkel when he broke the surface. He rotated but still couldn't see his group. Completing his circle, he pushed up out of the water just as the last rays of the sun from beyond the Temple ricocheted off the mask's wet lenses.

He thrashed to get clear of the light, knocking the mask from his face. The fins propelled him forward when he kicked wildly. Asher struck out, away from shore and the light. He dove each time he caught a glimpse of a boat in the distance, bending him to the right, southerly toward the salt marshes.

Asher was halfway across before he came to himself, and a deep shame covered him. The darkness now upon him! The moon not yet risen, he saw distant points of light from both the east and west shores.

"Hey," a voice called. "Are you lost? What are you doing out here in the dark?"

He turned to the sound and flung himself on his back. Asher kicked his fins to gain some distance from the long fishing boat bearing down upon him. His right hand felt a net. Before he could pull free, it wrapped around his arm like a snake.

He thrashed, but this time he became aware of where he was and tried to listen to the voice of the fisherman. Yielding to the directions, he lifted up a hand and grasped the net. Strong arms reached down and pulled him into the boat. Two looked down at him as they freed him from the knotted cords.

"I'm so sorry. Did I damage your net?" He rolled to the side and pulled off his fins, sitting in the bottom of the boat. He began to laugh. "Well," he lifted his head, "I see I'm in good company," he said as a small, silvered fish floated past his leg in the pools of water in the boat.

"Come on," a strong arm lifted him to the nearest seat. "Not from around here?"

"From across the way?" a woman's voice asked.

Asher caught his breath and nodded. "I'm Asher. Was at En Chaika. My first time snorkeling."

"Your mask? Lost that too, I see."

"Yep, probably near the bay." He felt embarrassment, but for the first time he knew he didn't need to hide.

"I'm Philip and my wife, Deborah. Tonight, we fish."

"Do you always fish at night?"

"Depends upon the catch. Lucky for you we were here to fish you out of the lake."

"Fishers of men," Deb said with a twinkle in her eye.

He didn't ask, but he knew they deserved an explanation. "Thank you for rescuing me." He stared over at the lights of En Chaika, wishing for a cell phone to let Owen know he was okay. "I had a panic attack."

Before he could explain, Deb sat near him. "We understand. My brother Lazarus has them too."

"Does he still wander?"

"Yes." Philip turned to the net and pulled it in.

Asher moved to the back of the boat, closer to the small trolling motor to stay out of their way. Together they pulled it into the boat and separated the fish into buckets. "When you get a chance, I'd like to call my friend to let him know I've been rescued."

Deb joined him in the back seat and pulled back a cover. She reached for the mic and activated the radio.

"We could have him back at the bay in the hour." Philip settled the net into its wooden crate.

Deb nodded, but she looked closely at Asher. Setting the mic on her lap, she said. "Lazarus, we…" Seeing her husband's confused look, she plunged in, "Could you help us find him?"

"Is he ready?"

She worked to keep her lower lip steady, "I don't know, but I do know that I had just prayed for someone who could connect with him. We've tried, but…it's like he's in a different world sometimes."

"I understand, and yes, all my friends tried to help, but I had to be ready to admit my need and accept healing." He found himself nodding. "I'm so glad they never gave up on me. I will try to help you find him; only pray I don't have another attack. That's why I'm at the center."

"We can drop him off tomorrow," Philip said.

Deb relayed the message to the water patrol.

Asher watched them fish. Once back at their home on the lake's eastern shore, he helped them unload the buckets and put them in a room-sized fridge. They sat at the kitchen table, sipping hot tea and munching on falafels.

Deb glanced at Philip. "He could sleep in the second room?"

Asher rose. The kitchen faced east, and the half-moon painted silvery lights along narrow twisting paths among the field of flowers and tall grasses bounded by large bushes and young trees. "Who settles this area?"

"The borders of the River and the Eastern Sea belong to all. Some from Arabia, some from Assyria have come."

Asher returned to the table. "What of the regions given over to desolation? Any due east?"

"Farther south."

"Have you discovered Lazarus' favorite places?"

Philip pursed his brow. Deb leaned forward. "Let me see, usually due east and a little south, but there's not much there—not yet."

"You are referring to settlements, civilization, growing villages and tilled fields, tradesmen and builders. But the deserted places are full of birds and rabbits, fields of flowers with trees. A person can see the Lord's Temple from afar and think of Him through the night." He finished his snack. "Thank you for the meal. The night is the best time, and with the moon up, I can start looking for him. Where did you last see him?"

They brought out a map. "You can take it with you."

Asher pushed it back. "That's okay. I will be relying on other guides and will return at dawn. The pillar of fire will lead me back."

Deb put round loaves, a partial cheese brick with a length of sausage in a satchel as Philip filled some water bottles. "From the nearby springs."

"Sweet water." Asher pulled on the light jacket they had lent him. "Please pray."

As they clasped hands, Philip said, "Oh, Lord, protect Asher, guide him, and if it be Your will, lead him to our Lazarus that he might be with us again."

Deb hugged him before he left. "Thank you."

—ᴠᴠᴠ—

Two angels, waiting just above the roof, silently followed Asher across the first pasture. They cast light along the path on the right leading down a slight ravine to a higher pasture. The field funneled into a wide valley. Asher followed the more brightly illuminated trails.

—ᴠᴠᴠ—

Asher walked along the paths, shifting from one to the next, following the one that seemed to catch the light. At a three-way junction, he paused and set his foot down. This walking in the dark felt familiar—but not like he was regressing and returning to his old ways. He pivoted on his left leg and looked behind him.

The gentle rise of the land had brought him high enough to see the shimmering Temple across the lake. That must be why he could almost feel the energy of the pillar of fire. It marked the sky with a warm glow. He remembered his walk north. *Wanted, sought out, chosen.* Soon, very soon, he would be healed, perhaps with a vision and purpose. He felt the stirrings of promise for his life and the land granted to him. Life was a gift; the land was a gift—all on loan for God's glory.

He turned back to the junction and took the left fork this time. So far, he had traveled generally southeast, and he feared he was heading toward the ruins of Edom. *What should I say to Lazarus?* Of course, the Holy Spirit would help. Praying as he walked, he stepped forward without hesitation.

The path wound around a slight rise on the left and followed its course to an unaccustomed landmark, a steep hill rising like a bump on a somewhat flat plain. He smelled the aroma of burning wood and heard the snap of the flames before he saw the occasional red tongue at the base of a hollow. A good spot. He tried to step quietly.

In time a figure came into view, sitting near the fire as still as the trees behind him.

———

The two angels with Asher acknowledged the two with Laza-rus. They formed an invisible circle in midair.

———

Asher whistled a few bars of a song and walked deliberately to the fire, praying it would be Lazarus. However, he knew, even if it were not, perhaps he could help, and joy rose up.

"Shalom," Asher said as he drew near. The man lifted his head. He stepped closer so he could be seen. "I'm Asher. May I join you?"

The man shrugged.

They sat for a long while without saying anything. Every so often the man added a stick or rearranged the wood to keep the fire going. *Lord, You must help me. Send Your Holy Spirit.*

"Did my sister send you?"

"Are you Lazarus?"

"So, she did send you to drag me back."

"No, to…" Asher prayed again, and he began to speak. "I bring an invitation. I am like you—one who feels as if I have been untimely born, without place, without home. But soon…" For some reason, he felt it best not to mention the center. "I will go to the Temple and see the Lord for healing. Does the past keep you from seeing your future?"

The man nodded.

Asher tried again, "Are you plagued by panic attacks?"

He nodded again.

Asher breathed and leaned slightly forward. "We are here in this place at this time for a reason. It's no mistake. God has chosen us to be in His world. We have the chance to start fresh, build something new, but we can't do this on our own. Where is your land?"

"Reuben." The man sat up and looked at him for the first time. "Near the Western Sea. I hate boats."

Asher laughed. "Mine is in Zebulun—almost in the center, and when I walked there after the lots were cast, it felt vacant, alone, foreign and desolate. I have not returned." He wanted to share how he had a growing desire to show it to Charlene. Then he would know how to make a home there, but he knew he had to be patient.

"I can't fish with them."

"God's plan might not involve boats." *What is God's plan for me?* The answer lay just out of reach, but this time with Lazarus seemed right. *Is this what I will be doing?* He laughed lightly.

"What so funny?"

"The two of us sitting here by the fire." He stood and extended his hand. "Look, the Lord sets His own fire in the sky." Asher turned to Lazarus, "He has a part for us to play. Shall we go together to find out?"

Lazarus stepped back. "Sure, I know He's got something for me to do, but I'm not fit."

"Lazarus, do you believe the Lord can heal you? Do you want to be healed?"

Lazarus stared at him, unblinking. Asher couldn't read the man's face. He looked back at the Temple in the distance and said quietly, "I need to leave soon. Tomorrow or the day after I will go see the Lord for healing. You are welcome to join us."

Lazarus stepped closer, and Asher reached out to hug him. "I am waiting for a friend to join me. It could be any day now."

"You'd be going to the center?"

"Yes, they've been very helpful."

"I've been there."

"Maybe you weren't ready."

Lazarus looked back at his pack and the dying fire.

"Deb packed a lunch for us. Let's eat first. I need to sleep a little. You can walk back with me—if you want to." They sat. He prayed over the meal. Lazarus was a quiet man, and Asher didn't mind. It felt good to be in a place where the night birds and owls could be heard.

They clasped hands and prayed. Asher began, but Lazarus bared his soul.

—⁓—

The Spirit of God encircled the men. The angels marveled again at the faith of men and their connections to the Mighty God and how He placed His peace upon them. The angels watched them sleep. The one who had sat with Asher up north sent a nudge to awaken the man shortly before the dawn.

—⁓—

Lazarus separated the last of the burnt wood and doused the coals. They packed in silence and headed toward the pillar of fire.

Asher nearly headed down the wrong path, but Lazarus corrected him. "Lead the way." He listened as Lazarus shared his story about his days in the army during the time.

They crested the last hill before heading for Philip's home. The sun was warm on their back.

"Walk west in the morning and east at night."

"Good advice," Asher replied. He followed Lazarus to the backyard veranda. Deb sat in a lawn chair with her coffee and Bible in her lap. Her face lit up when she recognized Lazarus.

In the day's light, Lazarus was a full head taller with broad shoulders and a slim waist. His long arms wrapped around his sister.

"Have time for a quick breakfast?"

"Coffee, anyway," Lazarus stated. He walked into the kitchen and poured coffee for both of them.

—⁓—

Asher's heart skipped a beat when he saw the crowd on the dock as the boat drew closer. Apologies, explanations swirled in his mind. A figure emerged from the group and stepped forward. His heart skipped a beat when Charlene came into view.

She met him with a hug and a kiss on his cheek.

"Charlene?"

"They let me visit for a little while." She stepped back to thank Philip and Deb.

Asher met with Owen.

"Please forgive me for not having your back out there. They said you were halfway across when they found you?"

"Yes," Asher swallowed. Before he could offer his explanations, the others from the group hugged him closely.

"Who is this with you?"

"Lazarus…he might be joining us. Have you heard from Kish?"

Owen shook his head.

Asher waited for Charlene to finish meeting Philip and Deb to ask, "Have you heard from your dad? When is Kish coming?"

"Oh, that," she laughed. "The crew who brought the sod didn't have a clue how to lay it. Dad saved the day. It took Kish and Dad to get the job done—probably around noon. So, Kish should be here this afternoon. At least, that was the plan."

"So, tomorrow?"

"Looks like it." Charlene looked at the older-looking, stern man approaching.

"Oh, Rabbi Zephath, please meet Charlene."

"We've talked," he said tersely.

"He told me I could come." Charlene extended her hand. "It's so good to meet you. I will be praying all works well today and tomorrow."

"You may stay for breakfast." He stared at Asher. "He'll be in my first session." The priest looked at Lazarus standing to the side. "You will be there? First session? Remember where my office is?" Seeing the man nod, he glanced at Asher and walked away.

"I see you have the pleasure of being assigned to Priest Zephath too."

Asher smiled. "Yes." He looked back at Charlene and realized how many times in the past few days he had almost said that Charlene was his fiancée. When their eyes met, he could not keep his smile from broadening. *Is it my imagination? Did her eyes light up when she saw me?* "I'll be a moment."

Asher stepped closer to Charlene, extended his elbow, and she linked her arm in his. She noticed that hers slid in perfectly and fit exactly right. They walked up to the courtyard and to the flower garden with broad stones. The sounds of a birdbath near a small waterfall blended with the birdsongs of the early morning. Just past a cupola on a widened circle lined with rose bushes, Asher stopped and drank in the sight of her. "Charlene, I love you." He swallowed.

She waited, her eyes studying his.

The question on his lips withered away as he realized that he had no ring, no home, no way to support a family. He shut his mouth.

"Yes?" she responded with puzzled eyes. Breathing in, she filled the silence. "Asher, do you have doubts that I love you with all my being?"

"No. The doubts are mine. I never wanted to hurt you, but I have… nothing."

She stepped back half a step, holding his hand in hers. She ran her fingers over the callouses and scars on his work-hardened hands. "We will figure it out together. I don't love you because of your wealth, or your fame, or your land." A mischievous smile crossed her face. "A new start and with the Lord's guidance, a new life, a family."

Asher returned her smile. *This is why I love her so.* "It is so good to see you. Hungry?" He moved as if to turn her to the direction of the dining hall, but she already seemed to know the way.

"You know, Asher, I am looking forward to seeing where we'll be building that house of ours."

―⁂―

Deb was the talkative one. Asher watched Philip and Lazarus exchange glances. The conversation between the women—Deb and Charlene—ran forward as if their men were there only to observe.

"Where is the territory for Reuben?"

"Center, north of Judah," she nodded at Lazarus. "And the family grant is near the Western Sea." She launched into the story of how they had set up on the eastern shore. "Just to get started."

"Isn't the fishing good on the west?"

"Somewhat, but not like in the Eastern Sea."

"The future will be in shipping. When infrastructure, manufacturing capacity and trade agreements are in place, our site in Reuben will be a boon." Philip ignored his brother-in-law's groan.

"What had been your profession, Lazarus?"

"I build computers."

"Oh, that's wonderful!" Charlene's eyes brightened as she discussed the latest innovations. "Liquid-crystal memories, next-gen batteries. I had a chance to tour two start-ups in Judah working on the latest advances. I know some feared the Lord's kingdom would stop innovation. It's merely shaped it."

"I didn't develop the hardware. I planned and assembled networks."

"Exactly what their global shipping business will need. And theirs won't be the only one."

"If that is what the Lord has planned for me," Lazarus snapped, his voice sharp.

"Of course, we want to do it all, but only with God's help and direction can we find the peace and contentment He has planned for us."

After breakfast, the visitors began to leave—Philip and Deb to the dock, and Charlene to the shuttle.

She breathed in the fresh air, the perfect temperature. "Strange that the brighter sun doesn't seem to bother my eyes."

They hugged. "Thank you, Charlene, for never giving up on me. That includes Elchanan and Zamira and Isaac…"

"Asher, you have so many devoted friends. I know I too can dwell in Israel with you…with them."

"God has blessed me," he found himself saying. It was true.

▶17

LAZARUS WAS ALREADY sitting in Zephath's office. The priest curtly acknowledged his presence. "Close the door."

Asher's hopes that the man would begin with Lazarus were dashed when he heard the question. "So, Asher, you have triggers?"

Something within him forced him to meet the man's steady gaze. Over the two years the Lord had peeled back excuse after excuse—he was alone, Charlene would not exist in his future. All lies. Despite his difficulties, he had true friends. Charlene had been returned to him. "If I have surrendered to the Lord's will? If I have found Charlene? If I think I am at peace and whole, why do I still have triggers?"

The two men looked at each other. "Lazarus, can you explain?"

Lazarus stated, "I assume yours went like mine—that in the beginning, along with everyone else, we were so relieved we had survived to enter a world where truth, peace and justice reigned. No one would ever again get away with lying about their wicked deeds when the Lord of Heaven's armies sat on the throne. But then, over time, little attacks grew more frequent. Trying to avoid our triggers, somedays, became a futile exercise, until…"

"Until the empty spaces became our home. And if we chose that, in time, there would be no room for us." Asher sighed.

"For many, the ghosts of past traumas melted away over time. Hopes and dreams coming into the light of day pushed dark memories into smaller corners. However, for some of us, the brain had hardwired itself to react to danger with fight-or-flight responses that overwhelmed our senses. To our brains, our triggers forewarn of mortal dangers. And thus, we are consumed by the past, unable to establish new lives in the Messiah's kingdom."

Zephath said, "It is more likely in those who had experienced trauma before in their earlier lives."

"I hadn't experienced abuse before but being in the army during the Tribulation—what I saw and what I was asked to do—I had to defect." Lazarus shook his head. "When everyone around you tells you that what is happening is fine and right to do and you know it's wrong at its core…" He shook his head.

Asher lowered his head. "Yes, I have triggers, and only the Lord can help me."

"Then you are ready." Zephath nodded and glanced at Lazarus.

"I am ready."

"I need to hear from Kish," Asher explained, "I promised he could go with us. He and Owen are seeking a life vision from the Lord."

"Who did you set this up with?"

"Uriah?"

"I'll contact him." The priest gestured to the door. "You may go."

Machir showed Lazarus his room. Asher took a nap. During lunch he filled his tray and saw Lazarus sitting by himself at a table.

"This seat taken?"

The man laughed.

"So, you're on a first name basis with Zephath. Friends?"

The guy shook his head. "I guess it's his job to force us to see that we need healing."

"Jesus always asked if they wanted to be healed. I'm thankful He's been so patient with me."

Lazarus slid over a schedule sheet. "We're on for tomorrow. Where's your friend?"

"I'll have to check it out when I go to Jerusalem this afternoon."

Seeing Lazarus' quizzical look, he added, "I have an errand." Having no idea what the rings would cost, he hoped he had enough in his account to cover his purchase.

"Errand? For what?"

"To buy rings so I can ask Charlene to marry me."

"Build her house yet?"

"No, figured we'd do that together."

Lazarus shook his head. "Usually, the groom gets the house ready, then goes through with the wedding."

"We're from the States. It's a little different there. The wife often wants to be involved in the planning. She can make sure the house has all the right features—walk-in closets, main-floor laundry, good-sized pantry."

"Just repeating what I've seen. But then, the Messiah did say He would join the new with the old." Lazarus smiled. "Mind if I tag along?"

"Not at all."

Asher discovered Lazarus was also a fast walker. His leisurely walk through the city had almost turned into a race. He didn't mind lagging behind, and Lazarus seemed intent on not getting too far ahead.

He skirted Elchanan's neighborhood market and headed for the central business district. "Have any business you need to attend to?"

"Not really. The center's not my favorite place."

Lazarus was good company. They both drew comfort in silence and didn't need to fill the air with chatter. Asher paused by a broad street with two-story buildings faced with decorative stone. The four-block section of businesses had been blocked off for pedestrians. In front of restaurants, cafés and meat markets, benches and round tables drew diverse crowds.

"Truly the nations flow to our city." Lazarus stated. "As the prophets foretold."

Looking at the crowds, groups of people occupying various tables eating falafels, bagels and pastries, shoppers walking by with bags emblazoned with the names of various dress shops and haberdasheries, a person would never guess that hard times had come and gone, and the age of the Messiah was upon them.

Asher had spied the jeweler's store on his way to Uriah's studies at the community center.

Sighing, he pushed open the door for the first jeweler. "I realized I at least needed a ring to ask her to marry me."

Three shops later, Asher sat on a table off to the side.

"So, you can't swing wedding rings plus an engagement ring. There is an older tradition that the engagement ring is a solid band with no diamonds or stones."

Asher stared off into the distance. A couple walking together hand in hand brought a lump in his throat. "Her parents are here, probably staying through the feast, I hope." He focused on Lazarus. "I was thinking of having the wedding at Elchanan's before they returned to the United States. Not much time to find a job and earn enough to buy the rings."

"If she's not intent on fancy, I might know a place."

"Lead the way." He followed Lazarus through the crowd, down a short flight of stairs, across another small courtyard and to the northern section.

The crowds thinned and swelled as they passed through blocks with open markets and some with grocery stores. "No more pharmacies, though," Asher noted under his breath.

Lazarus turned down a side street that followed the wall of the city and paused by a storefront with worn gray brick and rolled-up grillwork. Nearby vendors had tables out on the sidewalks, but the corner store almost resembled a pawn shop.

Lazarus opened the door. "Shalom, Baruch, you still dealing in precious stones?"

The stocky man with dark-gray eyes stroked his beard. "Now that would depend…"

"Wedding band for an engagement." Lazarus stepped to the side glass case. "One that would also work as the wedding ring."

Asher hovered a little to the side. The shopkeeper bent down and pulled out a black velvet tray with variously engraved rings, most of gold, but a few of gleaming titanium. He pointed to one that caught his eye—white gold with delicate vines and tiny clusters of grapes etched into the band. He swallowed his groan when he saw the price.

He ran his hand through his hair, knowing he also needed another haircut. Money. After months of not caring that he had so little, facing the realities of having a family brought up an overwhelming urge to run. *What have I been thinking?*

Asher clutched the edge of the glass case. His heart pounded and lungs struggled to draw in oxygen fast enough. He had to hold onto God. He could not let go. Not now—when he was so close. With all his will, he counted, *one, two, three, four* to slow his breathing.

"Baruch, you need to do better. Listen, he's a little short right now."

"No loans?"

"No loans." Asher surveyed the possibilities.

The owner knelt behind the cases, reached down and pulled out a small velvet-lined tray of gold bands bereft of markings of any kind. "This is traditional. Well, what's tradition these days? With so many marriages, people from all over, who can keep the old ways? So, to life!"

Asher leaned forward. At first, after having seen the beautiful bands etched with inlaid stones, these seemed too mean and small for the love of his life. He longed to give her the world with all its beauty, but an image of Charlene rose up of the first day they had met. She was warm and caring and altogether lovely with tousled, tawny hair partly caught up in a band, her skin tanned by the sun with freckles across her nose, in her junior year in high school. Simple t-shirts and worn jeans with scuffed runners suited her. The warmth of her gaze and her easy laughter had warmed his heart. He paused. If he loved her, he would choose a ring that suited her. Asher reached out and cupped his finger to his thumb. His hand hovered over each one. He reached for a slim ring that felt rail thin, and he pushed down the ash that rose up in his mouth. "The price?" Hearing the amount, he nodded, "Okay."

"Asher, once you're established, you can renew your vows and present her with the finest rings, unless you want to wait."

"No." Today he was certain of few things—the need to marry before Gary departed was one of them. *I can't go forward without her.* He repeated, "I'll take it."

Lazarus badgered Baruch until he brought out a small ring box.

"Your name?"

"Asher."

"Asher the burier? Do you know Elchanan?"

"Of course, my fiancé is with them now. Elchanan and Zamira are like family."

Baruch nodded, crumpled up the invoice and wrote a new one. "Discount for a friend of Elchanan." He laughed. "Don't want to have any problems with the head of the power authority."

"You know him that little?"

Baruch stared at Asher and laughed again. "Just my excuse to remember to be kind in the age of the kingdom."

Asher paused. "Thank you. I will not forget this."

Lazarus tried not roll his eyes. Baruch succeeded in business because he was also a consummate politician.

Asher noted their looks. "How did you meet?"

Baruch smiled. "He keeps my computers running. Simpler now, fewer worries, but I hear they are working on new machines. My friend, you must keep in touch when I need to replace this system. Reuben is not far."

Lazarus smiled.

"You have your bride and your home built?"

"Not quite." Lazarus shuffled his feet.

"We're both a work in progress," Asher added.

Lazarus lifted his hand to pat Baruch's shoulder. "You have been a true friend, and I'm so glad to see you found your way into the kingdom."

"Drop by with your bride when you are ready," he beamed a broad smile, "but first, put in your order for the engagement ring. I know several craftsmen who do fine work."

"I will. I will." Lazarus paused, his hand lingering on the edge of the case. "Tomorrow, we will see the Lord that He might heal us."

Baruch reached forward and grasped his shoulders. "Hallelujah. Deborah will be rejoicing."

"You knew?"

"Well, she would come here looking for you, but I told her not to worry." He leaned forward, "The Lord's angels kept you safe. And the time has come!"

"Here it is." Lazarus looked at Asher.

Asher remembered what Charlene had shared a few days before. *If God brought us through those times, He will be faithful to keep us through this one. We can live in His joy if we choose.*

Baruch came around the counter and hugged them both. "Thank you, Baruch," Asher said before he left. Shoving his doubts aside, they headed out into the street.

The crowds were not bad on their way to Elchanan's. Asher kept pace with Lazarus. His heart quickened when he thought he heard Charlene's voice mingled with others in the courtyard. They stepped through the open gate by the gnarled tree. Asher looked up—some of the branches were bursting with fruit.

He turned when a figure approached. "Charlene!" Suddenly shy in front of the company sitting at the two veranda tables, he almost extended his hand, but she drew near and hugged him.

"Look, Dad is here with Vera, Kish and Jael."

Asher forced himself to look away from her clear blue eyes. *Jael?*

Jael sat near Kish on the far end of the left table. Before he could make the introductions, Elchanan warmly greeted Lazarus and had him sitting at a table with a cold drink and a pastry from Zamira's platter.

Jael rose and headed to Asher. "Can I talk with you for a moment? Look, I realize I need to go with you."

"So, you're the fourth person." Asher studied the man's face. He had been so intent on his own troubles that he hadn't really noticed the changes in Jael.

"And I see Lazarus is the fifth." They exchanged greetings. "Everything's set. We'll meet you by the Southern Gate." He studied Asher. "Okay with you?"

"Yes, the Lord is Lord of us all."

"Listen, I've had a lot of time to think. I learned a lot from Shachna, watching him with Rebecca, sitting under the rabbi. I'm tired of trying to forge my own way. Kish and I…well…we've become friends, and I'd like to be able to call you friend."

"Yes." Asher extended his hand, and a surge went through his arm as he turned away from his dislike for Jael, and God's love for the man flowed through him. "May the Lord bless you." He stepped back. "Tomorrow then."

He stepped to Charlene.

She drew close to his side, took his hand, and they walked out of the courtyard.

Asher led her to the Garden of Dreams and found his spot where he used to watch the moon cross the sky. Shoving down his fears, he knew the time had come.

They reached the bench shaded by a tall palm tree that overlooked Benjamin. The scent of nearby rose bushes blended with a chorus of birds' songs. Charlene sat on the bench, but Asher did not sit next to her.

He dropped to one knee, pulled out the small box and opened it. "Charlene, you have always been my best friend. From the day I met you, I always wanted to be close, but I didn't realize…I had not understood that without you, life holds little meaning. Would you?

Could you walk these times with me? Will you marry me and build a home in Zebulun? I can't tell you what exactly it will look like, but I know that together we can serve God there."

She reached for the simple band.

He wanted to blurt out that someday her hand would be adorned with a more fitting ring.

She drew it from the velvet case, felt its smooth sides, curved and golden in the sun. "It's beautiful, Asher." Charlene slipped it on her finger and held up her hand. It fit like a glove.

"As if it was always meant to be." She peered into his eyes. "My heart broke when I thought I had lost you, and Colorado no longer felt like home." She slid to the side so Asher could sit beside her. Cupping his hands in hers, she said, "My God is your God. This is my home, my land, my people. And the awesome God has put us together! Praise His holy name! May He do great things through us. Yes, many times, yes." They sat together, shoulder to shoulder, drinking in the moment.

He traced the fine bones in her hands. "I know we don't have a place yet, but I'd like to have the wedding before your dad returns home. Will he be staying for the feast?"

"I think we can persuade him. They wouldn't want to miss the wedding."

"We have to be back at the center. Talk it over with Elchanan. Whether before or after. Just a simple wedding. And you?"

She leaned forward for a kiss. "My love, I think Zamira and I can handle the arrangements. Elchanan and I will see Uriah. He can do the wedding?" Seeing his nod, she almost dropped her secret, the big surprise, but she held it in and leaned forward for another kiss.

▶18

ASHER WOKE BEFORE the dawn. *The cost of the offerings! Is there enough in my account?* The events of the day before, so full of instructions from Machir and Zapheth and the coming of the day, had driven all thoughts of money out of his mind.

Asher reached for his Bible and tried to read and pray, sitting on a bench overlooking the bay. *I must trust God. God, I trust You.* He rotated back and forth between panic and a strange, settled calm.

Knowing that Elchanan often rose with the dawn at the first hint of pink in the east, he headed for the city and entered the courtyard. "Elchanan, hello! Sorry so early, but I haven't paid for the offerings. How does this work?"

"It's already paid, Asher. Be at peace. Everything has been arranged. The Lord is so gracious. Take no thought for any other thing."

"I will." He wondered who but doubted the man would answer that question.

"See you soon, my son."

—⁘—

Asher headed back to his small cottage, his head swirling with Zephath's instructions. How to bathe, what to wear, the steps for presenting the offerings. He shook his head to hold a rising panic at bay.

Asher sat and opened his Bible to Ezekiel to study the kingdom commentary. The whole burnt offering, *olah*, whose smoke ascended before the Lord, symbolized his entire surrender to God. A lamb had seemed fitting.

Lazarus approached his bench. "Well, it begins."

—⁓—

Owen, Asher and Lazarus waited at the center's main entrance for the driver to bring the van. Asher hadn't realized how hard the seats were. Lazarus tapped his heel on the floorboard, his knee rising and falling. At least he wasn't the only nervous one.

The road passed through the common lands of the Prince's portions with broad parks of graceful palm trees and olive and fig tree orchards. The early dawn cast long shadows, obscuring the base of the rise to the priests' portion—quiet neighborhoods with gardens and parks. The city's fields lay to the left.

The last road to the Temple rose steeply to a large plateau. The paved concourse was overshadowed by the Southern Gate entrance with its towering pillars and curved roof. They were let out, and the vehicle headed to the parking lot between the Temple Mount and the city.

White-robed Levites with turbans and sashes welcomed them. Asher paused when he saw a white canopy in the southwest corner covering a grouping of tables. He had seen the structures of boards resting between pillars at each corner of the outer concourse but had never seen them covered. "What is that for?" he asked their guide.

"A celebratory feast after a peace offering." He smiled. "This is only the first one for the day. They become more frequent as the feast approaches."

They changed in small rooms surrounding the outer courtyard. Asher emerged, feeling strange in the white linen garment. Asher, Lazarus and Owen stood close together like little boys waiting to see the principal. Priest Zapheth emerged from the western side. His sash and turban were a different color from the Levite's.

A crowd had already gathered for the morning offering. His heart skipped a beat when he recognized Charlene in a white robe next to Kish and Jael, standing apart from the crowd. Elchanan, near the outer edge of the worshipers, smiled and nodded in their direction. Their guide led them to the others in white robes.

The Eastern Gate to the inner court swung open, and the Prince stepped onto the portico and descended the steps. *"Give thanks to the* Lord, *for he is good."*

The people answered, *"For his steadfast love endures forever."*

"Give thanks to the God of gods."

"For his steadfast love endures forever."

"Give thanks to the Lord of lords."

"For his steadfast love endures forever."[54]

"Give thanks to the Spirit of God."

"For his steadfast love endures forever." Their voices melted away as a chorus of singers sang praise songs without accompaniment.

The Prince turned to the Levite bringing the lamb and laid his hands on its head. His lips moved with a quiet prayer that only God could hear.

The Levites prepared the morning burnt offering at the tables around the southern entrance. The Prince ascended the steps, led the people in praises to God, and the choir sang.

Through the east entrance, they watched the priest take the prepared offering and lift it toward the Temple in a wave offering before ascending the steps. A portion of the flour and oil was added, and the smoke of the offering rose to the heavens. All joined the songs of praises, rising with the smoke of the offering.

The Prince closed with a prayer, and the worshipers filed out through the Northern Gate.

Six Levites with lambs stood in a line by the southern inner gate.

The guide gestured for them to approach. "Are we all making offerings?" Asher asked him.

"Three burnt and three of thanksgiving."

Owen stepped close to him. "You, Kish and Lazarus will be making whole burnt offerings."

"Showing our complete surrender to God," Asher stated.

"Part of the thanksgiving offering will be returned for a fellowship meal."

Asher nodded, but they could say no more. The singers looked at the Prince, who waited in the portico.

Owen, Jael and Charlene accepted their offerings and presented them to the Levites who prepared them. They stood in front of the east entrance as the Prince led them in praise and songs of thanksgiving and fellowship with the God of gods and Lord of lords.

A Levite brought Charlene's portion of her offering, and she walked to the Southern Gate. Asher watched Zamira and Hannah join her as they exited the courtyard.

Hearing a rustle, Asher looked back at the gate. Owen and Jael had ascended the steps as the glory of the Lord, bright and dazzling, drew near to them. It was as if shining ones stood on either side of the presence of the Lord. Asher looked down, feeling the joy of the Lord, breathing in the praises of angels and men.

He risked a glance at Owen's brilliant smile when he reached the courtyard and accepted his portion of the offering. Owen's face glowed with peace and joy. Elchanan and Menachem met them at the entranceway, and they exited the courtyard. *What had the Lord shown them?*

Asher glanced at Kish. He knew his face also reflected the serious set of his friend's face. Theirs were burnt offerings, acknowledging their sin of resistance to the Lord's leading and healing grace. He reminded himself that he was saved, had been saved, and all his sins had been forgiven at the cross. This offering was how he would demonstrate his surrender to the Lord's will and lovingkindness.

Three Levites with lambs stood an arm's length apart. As if in unison, Asher, Kish and Lazarus stepped forward and laid their hands on the lambs' heads. The Prince led the prayer and fell silent. Each man had tears that fell. Each communed with the Lord of glory.

As one, they lifted their hands and walked to the first step until the Prince called their name.

"Kish of Dan."

Hearing his name, the large man stepped forward and ascended the steps. He fell to his knees on the edge of the portico. "I am not worthy, O Lord, to be a part of Your kingdom, but I thank You and praise You for Your lovingkindness. Show me my path. What would You have me to do, Lord?"

Asher's heart cried out with Kish's. The smoke of the offering rose, and as it did, the chorus sang. He found himself singing along with them, rejoicing that the Lord had accepted Kish's offering. As he glanced up at the end, he noticed the beings on either side of the Lord's presence were not the same ones who had been there for the earlier offerings.

They were of the 144,000 who had the name of the Father and the Son written on their foreheads, who sang a new song before the throne of God where the four seraphim dwelt. They followed the Lamb wherever He went.[55]

Lazarus was called next. The servants of the Lord who stood beside Him were different from the ones for Kish's offering. Asher noticed two off to the side. His heart skipped a beat. One was Daniel in his glorified body, whole and complete. Gazing into his former friend's eyes, he felt something mend within him. Everything that happened was as it had to be—as it was meant to be. Daniel, who would journey to heaven and see the angels before the throne and the servants of God by His side, and he, Asher, would live out his days, not in sorrow or fear, but in hope and joy.

A figure taller than Daniel stood to his left. Asher recognized the angel who had met him on the way north. Not one step had he taken alone—not even during his solitary hours of terror or times of falling in his distress. One had even been sent to keep him from harm on the roof, in the river, and on the Katuba. Tears ran down his face. *Truly the Lord loves me!*

"Asher of Zebulun," the Prince called.

He lowered his gaze before the Lord of glory, but he saw His gentle eyes and loving smile. Vaguely aware that he was on his knees at the top of the stairs, time stood still yet rushed ahead. The vision of the rock that had been made whole. He felt the healing. *I am complete.* The power of God renewed his mind—transformed by the renewal of the Holy Spirit as the Father provided.

———

He saw his land as if from the sky, as it transformed from a ranch to an estate. The city that grew along the small river through his land, and finally, the Shalom center in a gentle hollow a short distance from the roads—a place of peace and learning and healing and hope. From there the Word of the Lord would go forth to complete the kingdom.

———

With a start the vision ended, and he saw with his own eyes.

The Prince helped him rise. A Levite came to help him down the stairs. He walked ten steps and turned to see the Eastern Gate shut, but the canopied roof of the Temple rose above the entranceway and the pillar of the Lord's cloud went straight up into heaven—his home someday.

His strength returned, and he thanked the Levite. "And to think this is your job, every day."

"Every day." The man smiled and directed him to the Southern Gate.

Asher paused, feeling one draw near. Daniel now stood on his right. They did not need to speak. *It is good to see you,* Asher thought. He could see Daniel's peace and knew he would be as his friend someday.

They raised their hands as if to say goodbye, but Asher felt a whisper that in the future, sometime, he would be sent to him again.

—∿∿—

Kish waited for him right inside the southern entranceway with his hand extended. Asher had never seen him beam. In fact, he had never seen Kish smile. He realized that he also had a broad smile.

"From Dan to Beersheba." Kish's eyes studied Asher.

"From Dan to Beersheba," Asher replied. "What?" noting Kish's look.

"Oh, just you wait. They sent me to bring you."

Asher stepped through the long hall and down the stairs to head straight for the canopy. People crowded the area, with some sitting already. A small chorus of singers and musicians filled the air with sweet music. His heart tugged a little, longing for community, knowing it would come in time.

As they approached, people moved, regrouped, and stood behind their places. Once he drew close enough, he could see the tables had been joined with Elchanan at one end and Priest Zephath at the other. Charlene held out her hand for him to stand beside her.

"Welcome to our feast of thanksgiving to the Lord." She nodded at Owen and Jael.

Asher was almost flustered with all eyes on him, but he plowed ahead and stood behind his chair, Charlene on his right and Kish on his left.

Zapheth scanned the group. Seeing all were assembled, he said, "Let us pray." All bowed their heads.

Asher opened his eyes, and the tables bursting with food brought up a ravenous hunger. But all remained standing, looking at him.

"Asher," Elchanan said, "could you share your vision?"

He glanced at Kish. "From Dan to Beersheba? You will raise up a healing center?" With the nod of agreement, he grasped Kish's hand. "From Dan to Beersheba, may the Word of the Lord spread throughout the land. May we help spread the word that He comes with healing in His wings. That He would call us to establish healing centers," he said with a nod at the priest. "This is a calling that we could do only with and through the grace of God."

Owen added, "And to the plains of the Colorado. This I have seen."

"I have seen," Asher echoed. He glanced at Charlene. "And yours?"

"I did not need to ask for a vision, Asher. Your vision is my vision." She squeezed his hand. "But when I saw the trees by the River before the Temple, I knew that I would learn to help with the healing leaves." *A healer? Could I fulfill that task?*

Hearing her words of faith and trust filled his heart. He returned her squeeze and looked at Jael and Lazarus. "Would you like to share your visions?"

Jael spoke first. "He has a place for me back home in Simeon. What it will be, I will see as the years go by. But this I know: before He formed the earth and the sky and the mountains and the seas, He chose me for these days. Blessed be His name."

Lazarus said, "From the depths of the sea He called to me. I too will have a place—even if I live in many places, but I will never walk alone. This I have seen. Praise His holy name."

***

Music filled the air with a pleasant sound that undergirded the feast of community of the redeemed. When the musicians broke out with songs of the redeemed of the Lord coming to Zion, all stopped and joined in with them.

Asher noticed Zapheth with joy on his face, talking and laughing with Gary. He looked about and realized that he knew every person sitting around the table. Each one had played a significant role in helping him along the way. As the people finished their meal, Asher rose with a goblet in his hand. "I wish to toast to the Lord, but also to all of you who never gave up on me. Thank you."

Lazarus rose to make his own toast. Deb beamed at her little brother. Philip had to hold her to keep her from jumping up to hug him.

In time, they rose to leave. Asher thanked each one until only Gary and Vera, Elchanan and Zamira, along with Kish and Charlene remained. Elchanan went to bring the car. They loaded in the leftover food but not the meat from the offering—that had been consumed.[56] Zamira rode with him. Kish walked with Gary and Vera.

"They act as if they are close friends."

"They are now. You'd think they'd been working together for decades." Charlene grasped his hand. "I have so much to tell you."

"Do you have a date set for the wedding?"

"This Friday morning before the Sabbath? The feast begins next week."

He paused and held both her hands. "Of course. You had to make decisions while I was at the center." As if beginning to speak, he also said, "And I have so much to share."

"You're right—in time. But first, let's get back to Elchanan's. We have a wedding to plan."

►19

THE DAYS PASSED quickly. Asher rose with a start from his bed in Zamira's second guest bedroom by the back stairs. He dressed and padded down the stairs, more visible now with the earliest rays of the sun leaving boxes of light on the top steps. By the courtyard, he paused to look at the portable canopy.

Tears began to form, but he did not have time for them now. Chairs had been added to the tables, and flowing translucent curtains crossed the boards and traced the pillars with gossamer wings looking more like a fairytale than his life. He licked his dry lips. *It will be soon.*

Asher turned to the Southern Gate and stepped carefully across the courtyard, not allowing his sandals to slap along the pavement and perhaps waken his sleeping bride. They had been apart for only a day, but that was all the time they could lock away.

However, the day apart in prayer and Bible reading had not seemed enough—not as the day drew to a close. Asher paused at the portico of the Southern Gate, his eyes on the rising sun. Not once since he had gone to the Lord had the terrible visions returned. He could look at the sun, hear the distant cries of the hawk, or smell that musty-river odor without being thrown back into a vision not of his own choosing.

Instead, he lifted his foot for the first step down…his eyes not leaving the Garden of Dreams. *What do I seek?* He wondered in his soul.

Have I not had enough visions to last a lifetime? Asher's light laughter ran before him down the stairs.

He danced and twirled and sang quiet songs of praise, for he was alive in the joy of the Lord! The dam had burst. The rivers ran free! His eye settled on a tiny hummingbird drinking from the still open flower of a large, iridescently white lily.

Suddenly, he fell to his knees. "Apart from You, Lord, we can do nothing. Let us not take one step without Your leave. And let us…" He rose to one knee… "let us not linger behind or fail to keep up."

Asher sat on a nearby bench, studying the row upon row of lilies, orchids and peonies. The rustle and snip of the gardener drew close. They exchanged smiles. He was glad she hadn't seemed to recognize him from his earlier appearances. *When I was different—before I was made whole.*

His mind scanned the possibilities. In the midst of the planning, they had had time to go to the training center for healers with Charlene, Owen and Kish. Charlene had a seat waiting for her. Owen would study with the teachers of the law. Asher smiled, remembering the lovely Sallie on his arm. Sallie would attend the same classes as Charlene.

Of course, Daniel would have been Asher's first choice for best man, but he was detained. A slight laugh escaped his lips. From there, it had been easy to select Isaac. Elchanan, Leon and Kish had completed his list. Not to keep Charlene without a friend from home, Owen had arranged for Sallie to come. As if a bond had set that had been forming over the years, Owen had barely let her leave his sight once she had arrived. Asher smiled. He wondered how long it would be before Owen proposed to Sallie.

The trumpet sound announcing the morning offering brought his head around. It was time. The rest of the answers—when and what to build, the programs, would have to come later. He paused, his foot in midair. "Lord? How will we gather the people? Who will come?"

The call of God's trumpets to His lost ones would echo through the earlier years. They would come—some from the deserted places, others from their groups, and those who had hidden in plain sight. Turning from lesser things to their destiny, they will find their peace and purpose in Christ. Counsel for families, parents and children followed with a growing school for healers. And then... Asher caught his breath... the light of distant days was dim and fragile, but the Holy Spirit would lead, and their purpose made sure.

—⁓—

Asher set his foot down and faced the city. *It is time.*

—⁓—

Zamira, Bethany and Giselle completed the final touches on Charlene's gown and veil draped down her back. Sallie leaned closer to secure Charlene's hair before the veil was set in place.

"You are beautiful," Sallie said softly. Her smile widened with Charlene's nod. "Don't worry," she added, seeing her friend's furrowed brow.

"Oh, you'll be calm on your day?" She jested lightly, remembering to draw a breath and relax.

Sallie beamed with a glint in her eye.

"Has he asked you?"

"No," the assistant slid her eyes away.

"He will."

She nodded, not wanting to spoil Charlene's day. *Now that you are out of reach, he will see me.* Again, she pondered, but it seemed as if they all knew that she was meant to be with Owen.

—⁓—

Their ceremony would be simple, with plain rings and direct vows. *That is how our center will be—simple, complete, sufficient, enough. A fit place for spiritual growth and healing.*

Asher stood waiting for her to step forward, led by her father, Gary Benson.

He barely heard the singing and Uriah's measured tones from the Scriptures that they had selected. Asher only had eyes for Charlene as he held her lace-gloved hand. They joined, they spoke, they pledged their years to one another.

Asher and Charlene, as one, walked before the open courtyard while all cheered. The music started. He stopped, suddenly shy.

"We are to dance first," Charlene whispered. "It's tradition!"

He began to dance with his bride, and the rest followed. After a few token numbers, they sat and watched the festivities. Asher held her hand. "Our dreams can come true."

She smiled, grasped his hand, and wiped a few tears from the corner of her eye.

The dancers blended and separated until the music morphed to the traditional heel and step dance. Asher raised his brow when Kish led the way, outdoing all with top hat and a wine glass balanced on top. Before he could jump up and introduce Giselle, he sat back as the mixed dancing resumed, when she approached Kish.

"They make a fine couple."

"Oh, they do. Who is she?"

"Giselle, a friend of Zamira's. She was at Isaac's wedding. Invited me to dance with her a year ago." *Had it been that short a time?*

As soon as they could slip away, Elchanan arrived with his little car already loaded with their luggage.

"Where?"

"Come, my bride. Do you not know the man is to build the house for his lovely bride?" He smiled at Elchanan.

"Oh, that day—when you disappeared, leaving me at the mercy of Zamira and her sister to finish the details for the wedding?"

"Yes, that one. It's temporary. Keep that in mind, but it will be a place for us to take a day before the feast begins."

"And your renters? The ones with the goats or were they sheep?"

"They were ready to pasture them elsewhere and were going to ask to farm it, but they let me end the contract. Our land is open and waiting."

"We will see what the Lord will do."

—⁓—

The prefab home was small. But when she entered and saw the framed prints of the Rocky Mountains, her comforter on the bed and her Bible and journal by the bedstand, she swung her arms around him.

"We are home."

Charlene took Asher's hand and led him outside. In the distance, to the north, the Temple rose above the city. She stood close, letting their arms rest against each other. "To life!"

"To life!" he echoed.

20

CHARLENE ARRANGED THE extra dishes in the small cupboard of their pre-fab in Zebulun. She peered out the nearest window. Asher was still out for his early morning walk. She set the kettle to boil, made her own cup of coffee and pulled out her Bible and journal. They needed time to adjust to each other.

"Well?" she asked when the door slid shut. Charlene reheated the water for his coffee.

Asher placed his Bible on the table and sat, staring at her with an almost blank look.

Her hand tensed, but she willed it to open and poured the water over the French press. "Have a good quiet time?"

"Yes." Asher stared at her.

Charlene slid the coffee closer to him and sat down. "Honey, what's the matter?"

"You're leaving."

"You know I have to take the course. I thought we had discussed this. You could stay with Elchanan and take construction jobs in Jerusalem." She reached over and held his hand. "You don't have to stay here alone. Is that what's bothering you?"

He drew breath and rose to pace the small kitchen area, his thoughts swirling. *Where to begin?* "We have a calling to create a center and that means development, planning, construction." He resisted the urge to drop his head in his hand. *What must she be thinking of me?*

"Did you receive a timetable with your vision?" Charlene had discerned at least three calls in Asher's vision. "It almost seemed as if the Lord was showing you glimpses of the future over many years. Remember what Dad taught you? A simple house in a planned development could take over a year of preparation and permits to bring it all together. But to develop a neighborhood could take years. So…" She stood and looked over the acres of grasslands and rows of trees that followed the small river that ran along the western portion of their land. "We begin anew—like Noah and his family." Charlene looked back at Asher. "I don't think He expects you to bring it to pass overnight." She sat. "What do we focus on first?"

"You take that course at En Chaika." Asher's mouth went dry. "I… my heart wrenches when I realize that we're only going to see each other on the weekends, and that's if I can make it. I don't want to impose on Elchanan."

"Asher! He's like a grandfather to you. They are our family. Didn't Zamira say that they will always have room for us?"

He rose to pace again. *What was the real issue?* "Charlene, will they take me as I am now, or will they remember…?"

"Asher! Go and do what the Lord lays on your heart. Don't worry about what others think. They will learn in time that you have been truly healed. You're not the only former wanderer!"

"You're right. We can talk with them about it when we visit in a few days."

She smiled, sitting back in her chair. "Now, when is the best time to meet our neighbors? How many kids do they have? You said they're farmers?"

He looked over. "I don't know."

"Their names?"

"Uhh, guess I'd have to pull the contract."

Not surprised, Charlene rose and fetched their simple breakfast of cheese, fresh fruits and figs. "Well, I'm looking forward to walking over."

"We're going to have to drive. It's a long way. It took me a day to walk to and from their homestead."

———

The small auto they had been able to purchase came to life, and Asher drove it on the dirt paths. "We'll have to lay down a decent road before the next rainy season," Asher stated.

"I'll add that to the list. You'd hire that done and focus on building our center?"

Asher nodded, not taking his eyes off the path as it turned north to track a tributary from the River of Life that branched southward before making its way to the Western Sea. He smiled. "Your mom kept the lists, as I recall."

"Yep. Dad said he didn't need them as he had a good memory."

"He does."

"But she often brought up items at breakfast. I know he tried to hide that he was glad for the reminders. Mom's lists helped rescue him more than once."

Asher laughed, remembering the busy breakfasts that resembled open kitchen time—grab and go, along with the never-ending coffee.

Charlene gazed at the lush olive and fig trees that clumped around the river, and the myriad of flowers, blooming in deep reds and bright yellows. "Please stop!" She exited the car and approached a large clump of tender blue flowers—small effervescent blue cups that rode up slim stems. "Beautiful. May I bring some?"

"Of course, they're on our land." Asher watched his wife pick a smattering of smaller flowers, arranging them in her hand. Hope filled him. *Together, we can bring the Lord's vision to pass.*

Asher noted the additional barn at their neighbor's homestead. A fence encircled a large vegetable garden and more than a dozen rows of ornamental flowers.

Charlene drew in her breath. "Roses! Oh, Asher, they know how to grow roses!"

He smiled and parked in front of the house, now dwarfed by a large barn across from the center drive. Asher stretched and noticed the small irrigation ditch bringing water from the river—the same one that traversed his land. "Well-watered and giving life," he said quietly.

Charlene stood by his side. "Ready to introduce me?"

"Any time." They headed for the main house, now a sprawling two-story affair with a large front porch. "He's really expanded in only two years."

Hearing the cries of young ones, Charlene nodded. "Sounds like a growing family."

Asher rapped on the door and stepped back. A toddler approached, looked at them through the screen and ran away.

A woman emerged carrying a baby in her arms. "Yes?"

"Your long-lost neighbor, Asher, with my bride, Charlene."

"So glad to meet you. Come in," she held the door. "I'm Esther," she said to Charlene. "David's in the fields readying them for the next harvest. We can hardly keep up with it."

They followed her into the kitchen where a twin to the baby in her arms sat in a highchair. "Two for the price of one," Esther quipped.

"Your roses are beautiful. Are you the gardener?"

She pointed to the closest chair. "Yes, I always loved roses, but in this new world, without having to fight blights and infestations, they blossom and thrive." She brought a coffeepot. "Today's roses are magnificent and without thorns!"

"I'd like to see them." Charlene glanced at Asher. "When we build the house, could we add a flower bed?"

"Whatever you can handle," Asher said with a laugh.

"Right! Right! If I plant it, I take care of it."

"But it's easier now." Esther joined them with her cup.

Charlene extended her arms for the baby. "How old?"

"They're almost a year, Micah and Sarah. Ella's the oldest. I'd be happy to show you around, and then I need to finish lunch. David will be by soon. Can you stay?"

"Yes, wanted to drop by before, but…" He paused.

"I know, you just married. Newlyweds need time together. We had almost half a year, but then the children came." She smiled and let the older Ella climb onto her lap. Her eyes beamed as she looked at her daughter with dark, bouncing curls. "Here to stay now?"

"Well," Charlene glanced at Asher who seemed content to let her do the talking. "I'll be taking the healer's courses at En Chaika Healing Center. We have a few days before I have to go."

"What will you do, Asher?"

"Still figuring that out. Need to build a proper house. The pre-fab I brought in is just temporary."

"Right, we did the same thing. It takes time to discover the proper layout, placement, and then to decide the best way to build. I'm glad David had the foresight to design the house so we could expand easily."

"Could you show us?"

"Well, that's David's expertise, but I'd be glad to show you the gardens. The kids could use getting out of the house for a while." Esther glanced at Ella stifling a yawn. "Things work better if I can keep them up until lunch, and then they all nap together."

"Even Mom?"

"Even Mom."

"Great idea." Charlene rose with Asher, still holding the infant Micah.

Esther lifted Sarah from the highchair. She watched Asher extend a hand to Ella. "Do you remember her?"

"I think when we first met, she had been a sleeping infant."

They followed Esther to the circular drive and headed for the rose garden. "We would be interested in hearing your plans. I know David had said we no longer needed your pastures, but our goat herd has multiplied, and the markets haven't kept up yet. I know the demand will come in time. We're still building breeding stock. We were going to contact you, but we wanted to give you time to settle in."

He glanced in the large barn sectioned mostly for large equipment. He recalled the lean-tos in the fields that sheltered the goats and sheep. "You use tractors?"

"Yes. We managed to get in a good bid on tractors—leftovers from before."

Asher stared at the loader and skidder. "Do they work?"

"Temperamental, but they're serviceable. He uses those for clearing and grading."

"Asher is a good mechanic."

"I make do," Asher stated with a shy smile.

They walked the rows of roses of varying colors and sizes. The narrow path rimmed the perimeter of the garden, and Esther pointed out the various sections. Asher allowed the women to pull ahead. Ella's little legs worked to keep up, but he could see she was tiring. Scooping her up in his arms, he smiled as she babbled and pointed at the birds flitting past. His thoughts wandered to their own children that the Lord would give them in time. Perhaps it would be sooner than he thought. *House first.*

The air was light and fresh with a slight breeze sweetened by the roses, lilacs and flowering bushes along a hedgerow. He turned full circle, no longer having to fear facing the sun. Peace welled up—this was home.

They toured the flower beds and the garden. Charlene plied Esther with many questions, and she seemed eager to share her knowledge. They walked up the steps, and Esther headed for a two-way radio on a stand in the hall by the stairs.

Eventually David replied. "Tractor broke. I'll be a little late."

"Our neighbors are here," Esther stated.

Asher signaled for the radio. "Your wandering neighbor, Asher.

Could I bring some tools and parts?" He listened to David's answer. "I'll drive over."

Charlene played with Ella while Esther prepared the midday meal. Family, children, home had seemed so distant and out of reach, but she felt the stirrings of longing for her daughter. *What would her name be?*

"Were you in Jerusalem when God came?"

"No." Charlene told her story. "And you?"

"I was in Petra."

"Do you know Elchanan and Zamira?"

"Doesn't everybody?" They both laughed. "There are so few of us. But I had never heard of Asher."

Hesitant to share details about Asher's troubles, she said, "He was a burier searching for markers away from Jerusalem."

"What a privilege! I remember when we all cleared the land. David traded for a load of Armageddon firewood."

"I saw the pile." It would take time for the world to grow its forests to provide fuel for fires as well as lumber for building. "And you? Did you meet David there?"

"No, he lived in France. How he managed to survive! He hardly talks about his ordeals, but he lived near a series of caves where he managed to stay hidden after the desolation and everything changed. We met clearing the land and just knew."

Charlene laughed. "Everything changed for us with the disappearances."

"That too! But we didn't really understand until the Lord destroyed Gog and Magog and then led many to Petra." She rose, hearing David on the radio.

Charlene kept a watch on the children.

"They'll be here soon. Would you mind helping to feed the twins? Ella's such a big girl…" She smiled at her daughter. "She eats with us."

"Not at all. They grow so quickly." They talked of little things until they heard the vehicles return.

They ate and talked as if they had been friends for years.

Esther settled the children for their naps.

Charlene shared her dream for learning how to use the healing leaves, but Asher tried to dodge their questions about his plans.

"You were a burier. Did they send you to distant places?"

"No," Asher paused, reluctant to share. *Why am I ashamed?* Yes, he had resisted the Lord, but his story showed God's great love and mercy. It was only fair that they knew. He began.

"I believe the Lord wants us to establish a healing center like En Chaika here. My friend from Dan received the same vision." He paused, trying to gauge their reactions. The silence lingered.

David and Esther exchanged looks. "How soon can you begin?"

"You have lost ones?" Charlene asked.

As if a dam had burst, David and Esther listed ten wanderers they knew and the rumors of more in Zebulun and nearby Gad. "While the numbers might seem small, it's so hard on those who are left. How do we help them?"

"First, with prayer."

"Of course, but what if they don't come back? Will the Lord take action?"

"He waits for us to be ready. Yes, He makes them ready, but in time, I believe all will be brought in."

"And then what?"

Asher nodded at David. "An excellent question. The healing center will always be there with the leaves from The River to keep us whole and healthy through this time. But it will also be a place for us to worship, study, learn and pray." He sat back. "Where do you go to shop for supplies?"

"We barter among ourselves. There are some small outposts in Benjamin, but many make trips to Jerusalem."

"We can build a town here, near the river." Asher noticed their hosts exchanging glances. "What?"

"We already have a meeting place where we barter. Some bring items to share—ones they made, or supplies purchased from the north. It's on your land. Actually, where the three tracts meet. We've wanted to tell you about it but didn't know how to contact you. If we'd known, we could have left word with Elchanan."

Asher smiled. "Yes, that is what I saw. Probably there or close by the Lord showed me a town by the river. Have they named it?"

"Not quite. We've hardly set up a local council. Five of us tend to meet there every other month to discuss who needs help and how things are progressing. In two weeks, on a Wednesday, we'll probably gather."

"I'll try to make it. Charlene will be at En Chaika by then."

They discussed the possibilities, and the couple gave them two baskets of vegetables and a dozen ivory cream miniature roses.

▶21

THE DAY CAME, and Asher drove to En Chai-
ka. He had not been back since the day he went to the Lord for healing.
Somehow, he thought he would feel conflicted, but he remembered
the warm water of the Eastern Sea and its abundant life. The center's
white buildings gleamed like pearls outlined by a sparkling sea. Trellised flowers arched over the drive. Green and yellow parakeets flut-
tered among flowering bushes.

Machir met them at the entrance. "Charlene, Asher, your bunga-
low is ready. Bring your luggage—all of it."

Asher glanced at Charlene with furrowed brow, but she merely
smiled back and shrugged her shoulders.

He led them to a small cottage and opened the door. "You know the
dining schedule. Charlene, see Chilion; Asher, see Zephath in his office."

"Thank you," Charlene said and nudged Asher.

"Yes, thank you. We'll be right there."

Charlene placed her bag on the holder.

"What is going on? Did they tell you anything about me?"

"No, see what Zephath says."

───※───

He left her at the Healing Room. It took him a while, but he found
the hall that led to the offices of the priests, counselors and instructors.

He rapped on Zephath's door, and upon hearing his summons, stepped into the office to hover just inside the small room.

Zephath looked up from his computer. "Close the door. Come in." He watched Asher stiffly step to the side. "Please sit down." He attempted a smile.

Asher sat on a slightly padded straight chair. The bookshelves behind the priest's desk and along the wall overflowed with books, notebooks and papers. To think the man lived and breathed Hebrew, the language of God's Word! He nodded at the open testaments on his desk.

"They must be alive for you."

The man nodded slightly. "You love the Covenants, as I recall."

"Yes. I missed the latest division. Is that it? On your desk?" He accepted the paper from Zephath and read. "Beautiful, yet a warning."

"While we are privileged to live in God's utopia, we are not yet in heaven. What do the Scriptures say is to occur at the end of the thousand years?"

"*And when the thousand years are ended, Satan will be released from his prison and will come out to deceive the nations that are at the four corners of the earth.*[57] A rebel army will attack the Lord and His people."

"If all who enter the kingdom are believers, who is it that will rise against the one true God?"

"Our children."

"And thus, we must remember to persuade all who come after us to have believing faith in the Savior. This will be our job."

"Along with living lives that bring glory to the one true God."

"That too." The rabbi gathered his thoughts. "I heard the testimony of your vision. Your wife is acquiring the training to do her part. What about you?"

Asher tried not to roll his eyes. He forced himself to meet the man's direct gaze. "What I saw was so vast. How can I accomplish it? Yet I believe that where God calls, He will lead. But where to begin?" His eyes slid away, pondering the question. Looking back, he added, "In a perfect world, I would earn degrees in the Covenants and counseling. Yet, the study of the Scriptures is not finished with one degree or plan of study. No, it's a lifelong feeding on the Word itself, as the Holy Spirit reveals it to us, day by day."

The priest nodded, a ghost of a smile on his face. "And so it is. So it is. But the courses provide the tools, the foundational principles for that life of study. And counseling..." he swallowed a laugh. "Trying to guide men in the healing of their souls is as easy as catching moonbeams in your hands. Again, you help them see and then try to point them to the path, but each one is unique. Our Creator chooses different ways for us all. This also we must accept."

"God gives the increase. We are merely messengers." Asher watched Zapheth nod in agreement.

"I've enrolled you in the Testament courses. The one-year program—same length as your wife's course. And the counseling courses. You may stay at the Center. It will be best for your studies." He pushed some papers across the desk, "Here is a contract for you to help locate wanderers or assist at Hamonah." Zapheth cleared his throat. "If that is acceptable to you?"

"Yes, this is great news. I was concerned about how to finance everything and still pay for materials to build a house. But this is good. The first step." He recognized the standard contract he had signed at Hamonah. "Rabbi, God doesn't expect us to get everything done right away, does He?"

"No," a laugh rose up from his belly. "Not at all." Zapheth rose and looked out the window to the Temple's roof. "You worked on the Temple?"

"I built part of the western wall. It must have been a busy time."

The priest nodded. "And if you want to continue your studies, you will be welcome to do so."

Asher rose and extended his hand. "Thank you. Thank you for everything."

———

The next day, still settling in, Charlene emerged resplendent in her flowing gossamer sweater that trailed behind her as she walked. "Zamira won't mind us joining them for the feast?"

He laughed and pulled her into a warm embrace. "I think they live for these times. Remember our wedding? Their faces were nearly as bright as yours—if that were possible." Asher picked up their two bags. They were close enough that they could commute each day, but he didn't want to miss celebrating with dear friends his first feast free of dark memories.

They walked up the Mount to the southern city gate. Charlene paused to look back. The center gleaming against the azure blue of the lake in the bright morning light. "The new moon, each night a little brighter as the days progress," she said under her breath. "Home," she stated and smiled at Asher.

———

The markets pulsed, the streets breathed with the sounds of many footfalls, wrapping of food stuffs and gathering of palms, the chatter of bartering and the laughter, even of little ones. Asher wondered how crowded Elchanan's courtyard would be. Not disappointed, he paused by the old, gnarled tree. Gary, Vera, Menachem and Hannah were not there. Instead, he greeted several he had never met. For an instant he wondered if they should find other lodging or walk up each day. Charlene squeezed his hand. His heart settled. *The Lord will provide. I need not fear.*

"Oh, here they are!" Elchanan stepped past a group finishing the roof of the third booth in the long, narrow courtyard. "Our friends! Your booth is waiting. It won't build itself!" With a flourish, he introduced them to the group. "Our friends from Egypt."

"The Highway joins us in step as in heart," Asher said. They each hugged. He had never traveled to the far south of the highway. Perhaps someday they could. But as he cast about the three booths, all but one was finished. He turned back to Elchanan.

"My friend, since this is your first year of wedded life, look up and see!"

Upon the flat roof on the northern side of the house, the sitting and dining areas, stood naked logs tied together with the roof frame open to the sun now far up in the sky. One pointed out the piles of branches brimming with leaves, the drapes, curtains, stuffed mattress, pillows and rugs for a simple tent.

They set to work. Asher carried them up the ladder and Charlene pulled them up to lay them on the roof. She stepped back, marveling as he placed rugs and dividing curtains, covered the roof and walls, then creating a covered veranda facing the Temple. Providing each item as he called for it, she entered their tent—their home for the week. "But where will I cook? Where will we eat?"

"Oh," Asher directed her gaze to the now-erected awning jutting out from the main section of the house. "We will eat as a family. And your help will be expected." He knew she would be a willing participant.

—*∿*—

Asher joined the others setting up the folding chairs. He smiled, hearing Charlene's voice along with the other women helping Zamira in the kitchen. The age of grace continued, allowing each assembly to choose their own way to honor the gathering—some cooking on makeshift fires, others from nearby kitchens.

Zelkar from Faiyum, Egypt, asked, "So, what is the first day at the Temple like? This is your second feast, yes?"

The din had died down somewhat among the people standing on the far side of the court, waiting for the women to fill the table with the many dishes. Asher shifted his eyes away briefly, praying for what to say. *Speak truth!* Nodding, he smiled and faced the friendly young

Egyptian who also loved God and His Word. "I helped them build the booths. I helped them rebuild after the war, but the feast." He shook his head and glanced away. "I wandered. I couldn't face the press of people in the Temple courtyard." He met Zelkar's searching gaze. "I worshiped from beyond Hamonah—from the empty places. I was with them in spirit, even if I could not be there in person."

"And this year?"

"I came to the Lord for healing a short time ago. I married Charlene last week. We will experience it together."

"We must talk of this more," Zelkar stated. "So we can help our brethren who linger outside the gates."

"I look forward to it."

Hearing the call to eat, they turned.

—✦✦✦—

In the early evening, the air fresh and clean, Asher and Charlene made their way through the city to the Western Gate and down a gentle slope to the fields that supplied food for the city. The feast occurred after the harvest, and sections had been cordoned off for delegations from the nations.

"I think Dad said their booths were in the northeast sector." Charlene led the way, a rough map in her hands. "Owen and Sallie will also be there."

Asher followed her, holding back the reminder that they had three other booths to visit. He knew she had to stay in contact with her family, and it might be a long time before they were together again.

The women met and compared notes, almost talking over one another. Gary, Owen and Asher watched.

"Doesn't Zebulun have an area?" Owen asked.

"I guess, but I hardly know anyone there yet. Maybe on the western side? There's always next year." They all laughed at that reply.

"Nine hundred ninety-eight more."

"At least."

After sitting down for the obligatory iced coffee and donuts, they headed to the Temple Plaza, skirting past the Southern Wall and down to the fields bordering the Western Wall of the city. "Dan's section is right on the border with the priest's lands."

Asher nodded, noting the banners for the various tribes.

"Zebulun's is on the southern side, remember? We won't see it from here."

"I know." He glanced at her map and continued on. He swallowed a laugh, seeing Kish's tall frame beside many of the standard-sized structures.

"Wow, I didn't imagine his would be that short!" Charlene laughed lightly when the tallest pole structure, with woven walls, came into view.

"I'm guessing that's Kish's." Asher stepped onto the makeshift lot, but the large man who exited the tent was not Kish. It might have been his brother, but he was not certain. "Sorry, looking for a friend."

"Finally! Thought you'd decided you were done with us!" Kish approached Asher from the side.

"Not rid of us yet." He faced his friend. "Where's your tent?"

"You found it. Meet Andrew, my brother."

Asher stared, trying not to look as dumbfounded as he felt. Giselle emerged and invited them in. He looked back at Kish.

"First thing I did was make peace with my brother. We're still figuring it out, but we needed somewhere to plan the wedding away from wagging tongues and prying eyes."

"Wedding?"

"Well," Kish ran his hand through his groomed hair and beard.

"Ahh!" Asher smiled. "Following in our fine tradition. If it's right, why wait?"

"Exactly! What time will you go to the first offering tomorrow?"

"Start of the second hour from the Southern Gate."

"Wait for us. We want to join your group. With Elchanan?"

"Of course."

Without having to ask, Kish relayed their story. "You'd think I'd told him I'd cut him off when I signed over all my road contracts to him."

"Not the first time you had made overtures of peace only to gain more advantage." Andrew shook his head. "He hadn't even told me he'd been to see Yeshua."

The brothers shared their vision for Dan and their desire to raise up a people for the Lord, as well as send out emissaries to the lands north and east. Asher couldn't keep his broad smile from spreading across his face. With a little nudging from Charlene, he shared their dreams for the central region of Zebulun.

Finally, promising to visit them before the next Passover, the couple walked to the road and headed northeast. The Prince's portion had set aside an area for their brethren of Judah. "Isaac and Hannah," Asher stated, "will understand if our visit is short, but I wanted you to meet them. He was always a great help and encouragement to me. Do you remember them from the wedding?"

Charlene shook her head. Some parts of that day were still a blur.

Isaac and Hannah had a small tent for themselves. As the night deepened with no moon, they sat facing the pillar of fire by night. The men talked of the sacrifices to come the next day—the seven bulls and rams, and a male goat for a sin offering, with the grain and oil.[58]

Asher described their offerings to the Lord. He looked at Charlene. "She made a thanksgiving offering that day and held a feast in the courtyard of the Temple. Tell them what you said that day."

Charlene blushed. "That Asher's vision from the Lord would be my vision."

"Like Ruth," Hannah said.

She nodded.

►22

THE DAY DAWNED with the sounding of the trumpets. Charlene rose and joined Asher already seated on the rug facing the Temple, his covenant opened in his lap. She sat near him, praying, as she leaned closer to touch his shoulder. Angelic singing, blending with the Temple choir floated on the breeze from the Mount. Heavenly chords enveloped them, vibrating with pulses of light. Joy, peace, pure hope surrounded them, and Asher drank in the settled stillness in his soul, worshiping in the Spirit with the love of his life by his side.

The day had come—the day when the Lord Himself would greet the worshipers, and they would sing His praises. Asher opened his eye to read the New Hallel one more time, now seven Psalms of praise and thanksgiving for Immanuel. *What a gift!* God dwelt with men and His peace covered the world. Even the rustling of opening the bags and pouring out the granola merged with the angelic singing resonating from the Temple.

Charlene brought two plates for the short table. Asher smiled as she attempted to recline in the ancient half-sitting position. "I'm a modern man," he quipped, sitting upright on his pillow.

"I had to try it, having read about it shortly after we found Christ." Charlene paused. "Sorry." She sighed and sat upright. He was healed, and she no longer had to be afraid of triggering an attack. "Those days, as hard as they were…"

"We will always treasure," he finished as he reached for her hand. The dark fears were gone…the horrible memories silenced and buried in the depths of the sea. Now, they could recall their time together as the troubles had only brought them closer together. At times, they moved through their days with the certain knowledge that God had every minute under control. There was nothing they could not do with Him by their side—opportunities to share the reality of a living God, extending His love to others who also had experienced great pain and loss, and embracing his budding love for Charlene that he had not been aware of during those days.

She leaned close. "I have a secret. I loved you from the day I saw you in that rusty old Toyota that never quit."

"Oh, a stalker, huh? So that's how you caught me on Old Man Totten's land?"

She wrapped her hand around his, and they stared into each other's eyes before they remembered the time and the breakfast in front of them.

From the roof they could see the throngs beginning to grow and swell first in the market areas and then along the pathways up to the Temple plaza. "We are in the second group?"

"Zamira gave me an updated schedule this morning." She pulled out a folded page from a pocket. "Each contingent from a region presents itself before the Lord over the six days. The seventh—what they call the great day, is for Israel. Now that I am of Zebulun, we could join that group."

Asher accepted the sheet and spread it out on the table. Zebulun was second to last, only Gad lay farther south. An empty feeling within yielded no direction.

"Of course, only the official representatives have to appear at these times. The rest can take any ticket."

"Ticket?"

"Elchanan brought them late yesterday for all his guests. You were busy. This is the first year they've had to hand out tickets."

Asher nodded. A slight inner tension threatened to rise up when he thought of the crowds, but he felt it melt away, remembering a recent gathering at a daily morning offering. The jostling crowd and undertow of voices had seemed to focus his worship instead of bringing up past anxieties. Together, as one, they had sung praises and songs of thanksgiving. The priest's charge had touched his soul, as he had spoken on the third book of the new covenant. He glanced her way to take their pair of tickets. They would be in the last group.

"Elchanan said we could stay for the water ceremony."

Asher nodded, remembering last year's. He had hovered by the western branch of the River as it trickled from under the Temple Plaza. The priest, whose number had been drawn, was granted the privilege to lower a golden pitcher to draw living water from the River. He had turned, the crowd following, and made his way back to the altar before the Lord, joined by the one sent to the eastern branch of the River.

"Have you seen it?"

"Only the drawing of the water—not the Lord of Glory pouring the water upon the altar as He has poured the Holy Spirit upon us." He nodded. "Next year we will tabernacle with Zebulun."

Charlene looked puzzled, but she nodded.

Asher squeezed her hand. "During the weekends we can travel to our land, meet the people and worship with them." She nodded. "And maybe even to Gad, to search out…"

Their eyes met and as one they looked at the pillar of cloud, heard the swelling chorus.

"There weren't enough for all to attend the first sacrifice."

"The bull for the sin offering, by the Prince."

He nodded. "It is right they go before the Lord as a family."

They turned back to their Bibles and journals. To sit and study and pray in sight of the Temple seemed to add insight to their devotions.

Asher counted the rising smoke from each burnt offering—first the seven young bulls.

"We can make our way to the plaza with the first ram."

Normally, it took minutes to walk from the city to the plaza, but today, time would be a treasure to savor. The streams of people coming from all directions swelled the crowds as they ascended the steps to the Mount. All were one, unified in the Spirit of Christ. Spontaneous songs burst forth along with encouraging words of thanksgiving and praise.

"The seventh, which is the eighth for the day." Asher set his books aside.

Charlene stood beside him, and together they headed for the narrow steps along the eastern wall of the house. Asher paused for a moment and extended his hand. He felt her simple ring press against his palm.

The Levite in the courtyard on a pedestal proclaimed, "The fifth ram of the burnt offering."

Charlene glanced at Asher. They were on the plaza that surrounded the Temple walls on the southern side. He nodded toward the western wall. "We have time."

They wended their way through the crowds. Those waiting for the next offering were lined up, ready to enter the outer court through the gate. The swelling songs of praise as the sacrifices continued were muffled slightly when they rounded the southwest corner to walk along the long Western Wall unbroken by gate or window.

Owen and Sallie were ahead, standing next to a tall figure, glowing with the glory of the Lord.

Charlene paused, "That might be Millard. He's one of the 144,000."

"The one who led him to the Lord? The one he sheltered?" They stood silent, not wanting to intrude.

Feeling a heavenly presence, they both turned. "Daniel! Is this going to be a common occurrence?"

"No, during these days we are granted to mingle. It is good to see you whole, my friend. To you..." His dark eyes looked at both of them. "has been granted to live on this earth. While good, it has not yet been perfected. To us has been granted to lead and direct but observing as from afar. The day will come when we will be together again. Sorrow not for my brief pain. It was insignificant in the light of dwelling in the heavenly Jerusalem."

Gone was the desire to have died in his place. "Our path is set. We need only walk it, day by day. And in glory, someday..."

"We will see only the light of eternity, and these days will be past. For now, the Lord will raise up the rest of His people for the new heaven and the new earth."

They touched not, nor did they draw near. To speak of their daily life would only have cheapened the moment. Asher began to sing the New Hallel, and Daniel joined him. Charlene provided an alto harmony as their voices took on a cantor's rhythms.

Daniel looked to the parting cloud. "You are of the sacrifice of the goat. It is soon."

Owen and Sallie had continued on. They joined hands and headed to the Northern Gate.

"So, which group are you in?" Owen asked when they drew near the areas of worshipers waiting to form and enter the courtyard.

"The goat."

Sallie smiled and clasped Charlene's hand. "Us too! This is so exciting. An ambassador came and described it. They couldn't record the sacrifices, but he gave a whole seminar on the sacrifices and rituals. I never thought I would get to see it in person, but..." She cast a warm look at Owen. "Here we are!"

Owen stepped closer to her side. "The light pillars in the courtyard lit up the sky. I'd wondered if they could be seen for hundreds of miles."

"They are," Asher stated. The last feast, after watching the drawing of the water on the last day, he had retreated far to the north, having never witnessed the special offerings of the feast. "Will it be like our offerings before our wedding?"

"We will go through the near gate to the inner court and bow as they sacrifice the male goat. Groups will form to enter the Temple where we will see the Lord, Himself, surrounded by some of His chosen ones. Millard attended an earlier session, but he said He will speak to us."

"But He comes forth for the water ceremony?"

"He will." Owen took Asher aside. "Uriah was chosen to draw the water from the eastern branch. He said that a class of wanderers will be healed right after the Lord pours the living water on the altar."

Asher's face lit up with pure joy. "I'd like to see that. And so, He will bring all to Him. Not one will be lost!"

"And to think the Lord has granted us the privilege to minister with Him!" He smiled, glad that the two of them could attend some of the same classes in the coming months.

—∼∼∼—

Cleansed, ceremonially clean, they stayed to the side after their audience with the Lord of Glory. The glow lingered. The words He had spoken filled their souls with His presence.

Asher watched Zapheth lead the group that had come for healing. Seeing the hopeful looks of the men and women in white robes with sashes, his prayers welled up. His own tears streaked his face seeing them emerge with tears of joy and the glow of peace.

The four watched a Levite shepherd the group out of the inner court. Zapheth followed with a broad smile on his face. He extended his hand to Asher as he drew near. "The joy! No longer do we strive to help the wounded live out their days not whole or complete!" The priest tapped Asher's shoulder. "You and your wife must come to our sukka, our tent." He studied Owen. "Are you the other one—from Colorado? You also wish to build a healing center?"

Owen, standing close to Sallie, beamed. "We do. From Dan to

Beersheba to the midst of the coastlands. We're almost in the center of the continent."

"You come as well. There are others who would like to hear your vision."

"When, Rabbi Zapheth?"

"Why, now!" He leaned close to Asher's face. "Unless you have something more pressing?!"

Asher tried not to roll his eyes. It was a joke from his earlier days at En Chaika. "Not at all. My time is yours."

"I have some things to attend to. Meet me on the plaza in front of the Eastern Gate."

Zapheth, having changed from his priestly garments, greeted them warmly and headed down the stairs leading to the priests' lands.

"Had you any idea you were of Zadok?" Owen asked.

"Not at all. Didn't even know I was of Levi. I survived living in the streets, but when He delivered us from our enemies, making a way for us to escape to Petra, I followed the throng. From them I learned the truth—that Jesus had been the Sent One and that He was the Lord of glory! From there we waited for the end, growing daily in our knowledge and love of God, experiencing His provision—almost as if we were in the wilderness, completely dependent upon Him for living waters and manna from heaven."

A beautiful woman wearing a tan robe and jeweled sandals brought the lunch. She smiled. "Sit right there. I'm Miriam, and I am so pleased to meet you." Her broad smile rested on Charlene and Sallie. "Daughters of Light, may the Lord be with you."

They ate, saying little, in unity and fellowship.

"We didn't get a chance to really meet that day," Miriam said, looking at Charlene.

Almost blushing, Charlene nodded wordlessly. She knew their hostess was referring to their thanksgiving feast.

"You said that you did not need a vision because your husband's vision would be your vision."

"Yes."

"Yet God leads us as well. How is He leading you?"

"To love those He leads us to. To find them and share God's love for them. To give them a place where they can rest and seek, fearing nothing. To learn how to use the fruits of the trees and their leaves for nourishment and healing." She tilted her head, "But it is more than that." She encircled her fingers around Asher's broad palm. "Our children..." She nodded. "Our community...That ours would be a center where all can come throughout the ten generations."

Without thought, they all joined hands. Zapheth looked to the upper ceiling. "One by one in turn, the first, the second, on to the last generation..." He surveyed the group. "We are called to seek out the Lord's lost ones—those who know Him but are not yet ready to join us. In the future, we seek those who walk right on the outside but whose hearts are hard against God. All need to know that only through Jesus can we come to God and dwell with Him in the New Jerusalem for eternity on the New Earth."

They would remember that day as they helped at En Chaika and Hamonah, as they built their cities and retreat centers, and as they walked among the world now populated with millions and then billions, that all needed to be saved.

PART TWO

The Latter Days

►23

THE RANCH HOUSE near Paran River cast an arch across the courtyard. Slender limestone walls reaching up to chest level were topped by chiseled stones.

Charlene emerged from their home and surveyed the tan stone building that had stood for centuries. She held back her smile when Asher had the stable hand push their traveling carriage from the middle barn.

Asher emerged from the left-hand barn, leading her gray mare with a beautiful broad back and flowing tail that almost touched the ground.

"So, take the horses and not the car?" She approached and reached for the lead. "I thought we were stopping by Jael's for a quick visit. They are in New Tel-Aviv—in that condo overlooking the Sea."

"And a stable is a few blocks away." Asher retrieved his black gelding and glanced again at his beautiful wife, still so vibrant and full of life after 998 years. "Lester's coming with us, and he prefers riding horses."

Lester, one of their great-grandsons, was of the tenth generation. Charlene said, "I hadn't heard. The horses it is. But where is he?"

"We'll meet up with him at Isaac's."

"Oh, we're stopping at Isaac's too?"

Asher nodded. He had had a dream that night, and he needed to talk with his good friend from their burying days. Originally, he had thought about riding up by himself after their visit with Kish, but the Lord had changed his mind when Lester had phoned to say he could not meet them in Zebulun. And the dream…he couldn't let go of it. Had his friend had a similar one? Over the centuries it seemed as if the dreams and visions had almost vanished, or had life become so busy and full fewer were looking for them. Reminding himself that God works with purpose, he set about tacking his gelding.

They all had their place. They all had made their mark—himself, Elchanan, Isaac, Jael, Kish, Lazarus and Owen. Two years ago, they had visited Charlene's family in the States. However, for the first time, he realized it might have been for the last time. Ordinarily, they visited every two years, but he felt, as the end of the millennial kingdom approached, they would be busy with other tasks.

Clarice and Patrick began to load the carriage—suitable for carrying luggage or a group of people. Clarice was a transplant from Colorado and an expert horse trainer. Patrick, from Ireland, could manage any task Asher set for him. They were not only some of their best workers but also dear friends. However, as he cinched down the saddle, he wondered again if they knew the Lord directly—*were their names written in the Lamb's Book of Life?*

Shaking his head to distill the unsettling parts of his dream, he brought the horses to the water trough for a last drink. Following Clarice's lead, he helped put one horse by the left side of the carriage tongue. She needed only a short time to secure the tracings.

It should not have surprised him that, over the years, it had become harder to discern those who resisted the grace of God in their hearts. Everyone had seen the Lord Jesus, knew the words of faith, and because of an absence of outside forces to lead them astray, seemed to live the same lives as their believing neighbors. *Have I done enough to share the inner walk of faith with my beloved workers?*

Asher recalled what Sallie had said during their last visit to Colorado. None of them—neither he or Owen or the Bensons had experienced living in a "Christian" region. However, Sallie's hometown had had such a Christian worldview that it permeated all aspects of the community, including the schools. She had said, "Everyone put on a good show. I had no idea our next-door neighbors struggled with alcoholism. If you had asked them if they were Christians, they would have said they were—despite the fact that after the rapture they joined in on attacking Christians. Overnight, they exposed their true hearts. I couldn't believe it, but then I'd been left behind too. *Who was I to judge?* However, once I found Christ, I felt the difference—the change that came from within me—the transformation from the Lord."

The conversation had turned after that testimony. Each one shared their moment of decision when the Lord had opened his or her eyes. Asher had sat, unable to leave his train of thought—*In a "perfect" world with peace and justice, how can they come to faith? Hadn't it been the terror and destruction, the sorrows and heartaches that drove me to Christ?* Before he could even frame the question, their time was over, and they had to get ready for the trip back home to Zebulun.

On their way, Asher came to himself as his gelding pushed forward to pass Charlene's steed on a bend. Adjusting his seat, he tightened his legs and gripped the reins firmly to bring the two horses back into step. *You're not in heaven yet!* The thought rose up in his mind as if he were seeing with new eyes. The natural striving to be first, even in himself, existed as a suppressed undercurrent. Yes, it had been easier to live for Christ, but the muted stain and curse of sin still had a subtle effect.

Asher felt the steady strength of the stirrups helping keep his feet and heels in their proper place. Leather, examined for any rips or tears, tested and tried. His eyes widened. *It is only by the test of the release of the Wicked One can the Lord reveal the hearts of the people.* The phrase ran through his head. A test—a great test, and his heart longed for his friends, his many children, and those who followed in the carriage.

Save them, Lord!

—∾—

Traveling along the Western Sea and up to the center of Judah, where sweet scents of acres of vineyards in full bloom filled the air, took only a few hours.

Asher's gelding tried to increase his pace as they neared the barn and paddocks, but his firm hand on the reins held him in check. Before they could wrap the reins around the hitching post, a young man approached, looking them over. "Grandfather, Isaac said you would come. Are you the party from Zebulun?"

"We are." He extended his hand with the reins. "I'm Asher. What is your name? I haven't seen you here before."

"Asher of Zebulun—of the first generation." He paused then added, "I realized that I had to come home." The young man loosely tied the gelding to the wood railing and patted his front shoulder.

"How did you know I am grandfather before you heard my name?"

On his way to checking the front hoof, he turned. "That's easy, Grandfather, you have old eyes." His eyes narrowed, and the edge of his lips curled up. "You have lived a full life—hundreds of years—perhaps more than one thousand."

Asher nodded and met his gaze. The young man was correct. The only way to really guess at a person's age was his or her eyes. His appeared young, but with a cloud? A question formed, but Charlene drew near and extended the standard greeting—a full hug and a quick peck on both cheeks.

"Charlene, his *old* wife." Her laughter trilled, and all joined in. Through these years, long life did not need to be feared for sickness and infirmity no longer came with the centuries. They had had incredible opportunities to live and to learn and to do.

"Asher, are we staying the night?" Patrick asked.

"I'll check with our host." He glanced at the stable hand. "Are they at the main house?"

"All waiting," he replied and turned to his duties.

The four walked the stone path, bounded by flower beds and trellised morning glories. The long porch of Isaac's house faced south toward the Temple, and they could see Isaac and Bethany waving to them. Lester, his grandson, was not in sight.

Bethany's round porch table was already covered with a small feast. "I'll consider this an early lunch," Charlene said, slipping into a seat near Asher.

"Lester's not here? I thought he would come after the morning offering."

"They had another job that will take him into the afternoon. Our guesthouse is ready. You can leave early tomorrow."

"I'll have to call Jael. Let him know."

"Asher…" Isaac sat back with a broad grin. "Don't you think he knows? Lester works for him. In fact, he's up on the Mount with him."

"Really? Is it serious?" Asher shook his head. Jael, now the owner of the second largest computing company in the region, rarely visited worksites.

"Not that serious. When the Temple has a need, he always goes in person with the team."

"Of course." Asher should have known.

"We would love to show you around," Bethany said to Clarice and Patrick.

"I'll tag along. Check up on your latest varieties. My vines need to be rejuvenated with some younger plants." Charlene leaned toward Patrick. "You will love her flowers."

"After we eat, of course." Bethany, after making sure everyone had cold lemonades, nodded to Isaac to say the grace.

"You going, Asher?" Isaac asked as he filled his plate.

"No, I thought we could…catch up."

"Sure, same old, same old, right? Just try to have the harvesters keep up with the bushels and bushels of ripened grapes."

"And your processing operations? Still shipping worldwide through Lazarus and Deb's shipping operations?"

"Wouldn't work with any other." They turned their attention to Bethany who had Clarice and Patrick relaying their complete family and life histories.

"And you look so young, barely 100 years?"

"I'm not yet 100," Clarice stated almost blushing.

Asher marveled again at Bethany's perception and ability to lead a person to bare his or her soul to her. *I haven't been as diligent to really get to know my latest employees. Most passed through their time working for me as they develop their skills and move on—some to establish their own estates and pursuits.* He listened to see if he could discern their faith, but the meal was soon over, and they stood for the promised tour.

After the group had disappeared down the path, Asher looked at Isaac. "Your stable hand called me *old*. Never said his name. Does he resent us?"

"Does this surprise you? We have lived for more than a thousand years. He has two or three years left. Are you not aware that others also resent us?"

"Who?"

"How many walk the Highway of Holiness?"

Asher began to answer, then sat back. "But the coastal highway— that's why few walk it." He watched his friend shake his head slowly. "Okay..."

"Only believers can walk that path. In the beginning, I often saw the angels guarding it, but as the years pass, fewer use it, and the angels often choose to cover their presence. How many attended the last tabernacle feast?" He leaned forward. "How many countries are under the Lord's rain ban this year?"

"Fifty," Asher stated, barely above a whisper.

"What do you think those who never accepted the Lord in the first century are thinking? Would you imagine that they are resentful? Places they can't go. Imagine what they feel when they visit the Temple."

"But the gift of salvation is free! And they have seen His goodness."

"On the outside—yes! They have seen the Lord of glory, but His love does not dwell in their hearts." Isaac waved his finger. "No, they have benefited from a just and fair system. Poverty is no more. Their bodies are not diseased or sick. But unless they have admitted their sin and accepted Christ as Savior, they feel only dread and condemnation when they draw near." He sighed. "I've been studying the trends and watching my fellow Judeans. The numbers of those who resist the call of grace are much higher than we would like to admit."

Asher nodded. It's what he had feared, but hearing his friend speak of it openly sent a chill down his spine. "What can we do?" He stepped to the railing and watched workers in the distance tend the fields. An overwhelming sorrow drove him to his knees, his hands trembled on the railing.

"Asher, are you all right?" Isaac reached out to his friend.

"Jesus paid for their sins on the cross too. It's all covered. They don't have to face hell. That's why the Lord of Glory is on His throne in Jerusalem. They can come to Him. He would never turn them away." A few tears tickled his cheeks, and he wiped them away, surprised by their presence.

Isaac stared over the closest vineyard. "The way is wide, and many go that way. Did not our Lord predict that few would choose the narrow path?"

"Maybe they haven't suffered enough. Didn't our troubles send us to God?"

"Let's look at that reasoning. If that's true, why didn't more of them come to Christ during the Tribulation? Did you not meet those who hated God more with each plague?" Isaac helped Asher to the nearest chair and drew one close. Sitting down, he said, "God gives the increase. We are only the messengers. I know I'm not like you or Kish—not an evangelist or a healer. I'm a simple businessman, but all of us must not forget that our ultimate faith and trust is in Him—not us. It's not to ask what we can do to save them. We can't begin to do that. But we can say, 'Here, Lord, use me. I'll do whatever You tell me to do.'"

"And what has He told you?"

"To love all He sends my way. To share of the love of God that resides in my heart and tell them how much He loves them. That's it. I know the time is short, but if we're just now asking these questions, isn't it too late already?"

Asher's head shot up. "It's never too late. Friend, I didn't know why God sent us here, but this is why. Do you dream, see visions?"

Isaac smiled and shook his head.

"Your genuine faith is direct and pure and strong as bedrock. To call it simple seems to belittle it, but our faith is simply going to our Heavenly Father for He is the fountain of life itself. We remain sinners saved by grace." He leaned over to hug his friend.

"One more thing, Asher. Never forget. As good as life is right now, we're not in heaven yet. Just wait!"

"You saw?"

"I believe."

———

The group arrived, and they separated. Asher could not forget their conversation. When Charlene asked him later when they were in the guest cottage, he could scarcely gather the words. "I'm searching for answers. I think the Lord gave me some through Isaac, but I haven't put it together yet."

Charlene rose and kissed him. "Don't fret, my love. If the Lord is showing you something, He'll keep at it until you get the message!" She laughed, and they began their routine for winding down for sleep—sharing a verse, reading from the latest book, a memoir this time, and a simple game.

———

Visiting Jael in New Tel-Aviv was a whirlwind of activity—walking the shoreline, touring his latest division creating smaller battery chips, and dining in his favorite restaurant. Asher's only regret was not having taken the time to stop by and see Lazarus, but they had spent time together last year. They could meet again. He would find the time.

Two days later Lester led the way on his golden mare, and the three traveled beyond the carriage, leaving it behind. They took the coastal route. Asher almost thought of suggesting they walk it, but he knew they didn't have the time. He almost laughed, but held it in. *Are we truly running out of time?* For so long, it had seemed as if all of them had all the time in the world.

⁓

Kish's estate bordered his city named Gazelle. It glowed in the failing light of a moonless night. They had been there enough times that Asher's gelding seemed to know the way. Kish stood tall next to Giselle, his arm around his lovely wife. She waved enthusiastically when she saw them and called out to the staff to take the horses and unload the carriage.

"Welcome! Welcome! In one day! But you don't look exhausted."

"We are hungry, Aunt Giselle," Lester said, planting a kiss on his favorite "aunt." He smiled, knowing she would have a feast waiting for them. "Oh, Aunt Giselle, meet Clarice, our horse trainer, and Patrick, our field design wizard. They've never been to the border."

"Well, Clarice and Patrick, we will make sure that is included in the tour!" Giselle swept her hand toward their tall, stately front door. "Come in and dine!"

Kish stepped aside as Giselle led the guests to a long dining table set for eight.

"Who's the extra seat for?" Asher asked.

"Oh," Kish smiled, "Giselle invited a friend. She did hear that Lester is still single." He waited for the response, but Asher's face was pensive. "Distracted?"

Asher stopped. "Have you had any dreams lately?"

"You too?" Kish patted his friend's back. "We can discuss it later."

Kish sat at the head of the table and gave the blessing over the bread. Giselle blessed the fruit beverages. Their young friend seemed shy, but Lester never seemed to notice her. For that, Asher was glad. If his dream meant what he suspected and if Lester were to have a part, none of them would have time for socializing. His thoughts wandered until Lester's question to the young woman caught his ear.

"And you, Miranda, have you asked the Lord Jesus Christ to forgive you of your sin?"

Conversation stopped, and she began to redden.

"My apologies," Lester stated. He rose and stepped beside her. "Let's take a walk; perhaps you can show me the stars. Grandfather Asher is always saying it is easier to see the stars from here."

She dabbed her cheek with the linen napkin and rose, taking his hand. She led him by the back path up a small rise and onto a short plateau away from the lights of the city. "I love the stars. I took ten years at university to learn them all. That included traveling throughout the world to see how the constellations changed when viewed from different continents." Her voice faded away.

Lester stared. "They are marvelous. And you're right. They're slightly different from the southern region. But you see even more in the wilderness areas. I'm sorry if I embarrassed you. I only asked because just recently I learned that a dear friend of mine had never taken the Lord as his Savior."

"But why?"

Before he could try to venture a guess, Miranda said, "Why would he need to? I know that the earlier generations were wicked, but we have the Lord today. In our hearts? We have the ceremonies at the Temple. I go once a year for cleansing. Isn't that all one needs?"

"But it says all have sinned and have come short of what God has for them. If any does not have the Spirit of Christ dwelling within them, they do not belong to Christ." His voice faded. He couldn't bear to speak of her final destination if she did not believe. Even the thought of this beautiful woman with flowing black hair, alabaster skin and eyes as dark and deep as a pool, being thrown into the pit of hell clutched his chest.

"But what is this—*Spirit* dwelling within? Isn't it referring to our own joy at living in a good and just and fair and clean world? I couldn't imagine what life must have been like before He came."

Lester sought for the right response. *How can I describe something so personal, so intimate?* He cast up a prayer to the Spirit and heard himself say, "Miranda, let's walk to the Highway of Holiness."

"Oh, no. Um, that's for the holy ones. We're just people."

"But don't you see people walking it?"

"Yes, but they must have gone to the Temple and were cleansed. Right?"

"This far north?" Lester led her down the path and to the road that led to the highway. Step by step, they drew closer. She slowed, but did not stop. He reached for her trembling hand, and she held on as if drawing strength from it.

The glow of the path from the angels guarding it came into sight, and as they drew near, an angel became visible.

Miranda stopped, gasping. She looked at Lester.

"Miranda, do you want to know Christ within you? Do you want Him to save you?"

She opened her mouth to protest, but she knew in her heart that she was a sinner. As if seeing her life in pictures, she remembered tricking her little sister out of her candy, hiding a broken jar from her mother, and lying to her friends when she had failed a test.

"I'm…I'm a sinner?" She nodded. "I am." She stared at the straight road, and one part of her longed to walk it as she had seen others do.

"Don't be afraid. I also had to admit that I had sinned. I asked Jesus to save me, and He did. It's that simple." Lester prayed fervently, holding his breath.

Miranda fell to her knees and called out to God, tears running down her cheeks.

Lester looked at the angel who watched them intently. He smiled at Lester. As if he had heard the angel in his mind, Lester reached down and drew her to her feet. They faced the angel who stepped aside. "Welcome, daughter, and enter the joy of your Lord."

Miranda took one step, shuddering. Feeling Lester solid and steady beside her, she took the next step and the next until they were on the road and walking toward the northern border.

On a soft bend of a low rise, Lester turned them to face south. The pillar of fire of the Lord visible in the distance cast light on the Temple's curved roof. He heard her say, "Oh, the Lord of glory is my God!"

They walked for a while. "Miranda, what is the way back to Kish's?"

She nodded and headed down a side path.

They felt as if hours had passed. The four were now sitting on the porch, communing in the dim light. Their voices wafted along a cool breeze. "My grandfather helped me find God just a few years ago. He hadn't even known that I didn't have the Lord. God let him know and when he challenged me, I had to confess. Like you, I hadn't thought I needed it, but he said something that I could not forget." Lester laughed lightly. "I thought the sin thing was just a myth. Like you, I thought we had arrived as a race, and it would always be this way, but he showed me the second testament which predicted it would last a thousand years, and we were five years away from that. So, I tried to walk the highway—just as you tried, and an angel appeared. He was kind, but firm. I could not go because I did not believe on Jesus for my sins. My sins were my own and only I could pay for them. The verses Grandpa Asher had shown me returned to my mind." He paused. "Miranda, how many of us are there who don't know they need the Savior?"

"Lots."

"It will be okay, Miranda. It's your story, so it's yours to tell when you are ready. Aunt Giselle will be so happy."

"She tried to tell me months ago, but I wasn't ready to hear. Will she be angry?"

"No! She will be ecstatic! We all long for everyone to know the Lord as we do. He makes us spiritually alive inside."

She paused, feeling new life flowing within her that she had never felt before. "Jesus loves me! He really loves little me!"

"He does."

She quickened her pace, eager to share her story.

They all rejoiced, and Giselle led Miranda into the house with her and Charlene.

Lester sat in the chair next to his grandfather who couldn't stop beaming at him. "Grandpa, it was of God. I asked, we talked a little, and the Holy Spirit told me to take her to the highway. You know the rest."

"Like I said, it's never too late." Kish shifted in his chair.

Lester looked between them but hesitated to ask.

"My grandson," Asher patted his hand. "We love our offspring and wish them all to be saved, but we often fear there is little hope that any will find the Lord in time." He suddenly remembered a similar conversation 998 years ago.

"But the stories of His first coming prove that up to the day of death, there is hope. God can save, and none of His will be lost."

"See, even one under a hundred knows."

Asher nodded. He looked at Lester. "It thrilled my heart when you asked to go with us three days ago."

"What's so important about three days ago?"

"I had a vision, a dream. It had been so long that I had almost forgotten about them." Asher shook his head, pushing down inner regrets. No, he had to accept that he had done what God had wanted him to do over his long life. "I saw the multitudes as sheep running away from the shepherd and over a cliff into hell. Did they know where they were going? Why hadn't someone told them the way to God?" Asher wrapped his arms around himself. "For the last fifty years, it's as if I were blind to the fact that many I loved and cared about—many acquaintances and business partners were dwelling without God."

"It's hard to tell the difference when everything's good and right. Without the Devil or a wicked world system, many appear fairly good—most of the time." Lester remembered what Miranda had said as well as his own faith journey. His heart tugged, seeing Kish's and Asher's grave looks. For the first time he felt the fear of the loss of many he knew, cared for and loved. Yes, we have to do something! "We just have to make sure they all have a chance to be told the way. It's up to them to accept it. Free will, right?"

"It is that simple," Kish stated.

Asher looked at the both of them. "But it feels like a useless exercise. Why did they wait if they wanted God?"

"Miranda thought she didn't need it, but when face to face with the angel on the highway, she couldn't ignore her need."

"We can't march everyone to the highway to prove to them that they're destined for hell!"

"Asher," Kish looked at his friend. "We don't save them. God does. And if He chooses to send us out to spread the gospel—even if not one of them accept, our hands are clean before God."

"They will be without excuse," Lester stated.

"Where did you hear that?" Asher asked.

"I don't know. It just popped into my head." He smiled at Kish's laughter. "So, what's the plan. May I join you?"

"Oh, you'd better believe you have a part, young man."

►24

THE FEAST OF Tabernacles, Year 999, drew an even smaller crowd than the previous year. This time Asher was not surprised or mystified. After that evening a year ago at Kish's, their plan had morphed into first trying to revive the fellowships of the world.

Pulling in all their contacts, they invited believers throughout the world to join them for a special Passover celebration in Israel. Up and down the coast assemblies celebrated the Passover, remembering the sacrifice Christ had made, stressing the tragic end for all who had not yet accepted Him as their Savior. Had they done enough? Had they inspired them to evangelize their communities?

Talking with Owen and Sallie over the phone did not seem sufficient, but Asher and Charlene never had the time to return to the States to see the situation firsthand.

Charlene looked across the breakfast table. "You know, Asher, six months ago I was really upset I couldn't go home, but then I realized that I was home. This is home, and this is where we need to be. Nothing else matters."

Her dedication warmed his heart. She had been true to her word and had followed his visions.

"And remember to leave the increase or lack of it in the Lord's hands, Asher."

Just when he thought he was in the lead, sometimes she showed that, once again, she was ahead of him. He nodded. "It's simply hard not to judge by results. Handling a herd of horses is easier and, in some ways, more satisfying." He laughed, knowing it was a joke, nothing more. No, every time his motivation threatened to wane, it was as if the Spirit rose up within him, and he could barely rest. "We will have eternity soon."

She held his hand. "So, my love, as we preached to the assemblies, hadn't we also spread the gospel in our own communities? So, we continue, taking advantage of every opportunity He sends our way."

The silence hung in the air. Simple, direct, one message and remembering that the Holy Spirit would be with them, he began to share the next phase. "Again, we reach out during this last year. So, we call a meeting to make another plan for our eight cities."

"Will you go to Tamar?" The eastern city, lovely though it was in its remoteness, was too close to the perpetual salt flats and wilderness of desolation south of the Eastern Sea. Seeing the barren hills to the northeast from the town's center square still haunted her dreams. *Why?* She did not know. Probably it recalled images of how Asher had been before his healing—the deep, desperate longing in his eyes, and the haunted look of terrors past. A long time had passed since they had helped rescue the last of the wanderers. Now they were on a mission to find the wanderers in their midst—the ones with smooth smiles and bright eyes—who seemed blind to the danger bearing down upon them.

"Yes, if the Lord sends us. Remember, God can save anyone. He saved me!"

Charlene patted his knee, thankful once again for their long life together. Asher healed, whole and complete, at peace. Yes, if the Lord could so transform her husband, He could transform those still resistant to His saving faith. "Two by two, each team will pray for the best way to remind a town or village of the gospel and move on to the next."

She shook her head. "There are so many people now. Maybe reaching out for a second year will help those who weren't ready then."

"Lester and his friends have online video sessions and rallies for those under a hundred."

"I have a brigade of ladies ready to invite those crossing the highway to reach other paths to accept the Savior and walk the holy road."

Charlene heard a timid knock on their door. She opened the door. "Clarice! Come in. What's the matter?"

The woman entered and handed them a sheet of paper. "I've really struggled with this, but I have to go home."

"Clarice, take a seat. I'll make you a smoothie. Did something happen?"

She shook her head and verbalized. "No." Her eyes scanned the familiar kitchen with the large table where they had shared many meals together. "It's just time; that's all."

Charlene hugged her, read the letter of resignation, and handed it to Asher.

He rose and hugged her as well. "Of course, Clarice, we would love for you to stay, but we want what's best for you." He would have shared the gospel again, but the Holy Spirit held him back. He prayed she would find the Savior in her native land.

They watched her walk across the courtyard to the barn to turn out the horses. "Another one returning home." And they hadn't been the only ones experiencing that exodus. Many who had been in Israel for centuries were going back. "Does it mean they've turned their backs on God?"

"Perhaps, or maybe this is the Lord's doing to open their eyes. He works everywhere, my love. We must leave it with God." He had to remember that people didn't have to be in the land or standing on the Temple Mount to find the Lord.

Half the nations did not appear at the great feast. Some of the booths were empty. Asher and Charlene focused on worshiping Christ and fellowshipping with the faithful who had come.

They had held their breath through the last year. Thinking there was more to do, Asher tried to organize another gospel campaign, but it was as if the assemblies were frozen—praying within their groups and loving their neighbors as best they could, but organized efforts seemed to have been suppressed by the Holy Spirit. What decisions they heard of seemed few and far between, but a deep joy and peace kept them throughout the quiet year.

Knowing this was the last year, some came with questions. Asher tried to reassure them that they wouldn't simply vanish after the next Tabernacles. He had stressed the importance of knowing the one true God or they would be deceived. While the message he had delivered so many times came easily to his mind, his prayers did not abate. *How does God handle so many turning away?*

The feast of Tabernacles arrived, and all held their breath, but the worship services continued day by day. On the last day of the Feast, Christ Himself took the golden pitcher to the River of Life, drew the water, and declared, "I am the Way, the Truth and the Life. No one comes to the Father except through Me. Unless my Spirit dwells in you. Unless you have asked Me to save you, you will die in your sins. I am the bread of life. I am truth and knowledge and wisdom, and I am the light of life. I created this world and all that is in it. Come unto Me all you who labor and are heavy laden, and I will give you peace."

The angels sang with a contingent from the 144,000 who never left the Lord's side. The voices of the thousands filled the air. God's love in-fused the assembly as if for the first time all who stood in the courtyard were one in the Spirit. It was as if he were back in the first years, where all who walked the earth tabernacled with the Spirit. Asher closed his eyes, praying, willing his neighbors, friends, and many descendants to know the Lord.

Ten days later a deep moan escaped the very heavens. As if the fire of lightning had surged forth from the throne of God, a crack sounded that enveloped the planet and shook it to its core. As Asher and Charlene sat up in bed, their hearts dropped. *It has happened as the Scriptures have said. The thousand years has ended. Satan and his hordes of demons have been released!*

Asher recalled the years, long distant, before the disappearances of how subtle their influence could be and how unaware people had been of Satan's manipulations. *How long will it be before they sway the masses? It has to happen. It has been written.*

Although it was still hours before the dawn, Asher and Charlene rose and began to pack again. "We hadn't even put away our luggage," Charlene commented, trying to lighten the mood. "Do you really think we need to go back to the Mount now?"

"Let's just see what's going on there. I don't think they have pulled all our booths yet."

They left the car and readied their largest wagon. Charlene filled it with so many supplies that Asher began to object, but he reminded himself that his very capable wife knew how to listen to the Spirit as well as he did. He cast down a brief heart's tug for his home. A better home waited in the future—each day drew it closer.

They set out as the first rays of the sun crested the eastern horizon. He hoped the crews hadn't disassembled too many booths.

"Don't fret, Asher. If we don't have a booth to stay in, there's always Zamira's."

He knew that. They all were as healthy with as much energy as the day the Lord had invited them into His kingdom. But their eyes were old, and the youngest of them could pick them out. They were of the first—the smallest generation.

Asher encouraged the team up the slope and pulled back on the reins as they crested the plateau. For some reason few had taken down their tent villages. Row upon row of structures—some with partial coverings and branches waving in the breezes still stood. Few people were about. The morning offering must have completed, but crowds weren't gathered on the plaza in front of the Temple gate.

"Well, we didn't have to worry at all, did we, Asher?" Charlene asked, her voice flat. She almost tried to joke that she hoped he hadn't paid the breakdown crew, but if this was the end, it didn't matter.

Asher commanded the team to go, and he directed them along the roads to their section. Most were still up. Charlene climbed down from the wagon and walked the horses to their booth. Asher helped her unload, and they began to cover the walls with curtains, laid out the rugs, strung up the dividers and brought in the bedding, pillows and boxes, saying little.

Standing to stretch her back, Charlene smiled. "Asher! What are we doing? In a relatively short time, I will see my mother again. We will be as Daniel is now and will reside in the New Heaven and the New Earth. The glory of the Lord will light the world! We don't need to cling to this life. He gave us 1,000 years together, and how many can say that?" She began to sing praises to God, and Asher joined in.

They stabled the horses and backed the wagon beside the lean-to. "Let's seek direction at the Temple." Asher looked at his lovely wife.

Eliab and Helon, the resurrected saints who had watched over their little valley, walked around the corner of the booth. "You are summoned."

Asher nodded, and they followed the large shining ones who had once defended the tribe in the time of the judges. Charlene took his hand, and they turned to the raised plateau and gazed at the pillar of cloud still standing by the Western Wall—the signal of God's faithful continuance.

They headed up the steps. Their guardians led them to Uriah, who was standing in the courtyard. "Oh, good, you made it. Come with me." He led them to several tables at the southwest corner. Zapheth nodded in their direction. Asher noted more shining ones standing along the side closest to the Levite's quarters.

He recognized some from various tribes sitting at the long tables. Kish and Giselle walked over to greet them. They found seats near their friends from Zebulun as more came to join them. Asher noticed other tables under canopies in the next corner. He suspected similar gatherings were happening on the other side. "Did you see Elchanan or Menachem?"

"They're on the north side," Esther, their closest neighbor said. "Zephath called us here with this group. Yesterday, we simply knew we had to come. I insisted we take the time to bring supplies. You too?"

"Yes," Charlene whispered, squeezing her friend's outstretched hand.

Zephath called the group to order. "The time has come. The end of days is drawing to a close, and God will dwell with men on a New Earth. Before that, however, the Wicked One has been loosed and those who rejected the Savior will gather to attack the Lord and His people."

All nodded, some whispering, "As it has been written."

"God will be calling all the saints to His Holy Temple. We must prepare for a great gathering. All of you are from the more distant tribes." He pointed to a map on a board. "First, prepare your section for your people and lay up supplies. Dan, Asher, and Naphtali will set up north of the Temple. Issachar will be on the western side. Zebulun will occupy the fields east of the city and Gad in the western fields. Any of you who already have structures set up on the plateau, move them to your areas and prepare for the coming of the faithful."

He continued with his instructions but did not set a date for the attack. When two angels drew close to confer with the priest, the assembled talked among themselves. Some tried to predict how long it would take, but in the end, they understood that God knew. He would guide them. Seeing the shining ones and angels standing close by the canopy quickened their pulse. Soon death would be destroyed, and all would be one. The watchful care of their loving God would not fail them.

Charlene tried to smile reassuringly at the younger couples and singles who had not experienced God's miraculous deliverance through the Tribulation. She leaned closer to Sarin and Patty, close friends from the town west of theirs. "Where are Marge and Leon?" she asked.

Patty looked aside, and Sarin shook his head. David and Esther, their closest neighbors looked away, their mouths drawn down, saying nothing. Charlene knew she had to find out about Marge from Esther at the right opportunity.

"Are they coming later?" Asher asked.

David cleared his throat.

"Leon's from Kadesh Barnea, the largest city in Zebulun. Probably bringing his contingent with him." Asher studied Sarin's set face.

"Not coming at all. I sent Paul up to Kadesh Barnea to gather the faithful. He's telling everyone to stay put."

"But…" Asher stopped. He had known some would be revealed as tares—appearing to believe with all the outward works but lacking inward faith. However, not Leon. He glanced at Charlene. "And Marge?"

"I don't know. Maybe I could drop by and visit her."

Asher looked at David.

Sarin shook his head. "That might not be the best idea. If you go, don't go alone." He reached for Patty's hand. "This is only the beginning. We set up our booths in our area. Our regional guardians already have the layout and supplies' list—communal areas, dining tent, kitchen…" Thinking through what still needed to be done, his eyes unfocused as he stared into the distance.

"Let's see who can donate and what remains to be purchased…" Asher nodded and looked at Charlene and Patty. "Think you'll head up the kitchen?"

"Eliza, our shining one, along with the other three already have a plan. Don't worry, we'll be busy feeding the construction crews." Patty nodded at Charlene.

"And rounding up the children for activities," Charlene added. "We've got this, don't we, Patty?"

The quiet woman, petite with bright eyes, hugged her friend. "I wouldn't want to do it with anyone else."

Charlene embraced her, thankful for good friendships. "Tea times," she said quietly. Releasing her, she leaned close to Asher. "Well, we still have to move our booth. Will see you soon."

Zapheth raised his hands to give the closing benediction. "We walk by faith, not by sight. Meet with your watchers who will provide details concerning number of booths, the sizes of the communal tents and common areas."

Asher, David, Sarin and six other regional leaders gathered with the six shining ones who had administered Zebulun. Asher wondered where their faithful judges were.

Helon met his gaze and said to him without speaking. *They are busy elsewhere. There is much to do to prepare for the days ahead and what is to come.*

Asher nodded imperceptibly. Many found the overseers hard and unyielding, but to him, who had worked with them closely over the centuries, he felt the kinship of a shared faith—even if they had their glorified bodies and Asher's had not yet been given.

While no mention of the resurrection of the millennial saints could be found in the Scriptures, he knew that he would be transformed just as Helon had. Instantly, he relived the day of the disappearances— the day Patty, Frank and the rest of the Christians had vanished. So it would be. In God's perfect timing, they too would be transformed, as the hulls of a seed falling away, as a butterfly wresting free of its cocoon.

Charlene held his hand. "What, Asher?"

"I'll tell you later, but nothing…" His smile was broad and clear.

"…can stop God's love for His people." The settled peace and joy in his wife's eyes assured him that she was already there.

They headed for their booth and surveyed the peaceful busyness of many working toward a common purpose. Others were tearing down their booths. Asher walked over to the nearest one to see if they knew where to move it. After giving directions, he peered along the row and spied Mitchell, his missing worker, looking at the last booth in the aisle. Asher went to find and direct his crew.

By the time he returned, Charlene had their items boxed, the booth frame disassembled and stacked. "What? You didn't hitch the team yet?"

She squinted her eyes and teased back, "Can't leave everything to me!" She stopped there, recognizing Asher had been about his own responsibilities. "Well, we're going to need the long flatbed." She surveyed the growing piles of supports and standards. All had to be moved around the city and toward the Eastern Lake.

"David brought his."

25

BEFORE THE SUN set, all had been moved to their new "home." Their section was closer to the city and near the long rows of vines. *"No eye has seen, nor ear heard..."* Charlene said, her eyes fixed on the pillar, turning from a cloud to fire as it signaled the beginning of a new day.

Asher wrapped his arm around her shoulder, *"...nor the heart of man imagined,"*

"What God has prepared for those who love him,"[59] Arthur, their third-generation grandson, said. "I have found you." He melted into their warm embrace. "You can't believe what's going on out there! It's already begun."

"Mattie?" Charlene asked.

He shook his head. "And Rachel's brood refused to come." His eyes hollow with the fleeting memory of their rejection despite his pleadings.

"Arthur, remember, there's hope as long as they draw breath."

"I pray they don't wait until it's too late."

"Those of us who waited until the times of Jacob's trouble, some of us on the very day of His glorious return, and even those who repented on that day were welcomed into the kingdom."

Their beautiful grandson, seven hundred years old, who still looked young in their eyes, nodded. "That is why I go to the Temple to pray for our lost ones. Grandfather, I remember your tales of finding your lost ones—your generation's wanderers. But now it rests on us all to pray them into the kingdom."

"Do as you are led. Our prayers will go before you."

"I understand, as one of the chiefs of Zebulun, you both have much to do. I will seek you out as soon as I'm able."

The light of the four tall lamps of the Temple court bathed their area with a warm glow. Fusion lights strung along the edges of the canopies outlined the dining and cooking tents. Charlene went to check the tables—being set by an energetic group of under-hundreds. She paused to compliment them on their work and stepped to the portable kitchen with fusion generators, tables for prepping fruits and vegetables, along with bubbling soup pots. She headed for Esther and Patty.

Asher went to the main tent at the side of the dining area. Watchers Gadaliel and Benjamin were bent over charts splayed out on a large table in the center. No booths were to be assembled in the fields yet to be harvested. He wondered again how long they would be here. However, time was of no consequence as the Lord would provide.

As the watchers reviewed the structures still to be assembled for those still coming, Asher calculated the number. While at first glance it seemed as if they would be bursting at the seams, in reality, they would be housing barely three thousand. He stepped closer to David.

"We're hosting Egypt and some parts of northern Africa."

"Shouldn't there be more booths? If we add Zebulun, plus the southern regions of Egypt and her neighbors…"

"I would have thought so too, but truly the heart of man is dark even without the temptations of the Wicked One. And the children?"

Helon rose to his full height above seven feet. "Those too young to have understanding will be brought by their angels. Many of you will have the privilege of hosting them."

All nodded, and some wiped their eyes. "Esther and Charlene can find willing couples," David stated. All nodded in agreement. He was certain they would welcome all who could be rescued.

"Rejoice in King Jesus, the Lord of Glory, who makes all things new!" Eliab raised his voice in praise of God.

"Amen! And amen!" echoed through the group.

"In the morning, come for your assignments for your teams." Eliab gestured for Asher, David and Sarin to stay.

"Here are the remaining supplies that are needed. Tomorrow a few will go out for a last trip. None will be able to leave once the presence of the Lord surrounds the Mount."

The watchers withdrew, leaving it to the tribal elders to delegate the task.

"Just as some of us repented at the last moment, let us pray we will find some who will return with us."

"We must be careful. The shining ones have been recalled. That is what Eliab told me."

"But aren't the guardian angels still gathering the called ones?" Asher glanced back at Helon, standing just outside the tent. If the watchers had been withdrawn, most of them must be in the heavenly Jerusalem. He couldn't allow himself to think about what they were doing to prepare. He would see soon enough.

"We are the very camp of the Lord, and His presence will sustain us." Sarin's voice was deep and strong, like the steady words of a commander of armies.

They nodded their assent and headed to the dining tent. Asher wondered as he walked, Who should I bring with me?

The tables were laden with food. He walked over to the seat Charlene had saved for him. Their table was half filled with young children, each sitting by a couple. Asher smiled, remembering fondly the years, centuries ago when their fifteen sat about one table.

"I'm to go out for a supply run tomorrow." He paused, realizing she was occupied with making sure everyone had enough and helping the toddler sitting beside her. Amazingly, the young ones seemed at peace even though he hardly knew them. Asher's heart skipped a beat recognizing this little one had been the son of one of his workers who had left his young wife to wander the world.

Charlene wiped her hands and nodded at the young boy sitting across the table, eating the purple-red fruit. The juice ran down his chin. "Well then, I'd say, if we're going, we should swing by to check on Leon." The couple had been one of their first friends from Kadesh Barnea. Under Leon's leadership, it had become Zebulun's major city. Their little town near the river across from their conference center had remained quiet with a steady population.

She had never minded the slower pace of their area. It had been known throughout the three nations—Egypt, Israel and Assyria—as the place to go to, to get away, and seek the Lord. "After all he is one of the leaders of the second generation." *Surely, they believe. Maybe they are just gathering everyone.* She remembered how thorough he could be.

"David said that Leon told everyone to stay put."

Charlene worked at setting her cup down without spilling it. "What? But that's crazy!" She met Asher's gaze.

Despite his reluctance to see her put in any jeopardy, he nodded. "You can go with me, but we have to watch our backs. I want to find out what's up with them too."

—⁓—

Once all the dishes were done, the tables cleared, and the areas cleaned, the crew dispersed for their booths—some not yet assembled with beds and curtains.

They tried to relax in their booth. "Glad I never really unpacked," Charlene confessed. She looked about, trying to remember which bin held her family scrapbook. One look at the tired lines etched on her husband's face changed her mind.

"Sit, my love." Asher leaned over and pulled their snack bin filled with sausages, cheeses, and fruit closer to them.

They talked little, spreading hummus on crackers, munching on a few grapes. Asher drank the last of the tea Charlene had brewed earlier that day. She leaned her head against his shoulder to stop the tears. "Our home," she mourned just above a whisper.

"Our herd of Percherons."

Charlene tipped back her head. "It only took a few hundred years to convert you to rely more on horses and wagons. However, from Isaac's stories, I'm surprised that it wasn't donkeys."

"Nothing beats a horse."

She thought of trying to find Giselle and Kish, but she had already settled into a lethargy. Hearing a polite clap outside their booth, she called, "Come in."

Giselle entered, followed by Kish and his brother, Andrew.

"Where is Marta?" Charlene asked before better judgment could stop her. Andrew had waited one hundred and fifty years before taking a wife from Naphtali. A raven beauty with cream-white skin and dark eyes, as tall and willowy as Andrew. Once he had repented, the Holy Spirit had transformed the man's former rough arrogance, revealing a firm, yet gracious executive style that propelled him to leadership in Dan. In that position, he had worked closely with the judges and watchers assigned to their tribe.

Asher laid out pillows for their guests and pulled forward the bin of crackers, cheese, sausage and fruits.

Charlene poured the herbal tea. Prayers for their friends rose up in her heart. They were all more than 1,000 years old. The moments passed, but none fretted or tried to fill the air with empty words.

Andrew finished his cracker, drank the tea, and stared at the center of the breadboard between them. "The love of my life hid her feelings for Christ well. Being of Nathan's family, she was practically royalty. She knew the words of faith. I guess her naturally friendly, outgoing personality hid her rejection of Christ." He squeezed his eyes to stop the tears. "Two, no, three nights ago, she refused to bring in the Sabbath."

He sat back, shaking his head. "She said…she told me, 'You know, my dear. We do not share everything.' I was so clueless. I thought she was referring to her choice of restaurant or favorite auto or…"

Kish gently rested his hand on his brother's shoulder. They fell into silent prayer for Andrew and Marta.

"Bella? Your daughter?"

"The child of our old age." Andrew looked aside. "I thought her birth last century would have soothed Marta's pain of losing Lazar."

They all nodded. One of a small number to perish, he had rebelled and tried to rape a distant cousin. Marta had taken his loss hard.

He sighed. "Bella and her family are safe in Naphtali's sector."

"We can't count. I try not to keep track," Asher stated. How many of his descendants walked with God? It was deep into the second century before he could put that behind him. Why should he deny free will to his own when he had been thankful for the Lord's patience with him? "But there is great value in prayer—beseeching prayer. And in that, we will join with you."

"My beautiful wife." Andrew lifted his eyes, unfocused on the covering canopy. "It took me over a hundred years to move beyond the knowledge of my sins. I betrayed the love of my youth. I cast away the next two for their sins while blind to my own. One was careless, and the next one lazy. Miriam was beauty without grace, firm without mercy, and self-willed to the rejection of accepting her need. That day…" He looked aside. "When I begged her to take the Savior… That day when He had appeared, and we all confessed that which Isaiah 53 had spoken had been of Him and that He had come and we had cast Him away… That day I begged and pleaded, but she would not, and I saw her cast below into the underworld." He breathed. "Then I took the Savior, but I had been so blind."

"We both were," Kish said softly.

"But then you made peace with me, giving to me what I did not deserve. At first, I was embarrassed, then humiliated and then ashamed.

God pulled back the curtain to reveal my hard heart. I didn't feel that I deserved another chance, but then the Lord brought Marta into my life." His shoulders shook.

After a while, he accepted a tissue from Charlene and wiped his eyes. "I know that we all have those who should be here with us but are not. Together, we grieve these losses, yet the joy of the Lord is an undercurrent of peace. I guess we can be thankful for the times we did have together."

They sat in silence, centering on Christ and His love.

"We'll have to leave early this morning for that run north." Kish ignored Giselle's glare.

"Supply run?"

"Yes," Kish looked at his brother. "What are your plans?"

"I will go back to the Temple and plead for Marta."

"I will take Chaim with me. That will be enough," Kish said, trying to reassure his wife.

"I think the watchers will go along, somehow?" Asher asked.

"The watchers won't leave the border of the Temple Mount now. The angels will go forth and are patrolling even yet to bring in the last of the little ones and guard those who bear God's mark who have not yet been gathered in." Andrew shook his head. "I'm sorry I brought my troubles to you, though I know you are willing to grieve with me as I with you." He almost laughed. "To think that in the beginning we acted as if our lives would be as short as ever. Where was our faith?"

Giselle started to laugh lightly. "I remember those first hundred years. You'd think we hadn't known or believed the Word that foretold we would have a thousand years to live." She patted Kish's knee. "We had our first twenty children in forty years."

"Our fifteen in twenty-seven." Charlene added.

"Having two sets of twins didn't hurt." She sat back. "We were busy, but then…" She glanced at Kish. "How long before few were not having children until they were over a hundred and then maybe only three or four?"

"A couple of hundred years." Andrew sighed. "And now they are out of time. Many are gathering at the Temple to pray for those who have not yet come. The Lord Himself was with us along with a contingent of His 144,000 who are always by His side. Truly, how He loves us—even the stubborn ones." Andrew met Kish's gaze. "Soon, when the planes have delivered their passengers, and the ships have arrived, He will shut the gates." Andrew stared off into the distance. "Just as He shut in Noah and his family, and the masses who refused to believe could not come in. Nothing could be done to save them. They had lived through their 120 years of warning."

"Some had more than that," Asher stated. "But shut the gates? We can't all fit in the city or the Temple courtyard."

Kish breathed in as if remembering for the first time something their watcher had said. "God moved His pillar of fire between the Egyptian army and the people. From what I was told, it sounds like He will create a wall of fire from heaven to surround us."

"Then it's done?"

"No, they will allow us to wait by the wall. Angels will let in any who come to repent. To us is given the privilege to share our faith and pray with them."

All nodded, once again overwhelmed by the Lord's grace to include them in the ministry of rescue.

"They will come when it is time. Let us not decline such an opportunity."

"We will be hosting the Syrians, as we are pleased to do." Kish rose. "Well, we'll go out the last time and keep each other in prayer."

They rose to leave. Asher and Charlene stood and hugged them, holding them close for a time.

Kish embraced Asher. "I will pray for your safe return. Watch your back out there. Things are going badly very quickly—beyond what we could imagine."

Asher looked at Charlene. A tiredness threatened to overtake him.

Before he could discuss finding a way to get some sleep, he heard a knock.

Three stepped in. "Asher, could you help with the tent placements on the east side?"

Charlene watched Asher leave, turned, found her slim wooden box in the second bin, wrote a quick note and left to find Esther. She thought she knew where their booth was located.

Eventually, she found Esther sitting alone in her small enclosure. "May I?"

Esther slipped to the side and nodded toward the center curtain. "We have three little ones. They are finally asleep."

"I'll talk softly." Charlene sat and pulled out her large scrapbook from the box.

Esther pulled out hers. Their eyes met as they turned the pages, sometimes one page for each generation, until it took three, then four to trace all of their descendants. Their genealogies had joined and separated over the centuries. "Do you have your marker?"

She shrugged her shoulders "I forgot it. It was hard enough to find my book." She accepted the yellow highlighter and pulled out a pen. "What of those we had highlighted who have revealed they reject the faith?"

Esther turned to the tenth page of her fifth generation, tilted the page and pointed to a name that had been highlighted with a line drawn underneath.

"Nehemiah? Our favorite feed and supply store owner?"

Esther nodded. "His parents are devastated. Most of that family believed and lived their faith."

"They also had the best farms with exceptional fruit trees." She squeezed her friend's hand.

Together, they closed their books, turned to the first page, and stared at the names of their children, one by one. None lost, all with children of their own. They turned the page to the next with smaller rows and diverging lines as marriages created more offspring…century after century.

Charlene took a pen and underlined some as they surveyed the lists. They had done this year in and year out. While Asher had not encouraged it, he had not forbidden it. How could she explain it to him? Together they had prayed for both families, their destinies knit together not only from the closeness of good neighbors, but also as prayer warriors for their beloved children. "And yet, His love for them outstrips our own."

Esther nodded. "While we have a measure of grief for the lost ones, we still rejoice in what is to come for…" She leaned closer with a glint in her eye.

Together, they said with lifted voces, "We're not in heaven yet!"

"Amen!" David said, entering the sitting area in the booth. "They're finally done with your husband, and he is wondering where his wife is."

"I left a note." She rose, hugged them both, and left to find Asher, beyond tired. She prayed that she could sleep.

►26

THE NEXT MORNING, they retrieved their team and were soon traveling along the main road south. Charlene could not forget the news she had learned about Nehemiah. Before she could share it with Asher, he directed the horses to the Highway of Holiness.

"We're going straight to Kadesh Barnea. While Lamech at the feed store has his workers load the wagon, we'll drop by to see Leon and Marge." He waited for her response. "I thought you'd be pleased."

"I am, but it's not going to be easy. In fact, from what I've heard, we have to expect…"

Asher nodded. "God was with us through the Tribulation. He is with us still."

"Nehemiah has stayed behind."

"Yes…because they asked him to."

"No, it was his choice." She sat closer as he urged the four-horse team up a slight incline. "Esther told me last night." She gripped the seat tighter. "Get ready and pray the Holy Spirit will give us the words to win them back."

The streets of Kadesh Barnea were as crowded as always, but autos and bicycles darted here and there, crowding the carriage lanes. Asher slowed the team, bringing it to a stop whenever a wayward traveler cut them off. Thankfully, the supply and feed lots were on a quiet back street.

Asher halted the team by the large parking lot. "I'll get the order started. Stay with the wagon."

Charlene accepted the reins and slid over, talking softly to the team. The two horses in the rear were younger and a little skittish. The lead horses were also their saddle mounts—her gray and Asher's large black gelding.

She tried to make contact with the few rushing in or leaving quickly, but she hardly recognized anyone. The city felt foreign and dark—so different from their last visit only a few months ago. What had Marge said? That change would be welcome? She had thought the woman had been referring to eternity, but perhaps she had meant something totally different.

Shaking her head, trying not to imagine what she could not know, she prayed, focusing again on the people she could see. *Bring them to You, Lord.*

After what felt like a long time, Asher emerged with a set face. "Drive them to the fifth door." She flicked the reins on their backs, clicking and encouraging them to walk to the warehouse opening with a large "5" painted beside it. "Turn, Turn, gee, easy," she said. Once in position, she pulled lightly on the reins. "Back, back, a little more. Whoa." She leaned back slightly, but even the greener geldings had soft mouths.

What happened? We were to have ridden our mounts to Leon's! Charlene stepped down from the wagon.

Asher followed her. "Still a go for that side trip?"

"Yes." Tight-lipped, she watched him walk into the large warehouse, keeping an eye on the clerks bringing the order.

Charlene was surprised to see him jump up onto the bed to arrange and sort the load. Obviously, they would be driving the wagon to their friends' estate.

"Charlene, can you hand over the box of tie-downs?"

She scrambled up, felt for the box, knelt to get a good hold, and lifted it over to Asher. Climbing down, she steadied the horses, stroking the rear geldings and soothing the team with her voice. Everything felt wrong. Tension filled the air. *Praise You, Lord, for Your mercies. Praise You for Your wondrous gifts. Save our friends! Open their eyes.* Had not the Scriptures said that only by the Spirit of the Lord would they be able to discern the lies of the Wicked One? *Give us the words. Save them!* She reviewed their lost ones, lifting her prayers to heaven.

Asher rearranged the lumber, clipped in the bag of fastenings, and lined up bags of flour and grains along one side. "Ready. Hey, Charlene! We're ready." Asher climbed over the low back of the bench, gathered the reins, and extended his hand.

She climbed up onto the bench and grasped the side railing, holding her breath. Charlene glanced back at the load. It looked like half of what she thought they would be getting. "Did the order change?"

"They jacked up their prices just for us. They were going to add loading fees as well." He looked straight ahead, tight-lipped. "Let's pray Nehemiah won't do the same."

The hollow look in his eyes sent a chill down her spine.

"It's started already. So soon!"

Asher nodded. "I suspect Leon and Marge are going to feel very different." Slapping the reins on the team's backs to cross an intersection, he took secondary roads that avoided the main thoroughfares.

She recalled their warm and cordial visit with their friends only a month ago. Marge had said they could drop by anytime. Charlene continued to pray.

Leon's ranch on his estate formed a semi-circle that sat on the highest rise overlooking the rolling hills and plains heading south. Some of the Egyptian towns just south of Gad's territory could be seen in the distance.

Asher slowed the team as they drew close to the wrought-iron gate bounded by stone pillars that had been barred shut. He spied several cars parked along the drive near the large house. Two burly men approached them.

"Who shall we say is calling?" the trimmer one asked. His larger companion stood guard by his side.

Asher had not seen them before. "Tell Leon and Marge that Asher and Charlene are dropping by for a visit." Seeing their frozen stares, he leaned forward. "We're close friends. At least let him know we are here."

The men turned without a word, a nod or the courtesy of a standard greeting.

Charlene watched a couple in the distance make their way to a golf cart sitting on the side lawn. She clutched Asher's hand, reminding herself not to squeeze too tightly. She recognized Leon and Marge.

"Well, friend, we're dropping by to see how you both are doing." Asher stepped down and held up his hand for Charlene to follow.

Leon brought the cart to face them at an angle. He stepped out, holding onto the railing to keep his balance. Marge, still in her seat, stared at them stone-faced.

Asher's eyes narrowed. "I see you have company. Perhaps it's not the best time."

"You can say what you came to say!" Leon leaned his hip against the cart and crossed his arms.

"The Lord is calling all to the Temple Mount. When will your people be coming?" Asher stopped there, not wanting to share anything about the preparations underway near the city.

"*Your* people, Asher. *My* people!" He nodded his head toward the main house. The sounds of loud music and partying filtered along a soft breeze. "You know He doesn't own us."

Asher waited. Charlene held her breath.

"*Your* God…I hear His time is up, and He's leaving. So," Leon leaned to the side and smiled at his wife. "I'm not ready to run away— not for a mythical city in the sky!" He stepped closer, lowering his voice. "New management's here already and things will change, but they'll be better—fairer. No more sending hapless souls to that place they talk about—as if it ever existed."

Charlene held back her quick retort, feeling Asher's hold on her arm. She swallowed a rising anger and tried to pray. Marge avoided looking at her.

"He is called Satan, the Devil and is the Father of lies. You know you can't trust…"

"So, how do you know this? His book? Your God's truth!" Leon waggled his finger. "You know he has another name, Lucifer, and he is an angel of light. I submit he's different, but he's come to take what is his due after all that he has done for that God of yours." He dropped his arms and drew near to the closed gate. "All that nonsense—*being let loose to trick us into following him*—that's the lie. You have no idea what he has planned for us."

"And you think you do?"

"You know what, Asher? It's been nice knowing you. I never expected to be able to turn you, but many of your grandsons and granddaughters are more enlightened. There are many ways to meet the future. *Yours* is just one of many paths."

"Marge?" Charlene looked at her friend. "Do you agree?"

The tall, stately woman with short brown hair and green eyes, grasped the railing, put her leg over and attempted to stand. "This lady won't be calling Him holy, holy, holy for eternity or bowing and scraping before that God!" The spittle flew from her mouth.

"Marge was one of the first to perceive who the real enemy is!" Leon said proudly. He lowered his chin. "And you'd better get back to the safety of your God before some of my fine citizens realize you're here. I won't be able to protect you. Can your God?"

"And what of those who believe? They need to be allowed to come."

Leon shrugged his shoulders and turned away. "Free will, Asher. Free will."

The menacing gazes of Leon's guards sent a shock through them. Without a word they scrambled into the wagon, and Asher directed the team to trot quickly down the lane.

Charlene noticed that he drove past the road leading northwest. "Wait? Where are we going?"

"We are going to tell them." He turned his head, his face set.

"I'm in." She said and took the reins. Kadesh Barnea, built along a rise that hugged a tributary from the Western River, had a long, narrow main street. Charlene turned the team to the southern end and paused while Asher climbed into the back and wedged his feet among the lumber and boxes. He secured a short strap to the back of the bench and braced himself.

"What's the plan?"

"You drive. I preach. Remember those crazy street preachers we used to avoid when we visited Denver? Well, now, we are them! Go slow but maintain a vigilance. We might have to scramble to make it to the Highway. Ready?"

"Ready!" She brought the team to a slow trot, each horse's legs rising and lifting in unison, their tails lifted, their necks arched. The road curved and faced the main city district. She braced her legs against the footboard, gripped the reins tightly, and looked back for Asher's nod.

When they reached the first sidewalk, already buzzing with a steady stream of walkers, Asher lifted his voice.

"If you reverence Christ in your heart, come to the Temple Mount! If you do not, now is the time to believe on the Lord Jesus Christ! He is the way, the truth, and the life. Only by Him can you come to the Father and Mighty God. Only through Christ can you have a part in the first resurrection. All your sins are paid for! Free and clear! Go to the throne of grace and accept the free gift of salvation from the Lord of Glory—the Lord you have seen with your eyes, the One to whom you have bowed before the altar on His Temple Mount."

The crowds stirred, and a low mumbling began to rise up. Charlene urged the team to trot more quickly. She leaned forward, her head turning on a swivel. Shadows from side roads urged her to click and slap the reins along the team's back.

Asher continued, now almost in the center, he repeated the simple gospel. "Flee the wrath to come! There is no peace—no justice from the father of lies. Believe the Word of God. As it is has been fulfilled, this will also come to pass. Beware the second death! You cannot stand before God in your sins. Heed the call—come and be saved!"

Hearing a roar, Charlene cried out and leaned forward. The team jumped into a canter.

The roar of motorcycles coming upon them did not stop Asher. He raised his voice above the rising din, praying that some would hear, repent and believe.

The large black surged forward. The smaller gray ran swiftly by his side. Their nostrils flared; their eyes set on the road before them.

Some stood in the middle of the road, but Charlene urged the team on. She breathed a sigh of relief when the people scattered.

"Faster, Charlene!" Asher pulled himself toward the bench, climbed over its back and reached for the reins.

The team ran full out, but they would be no match for the jeeps and motorcycles. Asher glanced back, and it looked as if they did not know where to go. He noticed a bright, effervescent glow as of a pearl. The angels were guarding them. Even so, he kept the team at full gallop until they reached the Highway of Holiness, still patrolled by the guardian angels.

Charlene held on, feeling the presence of the glory of God that came with them.

Once they were a distance away, Asher slowed the team to a walk. He held his wife's trembling hand. Their eyes met. They had done what they could do. This might have been their last time to share the glorious gospel.

Asher tried not to think of his home, his estate, the city he had built, the retreat grounds or their gardens, fields and herds. He had to focus on the next world soon to come. This world was passing away. It had grown old as a garment. One more day. And then the next, until the last day. Only God the Father knew the exact day or hour.

His great-great-grandson had requested the ranch. Asher had agreed and asked him to care for the horses. The automatic payments to his employees were still in place. The farms were doing well without him.

Asher turned the team to the rightward road and across the river. Their little city gleamed in the light of midmorning. Fresh lilacs scented the valley, riding along the waves of the wind.

Charlene released a sigh. Home. Calm and peaceful, some waved as their team walked down the main street. "Stop by the park."

They climbed down, tied the team and headed for the main boardwalk. Looking, waiting for the Spirit to give them the liberty to share the gospel, but He did not give leave until they reached a young woman walking with a face of sorrow.

"Decorah, what's the matter?"

She lifted reddened eyes. "My little ones."

"They are safe at the Temple Mount. Don't you want to go with them?" Charlene reached out as if to hug her, but the young woman stepped back.

"I'm not ready."

"He will make you ready. Just as you are, Jesus will not turn you away." Charlene looked about. Already the darkness had fallen here as well. "Asher will be taking the team to Nehemiah's. Ride with us. We can talk along the way." Her eyes slid by her favorite pastry shop but knew those times had passed. *I will enjoy the feasts of the Lord in Jerusalem on the New Earth.*

Decorah went with them. Charlene shared the gospel. The woman wiped her eyes, bowed her head and prayed. Lifting a face tracked by tears, but lit with joy, she said, "I am ready now. Billie took the kids. I don't know why I had such a hard time."

She hugged the young woman. "We all must go before the throne of grace and surrender ourselves. It's not easy for any of us."

"But then we are clean—no longer fighting against our burdens of guilt." She lifted her eyes. "I had no idea that I'd been rebelling against Him all these years. How could He forgive me?"

"How great is His love for us!" Charlene hugged her close. Her own tears mixed with those of her friend.

The parking lot in front of Nehemiah's was empty. Asher sighed. He reached for Charlene's hand and led in a quick prayer.

The three walked through the open double doors. Nehemiah hunched over an inventory list for his next order with the distributor. "Ahh, Asher, Charlene, Decorah, it's good to see you."

Asher scanned the large board hanging above the register with the lumber and food sack prices. "Those still in place?"

"Sure. What do you need?"

He smiled for the first time, set his list on the counter and rattled off a large order. "We heard you chose to stay behind. Soon it will be too late to join us on the Mount."

The tall, broad man with short beard and dark eyes added the last figure to the total and swung the invoice around for Asher's signature.

Decorah stepped forward. "Uncle, don't believe what they say. Lucifer will not bring in another time of peace of safety. He brings only death. Don't die in your sins." She glanced at Charlene. "I believe now. It's not too late for you. Look around and see how everyone is changing so quickly. I wouldn't have believed it if I hadn't seen it with my own eyes."

"Didn't they take your family?" His eyes bore into her, then looked away. "Understandable that you'd choose God so you could be with your children. But don't you want to keep your freedom, your ability to decide about your life and not have it all dictated?"

"That's the lie, Nehemiah. That's the lie that Satan told Eve millennia ago—that we could be equal with God. Didn't we learn the history of his time before Christ came to rule? Remember the terrible, terrible murders and wickedness that nearly destroyed mankind?"

"God had a hand in that too."

"He allowed them to reap the consequences of their sins because they refused to repent. Please, come with us!" Seeing him turn away, she said, "I've always been grateful for your kind generosity. My family wasn't wealthy, but you never turned us away. I love you and will pray for you. If you do come, do it soon, and you can stay with us. I'm sure the kids already miss you, uncle."

Charlene led Decorah to the team. "Climb in, and we'll bring the team around. Remember, we are only the messengers; God gives the increase. We'll pray with you. We also love Nehemiah, the eternal bachelor."

"He's so settled in his ways—content to keep his store and do his own books in the evenings. When he would come with us to a festival, he would rather hold a baby in his lap or play with the toddlers than join in with the games."

"A very quiet, gentle man." Charlene untied the team and directed them to back up. "We will keep praying for him."

"I can't imagine what it's like for you and Asher and my own grandparents—the first ones. Doesn't the sorrow overwhelm you?"

"The joy of the Lord is a river of life to us no matter how bad things get down here. Remember joy and peace are from Him and His Holy Spirit. Seek it, ask for it and remember—He will never forsake us."

She wiped her eyes and nodded. "I will see Billie and the kids again!"

Asher purchased the last of the supplies, and Nehemiah walked back with him to help tie the load down. "You could come with us. Take the Lord and live for eternity," Asher said. It amazed him again that this nice man had resisted the Savior all these centuries.

Nehemiah only smiled in his usual way, went to get the receipt and began to talk of next year's crops.

"You think there will be next year's crop to sow, let alone harvest?"

"Who's to tell? Things have gone along for a long time. What's to change?"

"The wicked ones walk the earth as they did before Christ set up His kingdom. They will deceive all who do not know the Savior. Take His free gift. Let Him forgive your sins, and you can dwell with us forever on the New Earth."

"That's a myth. Come on, the King's just trying to scare us into joining His inner circle. What's the difference between you and me anyway? You say you're saved, but you still have to make an offering before you can appear before the Lord. We make an offering and worship Him. We're still here."

Asher listened to his friend's reasons. "The Spirit of God dwells within me. I have entered into His kingdom."

"Listen, you first-generation people have a great story, and I know you're trying to warn us, but we're not going to fall for that rhetoric. He can try to stir the pot, but things will continue on. We have evolved. See the civilization that we have built! The planet is at peace, and we will be able to keep it. Well, everything's loaded. Do you need anything else?"

Asher longed to repeat the invitation, but the man clearly was not interested. He hugged him. "It has been an honor to do business with you," Asher said. "God bless you, brother." He climbed up to the wagon seat with a heavy heart to join Charlene and Decorah.

As they turned, on their way, they saw the ships coming in the distance. Were they of the faithful coming to the Lord or the hordes who would soon descend upon the Mount of the Lord? His gut tightened. Things were falling into place very quickly.

►27

NEHEMIAH WATTCHED THE wagon disappear around the bend. He tore up his order and pulled out a clean form. Asher had cleaned him out of some key items. A slow anger rumbled, and he didn't like how it felt.

He trudged to the back warehouse attached to the general store front. *I almost raised my prices. I was ready to short his order. After all...*

He shook his head, amazed that he had harbored thoughts of cheating such a faithful friend and customer like Asher. Nehemiah froze in mid-stride, an inkling of something that he had never felt before. What had Decorah said and Charlene had repeated—that shiny, glorious Lucifer was a great deceiver?

But the pull to avoid the Temple... The urge not to bow to the one true God would not be denied. He shook his head and created a new order, finishing it this time.

After a quiet meal of reheated leftovers, Nehemiah gassed up his truck and backed it out to refresh his supply of fresh vegetables and fruits from David's farm. A twinge of jealousy rose up—his grandfather should have given the large farm to him and not those worthless grand-nephews. Again, he recoiled from the unusual thoughts running through his head.

However, the long gravel road to the farm drew close, and he slowed the truck, keeping an eye out for potholes. The last time he had come by the farm, they had been at the feast. The help had neglected to regrade the road after a rainstorm, and potholes had begun to appear.

Not surprisingly, he had to drive on the left shoulder to avoid the dips and rises that had seemingly developed overnight. Clouds of dark smoke didn't reach his consciousness until he drew closer. The smell of a combination of burning wood, tires and plastic invaded his inner musings, jolting him back to the present.

True crime accounts and the annals of the supreme judges who imposed the death sentence on the few who had the courage to rebel had grabbed his attention lately. What drove a person to take goods, or a life, or demand what didn't belong to them? Those questions had fascinated him.

Was he witnessing this rebellion now? This wasn't the time to burn the fields, and David rarely had resorted to that practice—few did since the King of Glory had removed all weeds and thorns. At first, he thought the fires were distant, but they appeared to come from the barns, including the one that housed the pigs and chickens. *Where are the workers? Where are Rick and Mike?*

Nehemiah ran up the steps, pulled open the front door and called out. "Rick! Mike! Laurie!" His pulse quickened; the rush of adrenaline that brightened his eyes made him feel alive—something that had been waning for decades.

The house was eerily quiet—far too quiet. He set foot on the staircase but decided to check the large, connected kitchen and dining room. Nehemiah stepped quickly, holding onto the door jamb to make the turn, and he nearly tripped over his feet when he froze.

The back of Mike's splayed head, with brains showing, faced him. The man had fallen onto a half-finished plate of eggs and sausage. Rick lay sprawled against the back of the chair—his chest separated as if by a cleaver. Blood spatter covered the chairs, table and had dripped onto the floor. Reddish-brown droplets even speckled the ceiling.

Their wives and daughters? Seeing Mike's mother dead on the floor close to the back door, Nehemiah released a strangled cry. He had to turn away. True, they lacked the weapons of ages gone by, but farm implements provided more-than-adequate substitutes.

His mouth dry, he recoiled from even thinking of pouring himself a drink in that room of death. Gasping, he ran to the first barn and there she lay—Esmerelda, fair and beautiful, disfigured with a look of dread stamped on her face from the blows of death.

Nehemiah knelt by the side of his favorite, close friend to cradle her in his arms. "I didn't save you!" They had joked about marriage, but both had been so settled in their ways. *Content? Have I really been content all those years?* The need to be with her…the need to have his own children rose up. He gently laid her down and stepped away, as if the distance would silence the emotions screaming within him.

One part of him told him to free the animals and put out the fire, but another whispered that he needed to leave before the mob found him. Common sense took over, and he exited the barn just as he heard loud boastful curses with the tread of many feet growing louder.

The horses had been taken or loosed. The bikes and four-wheelers had been stolen as well or smashed beyond usefulness. The wanton destruction took his breath away. *Is this my new world?*

A few voices grew closer. They argued over who would keep the corpse. He quietly stepped along the back field and peered down the hedgerow. It was clear. An inner voice urged him to run.

Slinking behind bushes and trees, he found his way to the roads but hesitated to walk them. In the distance, he could see the glow of the Highway. A pit within his gut wrenched. To go to them? Bow before the angels and beg for his life? The instant revulsion almost made him sick, but memories of Esmerelda lying dead and desecrated cast them aside.

His cheeks were wet. *Am I really crying?* Tenderhearted, they all said he was. His heart grieved as much for himself as for her. Now he knew… *If she had died here, she will not be in God's eternal kingdom. If I had died here, neither would I.*

Memories of his grandparents, David and Esther, Malcolm and Sonya. Nehemiah recounted the list until he reached his parents and recalled their patient teaching. "God is faithful, Nehemiah, and we must always thank Him for everything—all the good things."

"Even the bad things?" he had asked, a challenge in his heart even if he never spoke of it. What must they be thinking right now? Suddenly, his sins were laid bare before him. All these years he had assumed that he was a good man—certainly not worthy of the pit. Yet, here he was, refusing to surrender to the guardian angels.

The idiocy of his rebellion lay naked before him. Breathing in, he looked about, listened, and remembering his days of playing hide and seek with the children, and headed to the Highway of Holiness.

Let them be there for me, he found himself praying. Bowing his head, he continued asking for help, but most of all, repenting.

The lengthening shadows helped him avoid another gang on its way to ransack the next home. Cries of terror lingered on the wind. He wished he could help, but he knew he wasn't even able to save himself. *Jesus, deliver me!*

The distance seemed longer than he had remembered, but he pushed on until he made one last dash to the highway. Instead of an angel blocking his path, the gleaming one extended his hand and drew him onto the highway. *Why did I wait so long?*

The angel answered, *Not one will be lost.* The creature glowing with the glory of the Lord held his hand and turned him toward the Temple.

Nehemiah, with new life surging through his chest, smiled, stepped forward and looked back. The angel had disappeared from view, but he could still feel him. In wonderment, he turned toward the Mount and ran—not fleeing but running toward the eternal life that he hadn't tried to understand all those years.

Did it really feel this wonderful? Why did I wait so long?

Eventually, he slowed to a walk as the new day began with the setting sun and the first stars showing themselves. He saw the lights of a plane overhead. Earlier he hadn't taken the time to think about the two ships he had seen earlier coming into port. Having come closer to the Mount, he realized he no longer felt the oppression of the outer regions. Surely, other believers must also be arriving. However, they were most likely ones who had had the sense to believe before the turning.

Pushing those thoughts aside, Nehemiah continued on, thinking about what he would say to his family. "I'm sorry," he said, practicing his speech. As he recalled the pure joy on the angels' faces when they had welcomed him onto the road, he knew they would forgive him. Didn't the Scriptures say that salvation was something the angels desired to understand? Not knowing where that thought came from, he smiled to himself and walked more quickly.

Thankfully, his path did not have to intersect with the flowing stream of new arrivals. He would slip in on the southern side and work his way up to the city, and around to…*where?* The last set of stairs loomed before him, and he suddenly felt so alone.

Sensing a figure moving quickly toward him, he stepped aside to let him pass. But he didn't; he stopped and spoke, "Nehemiah! You have come!"

Overcome with gratitude, Nehemiah embraced his small father, his tears falling freely on his shoulder. "Forgive me! I'm so sorry."

"Of course, all is forgiven. Praise God you saw the light in time. Come! Soon the Lord will create a wall between us and them. You came just in time." His shining eyes took in his large son. "Of all my children, I am so pleased to know that we will have eternity together."

"So am I." Nehemiah glanced up the steps and noticed a crowd at the top. "Who are they waiting for?"

"You!"

►28

THE GREATEST FAMILY reunion of all time! Charlene smiled at Asher across the packed table in the dining tent. Now that all of their children were here—even the ones who had settled in Colorado, they could not seem to get enough of visiting with them. Children ran around, playing tag in the open areas. Groups, forming and shifting, met, swapped the latest news and continued on to find friends and family.

Charlene rose to meet Nehemiah as he headed for the tents surrounded by family as well. "Our prayers were answered," she said, clapping her hands in delight. His broad smile was all that she needed. On her way to the Temple to pray for the lost ones to come, she paused, seeing Asher's retreating back. He was obviously headed for the wall.

No teams were set or times posted. All seemed to know where they should be. Scores, hundreds kept up their prayers at the Temple. More hundreds kept up their vigil along the outskirts of the raised plateau, greater than 100 miles long and 50 miles wide.

Charlene stepped aside to follow groups of children led by several adults to the Temple. She watched the Lord of Glory step through the inner gate and spread His arms wide. He welcomed the children. All clapped, sang, and danced with songs of rejoicing.

—⁓—

Asher heard the rising praises to their Mighty God even close to the border's edge. One stepped through and looked about. Asher approached the bewildered-looking man. "Do you believe in the Lord Jesus Christ?"

"I do. Now I do. Help me find Him."

"Do you admit your sin and the need for His blood to cover you? Do you accept the free gift of salvation?"

"I do. Help me." His eyes pleaded his urgency. Remembering Nehemiah's hair-raising tales, he answered quietly and evenly. "Pray to God. He will not turn you away."

Asher listened to the effectual prayer of faith even in this last hour. He would have accompanied the new believer to the Temple, but a close friend stepped up and hugged the newcomer.

"Would you like to accompany him?"

"That's why I'm here."

Smiling, Asher stepped aside, wondering if someone he cared for deeply would step across the line. Feeling someone behind him, he turned and spread his arms wide. "Nehemiah!"

"What good works can I do now?"

"Whatever you can with the little time left."

"I watched the children, but they are asleep by now."

Asher grasped his arm. "Why the long face? You're safe now."

He nodded. "I am a child of God and truly adopted into His family, but none of my earlier good deeds will count for anything. So many regrets. What if I had listened all those years ago?"

"My friend. You are completely forgiven. Don't give into the temptation to miss the grace and mercy of God by wishing for what cannot be changed! Rejoice that you are here and with us. But if you do want to help, stand with me and talk with those who, at this late hour, will be coming to the throne of grace."

"How will I know what to say?"

Asher stepped away from the border and to a quieter spot. "You know the gospel, right? You've heard it all your life. You know the Scriptures. I remember when you won verse memory contests as a boy. The Word of God will sprout and blossom in your mind and heart. The Holy Spirit who now dwells within you will give you understanding of its precepts." He patted his dear friend's shoulder. "He will also give you the words to say. Just ask and believe."

"It's that easy?"

"No, it's that simple, but it's often never easy. So trust God and stand with me."

"It would be an honor, uncle." As they stood together, the woosh of angels' wings, the high-pitched songs of praise floating on the breezes, and the glory of the Lord seeming to fill every inch of the plateau blended with the cries of joy and words of encouragement for those crossing over.

Time seemed to stand still as the night deepened. Though the light from the Temple had dimmed the stars, many of them were still shining through. Fewer believers seemed to be coming in, and Asher was almost ready to head back to his tent when a tall, broad woman stepped over right in front of them. She almost looked familiar.

"Lydia!" Nehemiah stepped forward and wrapped her in his bear hug. "You have come!"

"Nehemiah! But I thought," she cast a glance at Asher. "I heard you had stayed behind." She stepped closer. "But I see we both made the same decision." She looked down the hill, trying to forget the scenes from which she had fled.

"Just in time." Nehemiah stared at her closely. "You believe?"

"Yes, I repented…" She shifted her eyes away from his. "It was so horrible."

He held her close. "I know. I saw what they did to those at David's farm."

"Oh, no! All dead?"

He nodded. "You too?"

Seeing her answering nod, he hugged her again.

Lydia stepped back and smiled, the light shining in her eyes. "But the love of God! You're right. We are here now, and that is what truly matters. Can I? Would you walk with me to see Jesus?"

"I would be delighted," Nehemiah extended his arm, and she slid her arm through to rest her hand on his forearm.

►29

THE SHIPS AND planes had released their cargo. The last ones to repent from surrounding districts had made their way to the upraised plateau. As the sun set, the pillar of cloud rose up and covered the area like a dome. Pillars of fire surrounded the Mount as an impenetrable wall.

The next event—Gog and Magog would assemble. The forces of darkness calling all who remained to their one task—to rid the planet of all who followed the King of kings.[60] The ships and planes now carried the hordes set on destruction, bringing with them whatever they could find.

—◌◌◌—

Many came and went from the Temple courtyard, but Andrew stayed on his knees, pleading for his wife, heedless of all else. Finally, he bowed his head. "Not my will, but Your will, Lord. Save her, but if not, I accept it."

An inner peace settled amid an emptiness that had threatened to overtake him. Sitting back on his heels, he stared at the tall lamp rising above the roof of the Temple that bathed the square with an amber light. The door had closed, and Marta had not come. Hope for her had withered away, but he knew the joy of the Lord would be his. It was sufficient.

Swooshing sounds of angels grew louder. He peered above the tall Temple wall as he stood.

Another delivery. It was late. Thirst thickened his tongue and cracked his lips. Hunger had dissipated hours ago. Although he knew that he should return to his booth and face his family, something held him frozen.

One angel after another landed with an infant or child cradled in his arms. One carried what appeared to be an adult. Narrowing his eyes and shaking his head, he refocused his eyes and spied long, flowing, black hair. His pulse quickened. Andrew stepped closer to where many of the angels were landing to hand over their precious cargo to those waiting to welcome the last of the arrivals.

Andrew moved aside to make room for two angels with children in their arms. He had not the heart to care for a child—not this night. He heard three land behind him, but before he could turn, the one with a woman landed to his left.

He turned and locked eyes. They widened, and with strangled cries, he stepped forward to welcome his Marta! *How is this possible? I thought…* He nodded in thankfulness to the angel, hearing the reply in his mind.

She clung to him, still shaking.

"I can take you to our tent…"

"No, I must see the King!" Marta released him and wiped her eyes, standing before him with a look he had never seen before.

Andrew waited. He knew his wife or thought he had known her.

She grasped his hands, cradling them near her chest. "You repented the day He appeared in the sky—at the Second Coming. That's what Elimelech told me. But you hadn't changed. He said you never deserved me; you'd been such a wretched, miserable person." She studied his face. "This is true? You never spoke of it."

What could he say? The old Andrew would have spouted lies about protecting her, but here at the Temple, knowing eternity was at hand, he tore down his inner walls. "To protect myself. Why I waited so long to marry. Even after I had received the love and mercy of God, I refused to let it change me. The hard, grasping, stingy, bitter road builder continued on as if new life in Christ had no bearing on how I lived."

"Listen, I want to hear your story, but I must make my confession…"

He grasped her arm gently and followed the people presenting themselves before the Lord of Glory. "I will walk with you."

She squeezed his hand.

They knelt before the Lord. Andrew couldn't hear the words, but he knew she was communing with her Savior. Joy rose in his soul, and he felt as if he could dance. He felt his wife shiver beside him.

The Lord laid His hand on her head, healing and strengthening her.

Thankfulness rose in his heart.

It was time. They stood, and Andrew walked with her to his booth, praying they would have some time together before the rest of the clan welcomed her return.

"Andrew, I desired you from the time I watched you arrange Father's contracts for the water system. I charmed you and won your heart—all the while denying the Lord that you worshiped. You had no idea?"

"None."

"Sad to say, I was pleased that I had deceived you so well, but after you left, when I saw what those who stayed behind were capable of doing, I was appalled. Assuming I was better, I could hardly believe the wicked thoughts, resentment and bitterness that almost overtook me, but I resisted, taking pride in my self-control. However, Elimelech almost succeeded in deceiving me. Did you know that even while he had been married to Katherine, he had been longing for me? I could hear his hatred for you. I knew what he said about you in the early years had been true, and I decided never to forgive you. But then I perceived Elimelech's hypocrisy. The Lord must have shown me that true salvation and faith had transformed you. I saw judging you by what you had been without considering what you had become was not fair." She reached up to kiss him. "And you, he couldn't begin to come close to you, my love! For the first time I understood the change that had been wrought in you was real. God was real and that He would forgive me."

He paused by a bench, and they sat.

She stroked his face and kissed him. "Because the man to whom I had been married for over 800 years was not the man he had described. No, he had been reborn in Christ. I had been so blinded by my own self-sufficiency." She looked away. "Even though I knew I had waited too long, I believed that the God who created the universe would preserve me to the day of glory the instant I surrendered to Him. He sent His angel to rescue me!"

"Not by your own strength!" A smile danced across Andrew's face.

"Absolutely not. Locked in a room, realizing my grievous error, I finally surrendered to God, and the angel swooped down to take me home." Her shoulders shook.

They huddled on the bench as the moon set, but the light in their souls never dimmed. Andrew rose, helped her stand, and they faced the east as the sun broke over the horizon. "Shall we join our family?"

She nodded and walked with him. *The Lord will give me the words to say.*

—⁓—

Light and glory filled the Mount. The gathering angels guarded the air space. No darkness or evil could penetrate the Lord's camp.

Outside, the forces gathered, frothing to attack, but the time was not yet.

On the seventh day, the sun's rays pinked the eastern sky and, within moments, blinded the hordes with the full glory of God. They rose up, determined to kill and destroy.

The protecting pillar of fire shielded the saints as fire from heaven destroyed all on the broad plain in a flash. As they had sinned with full knowledge of the glory of God and His mercies, so came His righteous judgment in an instant. They all died in one day with the coming of the Morning Star.

For the last time, Satan and his demons were cast into the lake of fire for all eternity.

Every living soul on the Mount was transformed...from mortality to immortality...from time to eternity...

Each and every one, all at the same time and individually, brought their works to the Lord of glory for the test of His cleansing fire. All the works of wood, hay and stubble burned away, but those of gold, silver and precious stones remained.[61] Their offerings to the Lord for what they had done in and through Him were presented, for apart from Christ they could do nothing.[62]

The end of the first resurrection... The end of the universe and days and time...

PART THREE

Day of Eternity

►30

JUST AS QUICKLY, the newly transformed believers, now glorified and in their immortal bodies, found themselves suspended above the earth with the angels and those who had gone before. They appeared to be standing on clear glass. Somehow, Asher knew it was translucent, pure gold that stretched out beyond his sight. Countless hosts of angels and the glorified redeemed stood with him.

Asher smiled at Charlene and reached for her hand. As he looked about, he realized that he knew the names and histories of the ones standing beside him. Daniel and Frank and Patty stood not far from Gary and Vera.

The sun bathed the planets with its light, but it paled before the light of the glory of God that spread out in every direction. A large, gleaming white throne appeared. The Lord of Glory sat on it in white splendor with flashing eyes and bronze boots.

Angels stood before pedestals supporting large books. Row upon row, in long columns, they stood at the ready. In the center a glorious angel stood before the largest book Asher had ever seen.

With a command the dead came forth from hades, the keeper of the dead. The sea and the earth yielded up all those who had not been included in the first resurrection and had not taken the Lord as their Savior, rejecting the free gift of salvation.

Each one was judged by his or her thoughts, words and deeds that had been recorded in the books. Before the Lord passed judgment, the large angel confirmed the person's name was missing from the Lamb's Book of Life.

Despite the Savior having paid the penalty for their sins, they chose to earn their own way—eternal torment in the lake of fire. This was the second death.[63]

With that, the Lord commanded the elements to dissolve, loosening the bonds that held matter together. It dissolved with a fervent heat. The old earth and heavens fled away and were no more.[64] Only eternity remained.

As the angels and redeemed watched, God made a new earth and heavens, reborn in purity and holiness, unspotted by sin's curse. The earth sparkled under the light of God's glory. Resplendent with green grass, tall trees and fields of flowers, they beheld a glistening orb with no sea.

The joy of the Lord poured forth from the throne, and the Lord of glory commanded the heavenly Jerusalem, as long and as deep and as tall as a continent to descend upon a waiting, upraised plain.

Its walls were constructed of fine jewels, and each gate was a pearl, white luminescence that welcomed all who came through.

Asher found himself on the broad plain before the towering cube glistening in God's glory.

All paused when they heard the voice of the Lord. *"Behold, the dwelling place of God is with man. He will dwell with them and they will be his people, and God himself will be with them as their God."*[65]

Daniel drew near, along with his parents and brothers. He said, "Eternity! No more crying or tears or separation or sorrow. The city is ready. Wait until we show you. The glory of the Lord lights the city with a river of life, and the tree of life is so large that a street passes through it."

"And the Temple?" Asher asked.

"No Temple is needed for God dwells with His people, and all sin has been removed forever. Now we will dwell with Him, and we will bring in the fruits of the earth. The days of sorrow are past. The day of eternity is here."[66]

Asher grasped Charlene's hand, and they followed Daniel, Frank and Patty to the gate. She paused. "Look, this is Zebulun's gate."

"So it is!" They entered the city with the redeemed and the angels.

And I heard a loud voice from the throne saying, "Behold, the dwelling place of God is with man. He will dwell with them, and they will be his people, and God himself will be with them as their God. He will wipe away every tear from their eyes, and death shall be no more, neither shall there be mourning, nor crying, nor pain anymore, for the former things have passed away... Behold, I am making all things new...It is done!"

– Revelation 21:3-6

► Timeline

Scattered throughout the Bible like bread-crumbs are verses describing future times that we can scarcely imagine—times of great distress and upheaval as well as times of paradise and peace. The Burier imagines what living through these future times might be like. These events are seen through the eyes of those who came to faith during the worst of times to find themselves in the utopia that man had always desired.

The Church Age — present day when all are called to place their faith in Jesus Christ as their Savior from sin.

The Rapture — a sudden event when all church-age believers are resurrected and taken to Heaven. They will return to earth with the Lord and will help Him administer the planet throughout the Millennium.

The Tribulation — a period of seven years when the Lord will judge Israel and the unbelieving nations. During this time, many will find faith in Christ, some are destined to be martyred or will die during this period. Also, the Lord will seal His 144,000 servants, sons of Israel, who will preach to the nations and serve the Lord for eternity.

The Second Coming — The Lord will return to earth to judge all who oppose Him. He will come with His angels and all of the resurrected saints. All who died in faith before the Church Age or during the Tribulation will be resurrected and help the Lord administer the planet.

The Millennium — The 1,000-year reign of the Lord Jesus Christ. Most of the curse will be rolled back. Satan and his demons will be imprisoned in hell, no longer able to deceive the nations.

The planet's surface will be reconfigured as the mountains are laid low, and a large plain created for Jerusalem and the Lord's Temple will be raised. This will be the highest point of the earth. A river of life will flow from the Temple. Eastward, the river will heal the Dead Sea. (In this novel, it is called the Eastern Sea.) The river also flows west to the Mediterranean Sea, which is called the Western Sea. Ezekiel chapters 40 through 48 detail the Temple, the city, and the areas on the Temple Mount as well as the new locations for the tribes of Israel. Dan will be in the far north, and Zebulun in the south.

Only those who came to faith in Christ during the Tribulation will be allowed to enter the messianic kingdom of Christ. It will be a time of peace, justice and joy. The nations will come to the Lord's Temple on the Temple Mount near Jerusalem to worship the King of kings. The Sabbath and feasts of Passover and Tabernacles will be re-instituted, along with daily sacrifices.

The Release of Satan and His Demons — At the end of the 1,000 years, Satan and his demons will be released to deceive many who were born during this time of peace. They will compel all who have not taken the Lord as their Savior to attack the saints gathered on the Temple Mount. When all the unbelievers are surrounding the faithful, fire from the Lord will fall to destroy all who oppose Him.

Day of Eternity — The millennial saints are transformed into their glorified state. The universe is dissolved. They watch the Great White Throne Judgment of the unbelieving dead from all ages. All who oppose God—men and angels—are cast into the lake of fire. God creates a new heaven and earth. The New Jerusalem descends onto a perfect earth; the city's size is about half of the continental United States. God will light the world. There will be no Temple in the New Jerusalem for all can come freely to Him. A river and the Tree of Life will be there. God will be with His people forever.

▶ End Notes

Unless otherwise cited, direct Scripture quotations are taken from the Holy Bible, the English Standard Version®, copyright ©2001 by Crossway, a publishing ministry of Good News Publishers. Used by permission.

Scripture quotation noted NKJV are taken from the New King James Version®. Copyright © 1982 by Thomas Nelson. Used by permission. All rights reserved.

Some endnotes contain the biblical references for a passage, event, or fact about things to come. This is a work of fiction—creating a story from yet-to-be fulfilled prophetic passages.

—◦◦◦—

[1]Zechariah 14:4-5 and 10-11 details the changes to the land when the Lord returns.

[2]The Highway of Holiness running from Assyria through Israel to Egypt was predicted in Isaiah 11:16; 19:23-25; 35:8-10.

[3]Revelation 4:8 paraphrased; Revelation 15:3 (ESV).

[4]Psalm 19:9 (NKJV) paraphrased; Deuteronomy 32:43 paraphrased.

[5]Lamentations 3:22-23 (NKJV) paraphrased.

[6]Ezekiel 39:15-16;Hamonah is the name of the city of the buriers.

[7]Isaiah 30:26 (ESV) states, *"The light of the moon will be as the light of the sun, and the light of the sun will be sevenfold...."*

[8]Jeremiah 25:33—shall not be buried with honor or remembrance.

[9]Ezekiel 39:11-16 describes the clean-up.

[10]Isaiah 55:12-13—Eden restored.

[11]Isaiah 19:23-25 predicts the alliance of saved Assyria, Israel and Egypt.

[12]The term for the raptured Christians and resurrected Old Testament and Tribulation saints who help the Lord administer justice and lead the nations.

[13]Isaiah 2:2-3 (ESV) says, *"the mountain of the house of the LORD shall be established as the highest of the mountains, and shall be lifted up above the hills; and all the nations shall flow to it...For out of Zion shall go forth the law, and the word of the LORD from Jerusalem."*

[14]Zechariah 14:8; the former Mediterranean is now fed by the River flowing from the Temple.

[15]Daniel 9:27, 11:31; Matthew 24:15.

[16]Ezekiel 48:26-27 places Zebulun's land in the southernmost section between Issachar and Gad.

[17]Ezekiel 44:1-3 states only the Prince can enter through the East gate of the Temple as this is the gate where the Lord God entered. Jeremiah 30:9 promises that King David will be resurrected.

[18]Zechariah 14 describes the changes to Jerusalem and the land when He comes for the second time to the Mount of Olives.

[19]Isaiah 4:5, *"Then the LORD will create over the whole site of Mount Zion and over her assemblies a cloud by day, and smoke and the shining of a flaming fire by night; for over all the glory there will be a canopy."*

[20]Zephaniah 3:9 prophesied the people's speech would be changed and be pure.

[21]Isaiah 65:22 (ESV), *"for like the days of a tree shall the days of my people be...."*

[22]Matthew 4:15-16.

[23]Revelation 16:20, Isaiah 2:2, and Micah 4:1.

[24]Joel 2:28 prophesied that God would send His Spirit to all and they would prophesy, see visions and dream dreams.

[25]Ezekiel 47:1-12—the living water from the Temple that heals the Dead Sea are bordered by fruit trees with healing leaves.

[26]Romans 12:19.

[27]John 5:22, 27; Acts 10:42 (ESV).

[28]Isaiah 55:13.

[29]Ezekiel 39:9.

[30]John 15:15.

[31]Isaiah 19:19 (ESV).

[32]Ezekiel 39:9-10 paraphrase.

[33]Kurt Kaiser, "Oh, How He Loves You and Me," 1975 Word Music, LLC (a div. of Word Music Group, Inc.). Permission requested.

[34]Isaiah 11:9; Habakkuk 2:14 (ESV).

[35]1 Corinthians 13:1-2 (ESV).

[36]Colossians 3:12-13 (ESV).

[37]Ezekiel 43:1-5; 44:2.

[38]Ezekiel 47:1-5; Zechariah 14:8.

[39]Genesis 2:2-3; Exodus 20:8-11 (ESV).

[40]MJL, "Shabbat Blessings for Friday Night: Lighting the candles, saying Kiddush and other Shabbat dinner rituals." https://www.myjewishlearning.com/article/shabbat-blessings/.

[41]Matthew 26:29 (ESV).

[42]The city of Jerusalem,is south of the Temple on the Lord's Mount (Ezekiel 40:2; 48:15-20).

[43]Ezekiel 46:1-3, 9-10.

[44]Psalm 128:2; 132:15 (ESV).

[45]Revelation 14:3-5, paraphrase.

[46]The Great Tribulation is 1,260 days, 42 months, or time, times and half a time. The abomination will be cleared away by day 1,290, 30 days later. Blessed are those who enter the Millennium 45 days lat-

er—1,335 days after the Great Tribulation began (Daniel 7:25; 12:11-12; Revelation 11:3; 12:6).

[47]Ezekiel 40:21, as estimated by the Holy Bible, New Living Translation, copyright © 1996, 2004, 2007 by Tyndale House Foundation. Used by permission of Tyndale House Publishers, Inc., Carol Stream, Illinois 60188. All rights reserved.

[48]Psalm 150 paraphrased.

[49]Ezekiel 43:7 paraphrased.

[50]John 17:5, 22, 24 (ESV).

[51]Joel 3:2, 12 paraphrased.

[52]1 John 4:18 (ESV).

[53]Jeremiah 29:11 (ESV); and paraphrases of Ezekiel 28:26 and Isaiah 65:22.

[54]Psalm 136:1-3 (ESV).

[55]Revelation 14:1-5 paraphrased.

[56]Leviticus 7:15; 22:29-30 contains the law of the thanksgiving offer.

[57]Revelation 20:7-8 (ESV).

[58]Ezekiel 45:23-25.

[59]1 Corinthians 2:9 (ESV).

[60]Revelation 20:8-9.

[61]1 Corinthians 3:10-15.

[62]John 15:5.

[63]Revelation 20:11-15.

[64]Colossians 1:17; 2 Peter 3:10; Revelation 20:11; 21:1.

[65]Revelation 21:3 (ESV).

[66]Revelation 21.

▶ Good Resources

FOLLOWING THE BREADCRUMBS through the Bible for the days to come has been an enchanting treasure hunt. Over the years of studying prophecy and teaching through it for ladies' Bible studies and Sunday school, I have been amazed at how the thread of the story of God's plan for the ages knits and weaves all the stories of the Bible together. I referenced the Bible primarily, but also read many books by those who had dedicated years to studying these future times. Below is a list of the most helpful resources.

Believers did not know that the Lord's coming kingdom of peace would last 1,000 years until John wrote Revelation. But this last book of the Bible barely describes what this period will be like. Those descriptions are scattered mostly throughout the Psalms and in the books of the Old Testament prophets, including Isaiah, Jeremiah, Daniel, Joel, Zephaniah, and Zechariah.

Resource List

Ervin, Matthew Bryce. *One Thousand Years with Jesus: The Coming Messianic Kingdom*. Eugene, Ore.: Resource Publications, 2017.

Hitchcock, Mark. *The End: A Complete Overview of Bible Prophecy and the End of Days*. Carol Stream, Ill.: Tyndale House Publishers, Inc., 2012.

Longman III, Tremper, and David E. Garland, eds. *Proverbs~Isaiah*. The Expositor's Bible Commentary. Vol. 6. Rev. Ed. Grand Rapids: Zondervan, 2008.

_____. *Jeremiah~Ezekiel*. The Expositor's Bible Commentary. Vol. 7. Rev. Ed. Grand Rapids: Zondervan, 2010.

MacArthur Jr., John. *The MacArthur New Testament Commentary Revelation 12-22*. Chicago: Moody Press, 2000.

Pentecost, J. Dwight. T*hings to Come: A Study in Biblical Eschatology*. Grand Rapids: Zondervan Publishing House, 1958.

Rydelnik, Michael, and Edwin Blum, eds. *The Moody Handbook of Messianic Prophecy: Studies and Expositions of the Messiah in the Old Testament*. Chicago: Moody Publishers, 2019.

Walvoord, John F. Edited by Philip E. Rawley and Mark Hitchcock. *Revelation*. Chicago: Moody Press, 2011.

_____. *The Prophecy Knowledge Handbook: All the Prophecies of Scripture Explained in One Volume*. Wheaton, Ill.: Victor Books, a division of Scripture Press Publications, Inc., 1990

Whitcomb, John C. *The Rapture and Beyond, Revised and Enlarged: God's Amazing Plan for the Church, Israel, and the Nations*. Indianapolis: Whitcomb Ministries, 2014.

Made in the USA
Middletown, DE
15 February 2022

61133833R00159